SHOWDOWN AT CHIMNEY ROCK

A FIVE ROADS TO TEXAS NOVEL

RICH BAKER

Edited by
SARA JONES

Illustrated by
AJ POWERS

COPYRIGHT

ISBN: 978-0-9988282-3-7

AUTHORS NOTE

With thanks to everyone who has joined the Phalanx authors on this journey. I think I speak for all of us when I say we're honored and humbled that you choose to spend your time with us and the characters we've created as they navigate the Five Roads universe. And now, once more into the breech, my friends...

Regards,
Rich Baker

SHOWDOWN AT CHIMNEY ROCK

Rich Baker

PROLOGUE

EL PASO, TEXAS, APRIL 24

"Dr. Sanjay, I trust you have good news for me," Nampoo Yi said in heavily accented English.

Sanjay was worried. The mercenaries who had shown up at the medical center had him shaken. They were never supposed to meet face-to-face, but he needed the satchel they rescued from the ill-fated courier. Until now, none of the teams who had been working for him had ever met him. This crew was quite resourceful, but they knew too much. He would have to have his security deal with them. He put that out of his mind for the moment, as there were more pressing issues to which he needed to attend. "I've been working diligently, Mr. Yi," Sanjay replied to Yi's statement.

He wasn't lying—he'd done everything they had asked and more. He oversaw the construction and provisioning of dozens of supply stations with everything the incoming forces would need—food, fuel,

1

weapons, transportation—all of which was outside the scope of his expertise. Still, he did it, and no one in the American government had connected the dots. And given the list of items he had to procure, it was no small feat. Sanjay felt he deserved some respect from the man on the other end of the connection. "I want to speak to my family."

Nampoo Yi gritted his teeth. He was tired of Sanjay's games, as if there weren't other people with his skills he could have coerced into performing the work for them. Sanjay was just the first to accept the offer, not that he had much choice. As time wore on, however, he'd been getting more petulant.

"I am a man of my word, Doctor. If I say they are fine, then you have to simply trust that I have done no harm to your family," Yi said with his best estimation of nobility while clinging to the mental image of his chambers that morning and the good doctor's eldest daughter chained to his bed, nude. He didn't typically like them young; however, the mother... she didn't hold up under stress well.

Sanjay sighed. He was becoming increasingly convinced that he was never going to see his wife or daughters again. He regretted ever getting involved with this cabal, not that he'd had any choice. It was too late for that now. He merely told the man what he wanted to hear. "I have the final components to the formula and should have the first batch completed shortly."

"That is fine," Yi answered. "I need you to start

mixing right away and send transcripts to my email via the encrypted server. Be certain to use the VPN so your transmission will not be traceable. No mistakes now, Doctor. We've come too far. Don't put anyone at risk at this late hour."

"Of course, Mr. Yi. It will be done as you say." Sanjay shut off the satellite phone and turned back to his computer. He dragged and dropped several files into an email, and after checking to ensure the VPN was active, he clicked *send*. He sighed, hoping that bought his family another few days of safety.

The PC beeped, drawing his attention back to the screen. A new email sat atop the rest of his messages. The subject read:

MESSAGE FAILED TO SEND

HE OPENED it and scanned the contents of the message. It listed a series of IP addresses and said the transmission failed after ten attempts. He tried to send it again, and again it failed. He banged his hand on the desk in frustration. He tried again, and once more it failed. He opened a browser and tried to access his Gmail account. He was greeted with the message:

HMMM... can't reach this page
   Try this:

Make sure you've got the right web address

"OF COURSE, I have the right web address, damn you!"

He grabbed an SD card from the lab station's top drawer and inserted it into the slot on the side of his laptop. He opened a folder on the PC and dragged several files into it. Then he started the word processor and typed a couple pages of information about the contents of the disk. He read it over, made a couple corrections and printed the document. He stuffed the paper and the SD card into a padded envelope, scribbled an address on the front, and took it down to the lobby desk. He gave it to the woman behind the desk, who put it in the outbound container marked for the courier. He knew that even if the US Mail wasn't running (was a pandemic apocalypse in their credo?), the courier from the company would come by as he did every day to see if there were any packages from Dr. Sanjay with the intermediary's address on them.

Now, Sanjay thought to himself, *time to deal with that arrogant prick, Ian McCollister, and the rest of his band of misguided loyalists.*

CHAPTER ONE

The six-man team checked their gear. The call came in two hours ago, and after months of training and waiting, they were finally going over the border. Kamal Baraghani moved from one man to the next and said the same thing to each.

"You've trained for this moment. You're ready. Allahu Akbar!"

Each of them nodded and exclaimed "Allahu Akbar" in response, but their nerves were showing. They were tense, jaws tight, shoulders stiff. It was their first real jump as a team for a real mission. Kamal knew from experience that once they were out of the plane, muscle memory would take over, and they'd be fine. They'd practiced HALO jumps hundreds of times. It was just a matter of getting them out the door.

The Pilatus PC-6 reached the drop zone on schedule. It was time to go. Kamal had practiced, over and over, the line he wanted to say. Now that it was time, it sounded inadequate, but he said it anyway.

"All right men let's go take our places in history. First Iranian boots on American soil!"

They stood in unison and gave their gear a final once-over. If they didn't have it with them, they'd have to locate it as they went. America had no shortage of places where they could obtain weapons, ammunition, and food, which would be their primary needs if the information they sought was not where it was supposed to be. One by one, the men went out the side of the plane. Kamal was the last to exit.

Directly beneath him was Ciudad Juarez. As much as Kamal hated the United States and everything the West stood for, he could understand why the Mexicans wanted to get there. Juarez was a cesspool. It was worse, even, than the slums of Tehran.

He watched the United States border glide by beneath him. At this altitude, he really could not see a difference in the cities of Juarez and El Paso, other than the US had more paved roads. He knew at lower altitudes, he would see a big difference—at least before the crimson plague began to spread. Now the cities were probably not that different. That thought made him smile.

They continued their descent. Kamal recognized Interstate 10 as it passed underneath. Ahead, he could see Beaumont Army Medical Center, their objective. The group Kamal was taking orders from was a mix of different nationalities, mostly Iranian and North

Korean. Their inside man was supposed to send them information critical to the ultimate success of their plot. It had been eleven days since they last heard from him, and there was no sign of the information. There was a Plan B for sending intelligence of this type, but it was courier-based, and the courier service had been unreachable as well.

The first man in their procession opened his chute. Landing atop the rectangular building was one of the trickiest landings they'd ever attempted. If they missed the roof of the ten-story building, they'd overshoot and end up in the parking lot or the desert scrub beyond. One by one, the chutes opened and their descent slowed.

The first man, Ario Pejman, timed his landing perfectly, his first foot landing close to the edge of the roof. Several strides later, he had his chute pulled in and was turning to help the next soldier. Ario spoke Spanish and was a good soldier. A master of few things, but good at a lot of things.

Javad Nalci landed next. His momentum carried him all the way to the walled structure surrounding the HVAC units, and it looked like he hit it pretty hard. Javad was their security system expert. Whatever information they could get from the system in the hospital, Javad would find it. He also spoke English, which could prove valuable on this trip if they needed to go beyond the hospital walls.

Zand Tousi stumbled and fell, tumbling on the rooftop. Zand was a generalist like Ario but also spoke

English. Kamal hoped he didn't break anything on that rough landing.

Marduk Pejman overshot the roof. He flared up, using the air current to gain some altitude, and pulled hard into a turn. He came back at the building and disappeared on the other side of the HVAC structure. Marduk was their demolition and transportation man. If he couldn't hotwire it or drive it, he could blow it up. He was also Ario's older brother. The Iranian military frowned on brothers serving in the same unit together, but they slipped through the system. Kamal found them both good to work with, so he didn't make an issue out of it.

Dariush Shojaee landed cleanly. Kamal intentionally overshot the building, maintaining some altitude, and executed a similar turn as Marduk. He could see Marduk on the roof, stripping his drop gear. Kamal aimed his landing at the east end of the rooftop, where there was more room for him to set down. Years before, he came in too hot and broke his leg on a rooftop landing. It took three surgeries to repair the bone fully. He wasn't eager to repeat that experience on hostile foreign soil.

He landed cleanly, keeping his balance and pulling his chute down. The four who set down on the north side of the building rallied to his position.

Kamal stripped his helmet from his head. They had just descended from 7600 meters, opened their chutes at twelve hundred meters, and traveled sixteen horizontal kilometers. "Whew! What a ride! Give me a status. Is anyone hurt?"

Zand raised his left hand. "I hurt my shoulder, but I'll be all right." He rolled it a few times. "It still works, but it hurts to move. I'll walk it off."

"I hurt my knee," Javad offered. "I hit that structure pretty hard. I'm sure it will be worse tomorrow, but I'm combat effective, sir."

Kamal nodded, assessing the team. "Okay. The hard part is over! We get that door open, go downstairs to Sanjay's office, collect his data, acquire transportation, and signal for extract. Allahu Akbar! We are the tip of the spear! The first Iranian forces to have boots on the ground in America. One day they'll be teaching this moment to school children. You're already heroes, men! Marduk, get that door open and let's execute our mission."

Marduk dropped his pack and retrieved the detonation cord and the electric detonator from inside. As he was getting ready to mount the det cord, he had a thought and pressed the thumb lever to open the door. It depressed, and the door pulled open.

Kamal laughed. "That's why you're the demolitions man, Marduk. You always think things through!"

Marduk chuckled. "I almost forgot rule number one—check to see if the door is really locked!"

The six men shouldered their packs and walked inside. After descending the stairs, they reached the door that would take them into the hospital itself. Kamal pulled the schematic from his jacket pocket. "Okay, when we get inside, we may be facing hordes of infected infidels. You've seen them in videos, and we fought some of them in Mexico. These will be no different. Small-caliber suppressed weapons only. Low noise. Understood?"

The men all signaled that, yes, they understood.

He continued. "Put on latex gloves. Any infected we kill will need to be checked to be sure they are not Sanjay, as the belief is that he was killed or became infected. Ario, Javad, and Zand, you three go to the security office and get their systems online. We may need the footage from the day Sanjay went dark. Whatever happened to him, we need evidence. Marduk and Dariush, with me. We'll go to Sanjay's office and see what there is to see."

The two groups headed in their different directions. Inside the hospital, the smell was pervasive. Not only were there infected wandering the halls, defecating and urinating on themselves, but dead bodies were rotting inside a building that had been baking under the hot Texas sun without working air conditioning.

They quickly dispatched the infected they sporadically encountered, checking each one to verify it wasn't Sanjay. Kamal had grown to like the suppressed .40 pistol allotted to him. It was chosen by the invasion force because American law enforcement widely used that caliber. Finding resupply on the fly would not be too difficult, and the 180-grain rounds were subsonic, which would help with noise discipline. They weren't as silent as Hollywood movies tried to make them sound, but they were quiet enough.

Kamal located Sanjay's office and tried the knob. It was locked, but it opened inward. He squared up and planted one of his massive boots directly next to the knob. The doorframe buckled, the edges of the metal trim work cracking away from the drywall. He kicked at it again, and the door broke loose, flying inward and swinging all the way to the limit of the hinges, driving the interior doorknob into the wall.

The smell of days of decomposition hit them all hard. Sanjay lay back in his chair, his head twisted to one side, leaving no doubt that his neck was broken. Fluids drained from his body, leaving a greasy pool in the carpet under the chair. Flies buzzed around the body in a thick cloud.

"We found him," Marduk said. "Now what?"

"We let the air clear out while we check the laboratory he worked in," Kamal answered. He consulted the building schematic and led the team to Sanjay's main lab. This door was also locked, but just as easy for the big man to kick in.

"After you," he said with a flourish. Marduk and Dariush walked in ahead of Kamal. They located Sanjay's workstation and began going through the drawers, looking for anything to do with the project while Kamal stood in the doorway, watching for infected. Dariush pulled a battery pack from his bag and plugged the laptop into it. It beeped several times, and the screen displayed the message *Boot Sector Not Found*.

Dariush looked up at Kamal and shook his head. "The doctor wiped his hard drive."

Kamal turned to him and nodded. "Covering his tracks. Smart. Can you get the hard drive out of it?"

Dariush closed the lid and flipped the laptop over, inspecting the screws. "Yes, I have the right tools with me."

"Good, then get it, and we'll take it back to the tech team. They'll see what they can get off of it. Marduk, have you found anything among his papers?"

Marduk was flipping through a notebook. "I don't know. It's all in English, and I don't read it well. Nothing jumps out at me."

"Okay, toss it in your bag. Javad, Zand, or I will review it later. If he had the foresight to wipe his hard drive, he probably wouldn't leave a notebook with critical information in it just lying around, but you never know."

Kamal's radio crackled, then Ario's voice was in his ear. *"Security has its own uninterrupted power supply but is down to ten percent. If you want to view the tapes, you need to get down here."*

He pressed the button on his mic. "We're on our way."

Kamal rechecked the hospital schematic. "This way," he pointed and led the men down the hall to a stairwell. In a few minutes, they were at the entrance to the security office.

Ario rushed the three men into the room. "Come, come. We don't have long with this power. We have some things ready."

He nodded to Javad, who began working the controls. On a thirty-two-inch screen, a video started playing. It showed Dr. Sanjay walking away from a group of two armed men and one woman in the lobby outside of Sanjay's office.

"Get a picture of those people," Kamal directed.

Javad paused the video, and Ario took a picture of the screen. Javad started the video again as Sanjay walked out of frame. Javad clicked away at the keyboard, and another camera picked up Sanjay entering his laboratory. Javad switched to a different camera inside the laboratory, which captured the entryway and most of Sanjay's station. They watched as Sanjay sat down.

He pulled a satellite phone from a drawer and made a phone call. It lasted about a minute, and his body language was animated.

"This must be the last call he made," observed Zand. Kamal nodded.

Sanjay then turned to his laptop and typed for a few minutes, which Javad fast-forwarded through to a point where Sanjay pounded on his desk. Javad slowed it to regular speed, and they watched as Sanjay moved his fingers over the trackpad, clicking a few times and getting angry again.

He dug through a desk drawer and pulled out an SD card. After he popped it into the slot on the side of the computer, he worked his fingers over the trackpad again, clearly dragging and dropping files onto the memory card. He got up and walked out of view for a moment, then returned with several printed pieces of paper. He sorted through them, reviewing the text, then folded them in half and stuffed them into a padded envelope. He ejected the SD card, placed it in a protective plastic case, and put it in with the papers. Then he hurriedly scribbled a name and address on the envelope and left the office.

Javad typed some commands, and the screen switched to another camera. Sanjay walked to an elevator, where he swiped a card then stepped inside.

"Where did he go?" Kamal asked.

More keyboard clicks, and the camera switched to the interior of the elevator. The **L** on the board was lit.

Javad typed some more, and the camera switched to the lobby. He fast forwarded until Sanjay came out of the elevator and approached a woman at the front desk. He handed her the envelope, and she placed it in a bin marked COURIER.

Kamal turned to Dariush and Marduk. "Go see if that package is still there. We haven't heard from the couriers in more than a week, so it's possible it's still in that bin!" He turned back to Javad. "Go back to the room where the Americans were talking with Sanjay. I have a feeling they killed him."

Javad switched back to that camera and scrolled ahead. They watched as Sanjay came back into the lobby and talked with the Americans. They began yelling at each other, and the big one—not the leader—started manhandling Sanjay.

A second woman showed up, and while she didn't appear to be with these three, she left with the woman who *was* with these men. The two remaining men forced Sanjay into his office. They were clearly interrogating him, and at one point they removed some papers from his desk.

Black-clad men showed up, and there was an exchange of gunfire; this group quickly and easily killed the ones in black. Then the two women came back with yet another man. The group exchanged a few words, and the big man broke Sanjay's neck.

Kamal was shocked at the brutality of what he'd just witnessed. Not at the act itself—he'd done worse in his time, and they already knew how Sanjay's story ended. He was surprised because this wasn't what he'd expected from Americans. They were not as Kamal, or his compatriots had been told. This group killed with no remorse. Americans always played by the rules, and that was one of their weaknesses. This group was different. Also, they had women fighting alongside them. *Shield-maidens*, the Vikings called them.

Kamal pointed at the screen. "Take note," he cautioned his team. "The Americans are more brutal than we've been led to think. And their women fight. If we get into combat, anyone could be a soldier. Do not make assumptions that anyone is not a combatant."

The radio crackled. *"Kamal, the package is not here."*

"Thank you, Dariush. Wait there." Kamal turned to Javad and started to speak but was cut off.

"Switching back to the lobby," Javad said as Kamal smiled.

The camera in the lobby showed the woman behind the counter. Javad sped up the video. The woman typed for a few minutes, fidgeted with some papers, put a few things away, then checked her watch. Several men in black uniforms came through the entry. They exchanged words with the woman, who seemed almost relieved when they pointed at the exit. She grabbed a bag from under the desk and left while the men disappeared down the hall.

After a few more seconds, a young dark-skinned man in a military uniform came into view. He retrieved the package and exited the hospital. Before Kamal could say anything, Javad got a picture of the young man then switched cameras to the external entrance. The man got into a military ambulance and drove away.

"Go back to the internal view," Kamal directed.

The internal view showed no activity for a few minutes, then a woman in uniform came out. Javad again got a picture of her and switched to the external camera. She stood outside for a few moments, looking like she wasn't sure what to do, until a Mercedes SUV pulling a small trailer approached. She talked to the driver, got in on the passenger side, and the vehicle drove away.

"Wait, go back!" Ario said. "Someone was in the caravan."

Javad wound the video back and played it in slow motion. The curtain on the side window peeled back, and a face appeared through the glass.

"Where's the picture of the young soldier?" Kamal asked.

Javad held it up next to the screen. The image was the same—the young man who took the package left in the trailer being pulled by the Mercedes with the woman in it.

"Keep the video rolling," Kamal ordered. A few more minutes scrolled past on screen when the Americans who killed Dr. Sanjay left, disappearing from view as they headed for the parking garage. The battery backup beeped, and Javad looked at it.

"We're down to one percent battery," he said.

"Just let it scroll," Kamal responded.

Another twenty minutes sped by with no one coming or going from the main entrance. The battery beeped again, and the system shut down.

Ario put a diffuser on a flashlight and illuminated the room. All eyes turned to Kamal, who clicked his mic. "Dariush, Marduk, return to security." He turned to Ario and Zand.

"Okay, Sanjay's office has cleared out as much as it's going to. Go and check his body. I'd like to know what those papers were that the Americans took. See if they left anything useful, then come back here."

The two men left, and Kamal continued talking to

Javad. "We'll stay here tonight and leave in the morning at first light."

"Where are we going, Kamal?"

"I don't know yet."

Dariush and Marduk returned a moment later, and Kamal repeated the plan to them. "Now, Dariush, we need you to work your magic. You have the satellite uplink, correct?"

"Yes, Kamal."

"Set it up and get us connected. We need to send the pictures of these people to the tech team so they can run their facial recognition against the department of motor vehicles databases. With luck, they'll get us an address, and we can start tracking down that package."

"Yes, Kamal. But—they wore military uniforms. Wouldn't they be inside Fort Bliss?"

"I don't think so. They were in a civilian vehicle pulling a caravan. I think they were leaving town."

"Got it. I'll get it done." Dariush set about getting the uplink going.

Ario and Zand returned from checking Sanjay's body.

"If this keeps up, I'm going to run out of these gloves," Ario said. "That was gross."

"Did you find anything?" Kamal queried.

"No. Just a set of keys, a hospital badge, and a wallet. It had credit cards, a driver's license, some cash. Nothing else."

"Uplink established and photos sent, Kamal," Dariush interjected.

"Okay. Listen—everyone get a few hours of sleep. We have a long day tomorrow, I fear." Kamal set his pack down against the back wall of the large office, where he lay down and put his head on it. He started lightly snoring within a few minutes.

CHAPTER TWO

Sarah Washburn scanned the length of Highway 160. The moon, full two nights before, provided plenty of light. Nothing moved on the road ahead.

"See anything?" Charlie Washburn asked. He was looking along the length of Highway 151. "Because I don't."

"No, nothing."

"Do you get the feeling they sent us out here to get rid of us?"

"Yes."

"Really? I was half joking!"

"No, it's true. I heard Leonard's dad and grandpa talking about it. Dominic said they should put us up here until he can get people on board with us being here."

Charlie chuckled. "Dominic has his finger on the pulse of everything in this area, I think."

"That he does. You can't get anything past him, that's for certain."

"Hey, I think I have something. Check the junction of 160 and 151."

Sarah swung her binoculars to the northeast. "I don't see anything, Charlie."

"Coming out of the woods, just north of the interchange."

She moved her view a little left. "Got 'em. Looks like they're just wandering, not hunting anything. You want to call it in? You spotted them."

"Sure." Charlie keyed the button on the police radio Leonard's dad had given them. "This is, ah..." He let go of the button and looked at Sarah. "What are we called?"

"Chimney Rock watch station."

He keyed the button again. "This is Chimney Rock watch station. We have a half dozen infected coming out the woods at the junction of Highways 160 and 151. Heading..."

"South," Sarah answered before Charlie could ask.

"Heading south." He released the button and waited a few seconds.

"Roger, Chimney Rock. We'll intercept on 151."

They both turned their focus to Highway 151. A couple minutes passed, and Charlie said, "Here they come."

A dark shape moved up the road at a slow pace, lights off, heading toward the group of infected. The radio squelched, and a voice came through the speaker.

"*We're northbound on 151. Do you have eyes on us?*"

"Uh, roger?" Charlie said. Sarah laughed at the way he asked it like a question.

"*How far are we from the infected?*"

Charlie swung the binoculars back and forth a couple times. They had noted some landmarks earlier to estimate distance, but in the dark, he couldn't see them. "A half mile, I think," he said. "Hard to tell because of it being, you know, dark."

"*Close enough, Chimney Rock. Intercept out.*"

On the road, the dark vehicle slowed and stopped at the curve where Highway 151 turned southwest, and they waited. Sarah and Charlie could see the infected getting closer. Charlie keyed the button. "They're getting closer. Maybe a few hundred feet in front of you."

"Roger, we see 'em."

In the distance, Sarah thought she saw the driver's side door open, but it was hard to tell on the all-black SUV. They saw several muzzle flashes from a pair of rifles, and the infected on the roadway collapsed. Sarah was waiting for the sound of the gunshots, but they never came. Their rifles must have been suppressed, which was good. Any loud noise was like a homing beacon for the infected.

Her watch beeped. She looked at it. Two AM. Time for shift change.

They watched the SUV on the road make a three-point turn and head back south.

"Chimney Rock, infected are down. Clean up crews will deal with them in the morning. We're headed back. Intercept out."

When they started the night's watch, they agreed to rotate every four hours so they could get some decent sleep, if that were possible. Gravel crunching underfoot let them know the next shift was coming. Susan Red, an officer with the Southern Ute Indian Police Department, was the first to show up to relieve them. It seemed a lifetime ago that Sarah met Susan when they were heading to El Paso. The situation was much different then than it was now. Back in March, Sarah, her husband, Jack, and his father, Charlie, were fleeing a wave of infection, headed to a government safe zone. Jack had been infected but was seemingly immune to the disease. Cedric Naranjo, another officer with the SUPD, had sent his son Leonard south with them to gather information about the outbreak.

Things had gone very wrong in El Paso, and Jack died—not so much from the disease as from the doctors at the Beaumont Medical Center experimenting on him. A massive horde of infected, estimated to be over a million strong, was headed to El Paso from the east, so their group left the West Texas town for the relative safety of the remote Colorado Southern Ute Reservation.

"Shane is right behind me," Susan warned them. "We'll hold the fort until six. Then the next crew should be here to relieve us."

"Thanks, Susan," Sarah replied. She liked the

heavyset woman. She was friendly and matter-of-fact about everything.

They passed Shane Frost on the path back to the thousand-year-old ruins spread out on the mesa of Chimney Rock, getting little more than a nod from the sleepy nineteen-year-old.

The masonry walls and sunken floors of the kivas helped hide any light from their small fire, built to keep them warm and cook soup over. Leonard had let the fire burn down to embers, only adding pieces of wood every now and then to keep the heat coming.

"It's Sarah and Charlie," Sarah called out. Everyone was nervous with the infected running around, and she didn't want any of the people in the kiva to get jumpy with their weapons.

Leonard was excited to see them. "Hi, guys! Come and sit down! The fire's really warm, and we have soup and coffee going."

"Thanks, Leonard," Charlie said. "Soup would be good. Hi Aaron, hi Lori."

Aaron and Lori returned the greeting. Aaron Valdez was Leonard's friend from childhood. He looked very similar to Leonard... so much so, they used to tell people they were brothers. In a town where everyone knew everyone else, no one believed it, but sometimes people would act like they were confused to humor the boys.

Lorelei Branch, who went by Lori, had been a nurse at the Beaumont Medical Center. When Leonard was working there to keep an eye on Sarah's husband, Jack, Leonard and Lori hit it off, and when the group fled El Paso, she left with them. She hadn't been far from Leonard's side since they arrived in Arboles.

Leonard poured some soup in a camping cup, put a spoon in it, and passed it to Charlie. He looked at Sarah, who was holding her hands over the fire to warm them. "Sarah, you want some soup?"

She thought for a minute, then said, "Yeah, it would probably be good. I'd like some coffee too, please."

Lori poured the coffee while Leonard dished out the soup.

Charlie finished his soup and scraped all the thick broth out of the cup that he could. "What do we do with these, Leonard?" he asked, holding out the empty vessel.

"Here," Aaron held out his hand. He took the cup from Charlie and wiped it out with a paper towel he retrieved from his duffel bag. He put the used towel in the embers and pushed it down with a stick. The moisture hissed as it evaporated in the glowing coals, and the paper burst into flames deep in the fire pit. It cast a flashing light in the kiva, throwing shadows on the masonry walls, then disappeared almost as soon as it flared up.

"Tell us more about this place," Charlie said. "I've lived in Colorado most of my life, and I've never heard of Chimney Rock."

"Okay," Aaron started, "so, I already told you it's

named for the massive towers of rock sticking up into the sky. The taller one is Chimney Rock; the other is called Companion Rock. Every nineteen or so years, the moon rises between those towers. It's an astrological thing. The ancient Puebloan people were stargazers, and they built this place around that event. About a thousand, maybe twelve hundred people were living on and around this mesa for a couple hundred years, from, like, the late nine-hundreds to the early eleven-hundreds. This was an outlying community that was part of the larger Chaco Canyon community.

"The kivas, these big round rooms, were ceremonial houses. Back then, they would have had roofs over them, and the fire would be enough to heat it during even the coldest winter nights. The square rooms surrounding them were probably storage rooms, or the larger ones were maybe family dwellings. This site was important to the Chacoan culture. The astrological information from Chimney Rock was passed to the other communities. It told them things like when to plant certain crops and when to harvest them, stuff like that. They would light signal fires that could be seen on mesas all around, and the people on those mesas would light their signal fires, and so on until the news reached all the communities."

"Like in *Lord Of The Rings*," Leonard added.

Adam scoffed. "Yeah, the Hobbits straight ripped off our culture, yo!"

"So, the people who lived here were your ancestors?"

"I don't know. Probably. Maybe. The Ute didn't always live here. That was a later arrangement."

"More likely to be ours than yours, paleface," Leonard said, smiling.

Charlie let the comment pass. "So, these structures we're sitting in are a thousand years old? What are we doing touching anything in here? I feel like we're breaking an antiquities law or something."

"The world is ending, man," Aaron said. "Sitting in here hides the fire and gives us some protection from the wind. None of the infected can see the light unless they're here on the mesa. I think the Ancients would be cool with us using this site to help protect our people. I just wish their roofs would have lasted as long as their mason work."

"It is a good vantage point, that's for sure. Three-hundred-sixty-degree view, a line of sight for miles. Only one road leading up here, steep sides—not impassable—but enough to make the ascent hard. Could be a lot worse places to make a stand."

"So, your turn," Aaron said. "Tell me more about El Paso."

"Well, there's not much to tell. We went there to get away from the infected. The folks I talked to on my ham radio said it was safe there. It was, for a while. When we got there, we were given a choice to join the Army's new Civilian Division or go to the FEMA camps. *Service or citizen* was how the Army kids put it. We chose service."

"Yeah," Leonard picked up the tale. "And I went to

Beaumont Medical Center with Jack, Sarah's husband. They tested everyone for the disease at the checkpoints going into the city, and he tested positive even though he didn't show the classic symptoms. Hundreds of people came to Beaumont, and we had to put most of them down." He said it matter of fact, like a shelter worker dispatching a rabid dog.

"*We?*" Sarah asked. "You mean you helped with that?"

"Sometimes. I had to, Sarah. We couldn't have infected running around the halls, even though that's exactly what happened eventually."

"No, it's just—I didn't know you were in that much danger."

"It got crazy sometimes. It was nasty at the end when some of the doctors got infected."

Sarah's voice got an edge to it. "I can't say I feel sorry for the 'doctors' there. They kind of reaped what they sowed."

"They weren't all involved in the... experiments," Lori interjected. "There were only a few who did those things, and they reported directly to Dr. Sanjay. The others were really trying to help people. And it was only toward the end that I found out what Sanjay's people were up to. Once the size of Sergeant Duckett's security team began to dwindle, protocol and secrecy started to break down."

"And that's when we came and got you," Leonard said.

Aaron looked at Sarah for long few seconds. "I'm sorry about your husband. It has to be tough."

Sarah sighed. "The morning after Jack and I left the city, after we arrived at Charlie's cabin and had that gunfight, that one hillbilly kid—what was his name?"

"Rollie," Charlie answered.

"Yeah, Rollie. When he got sick, and the only blood he'd come in contact with was Jack's, I knew what the end would be. I didn't want to admit it, not even to myself, but I knew we'd never kiss again, he'd never hold me in bed again, that we'd not be growing old together. I thought El Paso would offer us hope, that they would have a way to at least stop it, if not cure it. To find out that prick Dr. Sanjay was trying to defeat Jack's immunity, well, that was a kick in the gut. Sanjay worked for the *US Government,* for Christ's sake. How could they be doing this?"

Leonard and Aaron traded a glance. "You're asking *us* about the government doing horrible things?" Aaron said. "We have some history with that. I don't think many folks around here would be surprised if the government was behind this whole thing, if you know what I mean."

"Sorry," Sarah said. "Anyway, once Jack... succumbed, that's when we left."

"Well, that and some other things," Charlie added. "Sarah and I were working on perimeter defenses, putting miles of concertina wire around the city to slow the infected that were coming in from the east, helping fortify the cargo containers they used to wall off Fort Bliss."

Aaron tilted his head. "Cargo containers?"

"Yeah, double stacked, welded together. That made the walls seventeen feet high, completely surrounding the Fort. They moved in massive piles of dirt against the backs of the containers, in part to make them stable, and in part so the Strykers could drive right up on the walls and open up on the hordes."

"There were hordes of the infected?"

"Not yet, but the city itself was getting bad, more attacks every day, and the intel from the recon flights was that there were millions—*millions*—of them headed at the city like a battering ram. If the walls held, Fort Bliss and all the people inside would be surrounded. It would be a siege."

"So, you left them? What if your guns would have made the difference?"

"There's no way I was staying with the bastards who murdered my husband," Sarah interjected. "I couldn't do that."

Charlie shook his head. "I don't think the Army knew about Sanjay's hijinks, Sarah."

"Sergeant Duckett did," she replied. "Or he figured it out. I wonder what happened to him... If he let that other guy, Ram, go. In the end, I think Duckett was trying to make amends for his part in it."

"Well, I don't think any of the guys we worked with knew," Charlie continued. "In any case, we promised Leonard's dad we'd look out for him, so bringing him back here made the most sense. And without us there, they'll have more ammo and more food. That's going to be their biggest problem. They estimated there'd be four million or so refugees in there. When the food runs out, it's going be as ugly inside as it is outside those walls."

"Yeah, Aaron, it was bad out there. If you saw what we went through getting back here, you'd never think about going to El Paso," Leonard added.

They fell into silence. Lori leaned against Leonard. Aaron stirred the coals and added a couple small sticks to the fire.

Sarah felt her eyes getting heavy, so she got a bivvy sack out and crawled into it, reveling in the way it trapped her body heat. She laid her head against her pack and looked at Charlie. He seemed weary, the flickering flames casting deep shadows in the lines on his face. She saw Jack when she looked at him. An older, weather-worn version, but the resemblance was unmistakable. She drifted to sleep with memories of happier times floating through her dreams.

CHAPTER THREE

"We got him," Dariush said.

Kamal looked up from his breakfast of protein paste—his name for the ready-made meal—and smiled, his white teeth showing through his heavy black beard. "Go on."

"His name is Leonard Naranjo. Twenty-four years old. Lives in Arboles, Colorado."

"Arboles means *trees* in Spanish," Ario interjected.

"Thank you, Ario," Kamal said. Ario began studying Spanish when he learned they were going to be deployed to Mexico. He had learned enough to get them into trouble with some of the locals in Juarez. Much Mexican blood was spilled that night. "Dariush, please continue."

"The plates on the vehicle tie it to a man named Gilroy Johnson. Lives in Highlands Ranch, Colorado. But his DMV picture doesn't match any of the people we saw in that video feed.

"The driver's picture matches a man named Charles Washburn. Fifty-nine years old. His DMV record lists an address in Grand Lake, Colorado, but the property records say he sold that house a year ago. No other address listed."

Kamal stroked his beard. "There was a Washburn as a patient here. One of Dr. Sanjay's status reports mentioned him. Could be a coincidence, but I don't believe in coincidences. What about the woman?"

"No match in the facial recognition program. The image wasn't clear enough."

"Okay, where are these cities? Highlands Range and Arboles, the city of trees?" Kamal shot a sideways glance at Ario, who smiled at him with a mouthful of protein paste.

Dariush consulted his tablet. "Okay... Grand Lake is just over eleven hundred kilometers. Highlands *Ranch*—not *Range*—is a thousand. Arboles is just over eight hundred."

"That's where they went. Arboles."

"How can you be sure, Kamal?"

"Because why would they take the vehicle back to the owner's city if the owner isn't with them? And why would they go to the city where the Washburn man *doesn't* own property? Besides, if I'm wrong, it's only another two hundred kilometers to Highlands *Ranch*. What about the people who killed Sanjay?"

"The woman and the big man did not have a match. The other one is Ian McCollister. He runs a team of mercenaries. Sanjay employed them as one of the teams setting up some of the supply sites."

"So was this a business disagreement? They didn't seem to be interested in anything other than Sanjay and some papers that were on the table. Let's stay on task and focus on Leonard and his friends. Plot a course, Dariush. Ario, wake the others. We need to secure transportation and let Command know what our next move is."

Ario went to the outer room of the security office and found Zand and Javad in large chairs, and Marduk stretched out on the couch, all of them still sleeping. Outside the windows, the gray of pre-dawn twilight was illuminating more of the city. He could see silhouettes of infected wandering the streets around the hospital. The sun would be up within the next thirty minutes, and they needed to be on the road by then. It would not do for six Iranian nationals to be caught in the streets of El Paso by the American military.

"Wake up! Javad! Zand! Marduk! You've slept enough!"

He kicked Zand's leg, startling the big man.

"Ario! That's how people get shot," he lamented.

Ario laughed and did the same thing to Javad, who just yelped and gave Ario an angry look. "Ass! My leg still hurts from the drop in!"

"Oh, yeah, sorry," Ario said, though he laughed as he said it.

He walked to the couch and reached down to shake Marduk.

SHOWDOWN AT CHIMNEY ROCK

"Touch me, and I'll break your hand, little brother," Marduk said without opening his eyes.

This got a laugh from Ario. "Ever the morning person, Marduk. When you're feeling up to it, Kamal wants you three to find transportation for us. He wants to be on the move in twenty."

"So we should go now."

"Yes, you should go now! Did my sarcasm not come through?"

"Neither did mine, apparently. Tell Kamal I've already picked the vehicle for us. We'll go get it now. Be ready at the emergency entrance in fifteen minutes."

Marduk sat up and stretched, rolled his head around to loosen his neck, and yawned. "Javad, Zand, are you ready?"

They both got up and put on their packs. "Yes, Marduk. Let's go," Zand said.

Marduk smiled and put his hand on Ario's shoulder. "Don't worry, little brother. I've picked a good ride!"

Ario walked back into the security control room and found Dariush packing up his satellite datalink equipment. Kamal was using a satellite phone and held up a finger to his mouth, indicating Ario should be quiet.

"Of course. We are doing just that. Yes, yes, understood. Yes, I know what 'discreet' means. Of course, we will." Kamal disconnected the call and powered off the phone. He looked at the other two men. "I am thrilled that people in a conference room half a world away know what we should be doing on the ground here in America. Did you know we are supposed to be discrete on this mission?" He laughed. "I'm glad he said something. I was getting ready to start randomly blowing things up like a cowboy!"

Dariush and Ario laughed too.

"What else did they say?" Daruish asked.

Kamal zipped his pack and checked his rifle and pistol, ensuring they were loaded. "I'll tell you all once we get in whatever vehicle Marduk got for us. I don't want to go through it twice. Ario, what's the status on that?"

"They left right before I came in here. Marduk said to be at the emergency entrance in fifteen."

Kamal shouldered his bag. "Okay, let's head down.

A BLACK TOYOTA SEQUOIA rolled up to the emergency entrance. Kamal, Ario, and Dariush hustled out of the hospital to the vehicle, opened the doors, tossed their bags to the other men, and climbed in. Despite the shrieks from nearby infected, Kamal walked around to the driver's side and motioned for Marduk to move over.

Once he climbed in the driver's seat, he adjusted its position, moving it back a few inches. He put the vehicle in gear. "Which way, Dariush?"

"Ahead, then left. The Americans have built a

perimeter around the base. We must go south and get on I-10. There should be plenty of signs, but I'll tell you when to turn."

"Okay. Nice ride, by the way, Marduk. It's no Toyota Hilux, but it will do."

Everyone smiled at the mention of the omnipresent truck persistently utilized by militant upstart groups across the Middle East.

Dariush buckled his seat belt. "Yes, this one has safety restraints for all of us! So, Kamal, what did Command have to say?"

The other men sat up and paid attention at the mention of Command. Kamal looked in the mirror at the four men in the rear seats and cast a sideways glance at Marduk.

"Okay, our mission parameters haven't changed. We still must find the package. They stressed that we must be as discreet as possible. Dr. Sanjay's death has complicated things. Nampoo Yi has been executed, and Hamid Sari is our mission commander now. We check in with him in twelve hours."

Kamal swerved around several infected that were shambling around the street. A glance in the mirror showed many more coming from side streets and emerging from hiding places. He almost felt sorry for the Americans who had lived in this city, which now belonged to the infected. Almost.

"Why was Yi executed?" Dariush asked from the back seat.

"I didn't ask. It has no bearing on the mission, and

I've found when dealing with people of this type, the less you know, the better."

Marduk scoffed.

"You don't agree?" Kamal asked.

"It just seems like it would be wise to know what the offense was so we can avoid the same thing. I think you did ask, and you just don't want to tell us."

"All right. Unless you're going to take hostage the family of the only doctor who can provide us with protection from this disease, then fuck his wife and daughter to death, then lose control of a mercenary group that kills that doctor, you're not likely to commit the same offense."

"Really? Yi did all that?"

"Yes. Well, I think Sanjay lost control of his own mercenaries, but yes. Yi was bad, even by North Korean standards." Kamal meant this to be a joke, but no one laughed.

Javad shook his head. "Can I say, unofficially, that I am not one hundred percent on board with the North Koreans?"

Kamal looked in the mirror. "Keep that unofficial." He looked around at the rest of the group. "That goes for all of you. Yes, we all know that the NorKos are a shadow of what we are. Their people are starving. I mean, they're shorter on average than their southern countrymen. But their leadership and their RGB staff are ruthless. Never say anything aloud against them outside this group. You understand?"

The men nodded.

Dariush pointed at a split in the road ahead. "This road curves to the west. Follow it to where it dead ends, and we'll go left."

Kamal followed the instruction, weaving around several abandoned vehicles and shrieking infected. The sky was now gray and getting lighter by the minute. The sun would be up soon.

The infected were not as plentiful here as they had been closer to Fort Bliss. The activity on the base must have been drawing them from the outlying parts of the city.

"Here," Dariush pointed. "Go left, then in three hundred meters, go right. This will be Interstate 10 and will take us out of the city."

They drove for few minutes before encountering an abandoned roadblock that forced them to exit the interstate, find an alternate route, and re-enter the road at another on-ramp. Finally, after thirty minutes of this, they passed a sign proclaiming *The Outlet Shoppes at El Paso*, where they had to divert around the last of the military barriers.

Far behind them, a black SUV pulled on to the interstate, using the same on-ramp the Iranians had used. It stayed far enough back, so it didn't raise their suspicion, but close enough to see all the moves the Toyota made. With no other cars on the road, it was pretty easy to track it in the distance. The driver knew he must not let them out of his sight.

THEY WERE out of El Paso's city limits before the sun rose, the smoke and haze from the nationwide destruction making the sunrise a deep red that turned more orange as the minutes wore on. Dariush stayed awake to provide directions to Kamal while the others fell asleep. They had to stop for fuel in a town that was empty of all humanity. The team formed a perimeter around the SUV while Marduk siphoned gas from a pair of abandoned vehicles.

Kamal traded off driving with Zand and napped in the back seat. Zand noted that many of the smaller towns they drove through had no infected, but he didn't see any people either. Either they were in hiding, or the disease had taken them all. The route they were using was a little circuitous, but Dariush insisted it was necessary to avoid the larger cities, where they would undoubtedly get entangled with large populations of the infected.

Zand slowed the Sequoia as they approached the town of Tierra Amarillo, New Mexico. He looked over at Dariush. "Wake them up."

In a moment, the group was all awake and alert. Zand stopped the SUV fifteen meters behind a teardrop-shaped trailer, abandoned on the side of the road. The driver's side tire was flat, so the trailer listed to the left.

"Is that the same caravan that the Washburn man towed away from El Paso?" Kamal asked.

"It sure looks like it," Zand said from the driver's seat.

They could see the glint of hundreds of brass casings littering the ground around the trailer. Bodies were strewn all around.

"There are dozens of dead, maybe fifty or more," Marduk said. A hint of awe came through in his voice. "They can fight. When we catch them, remember that."

Kamal opened the door and started to climb out. "We need to search the bodies and see if any of them match the people we saw. Ario, Javad, you two search the caravan. See if the package—or anything useful—is still inside. The rest of us, check the bodies."

The search turned up nothing other than a ham radio in the trailer and some clothes. None of the bodies matched the pictures from the hospital.

Kamal checked his watch. "It's time to check in with Command. Let's move up to that gas station, secure it, and get some food."

Zand drove the Toyota under the canopy of the Chevron station. The team moved quickly through the interior of the building, securing it for their use.

Kamal retrieved the satellite phone from his bag and dialed the number for Command. He looked around at the rest of the team while he waited for the call to connect.

Zand had a stove going and water heating up. The men were retrieving their food packs. Hot meals were sometimes hard to come by while on a mission, so they took every opportunity they could to have something other than a brick or tube of "nutrition."

The call connected, and Hamid Sari was on the other end of the line.

"Sir..." Kamal began but was cut off. "Yes, sir. Understood. We'll go all night if we have to, sir."

"That didn't sound good," Zand said.

"No, it's not. The NorKos had an encounter at the airport in Phoenix. There's a faction of the US military there, so now they're aware of foreign operations on their soil. Also, the locations of all supply depots and safe houses have been uploaded to the Internet. Our tech teams are scrambling to hack the servers and take them down, but the information is replicating faster than we can get to it."

"Who has that information?" Marduk asked. "Only a handful of people have those locations."

Kamal smiled. "We know the answer. We saw on the security cams at Beaumont that the mercenaries took some papers. I thought they looked like maps, but I didn't make the connection until now. Now those maps are online. Again, I don't believe in coincidences."

"Those plans could have been in the package Leonard Naranjo took, too," Ario added. "We don't know what was in there, but they could very well be on that memory card. It could be he did it."

Kamal nodded. "All the more reason we need to get that package. Who knows what else is in there?"

Dariush tipped the package of food up and dumped the last of his meal into his mouth. "Okay. I'm fueled up. Let's go get this Naranjo kid."

CHAPTER FOUR

Smoke from the bacon and eggs cooking in the iron skillet penetrated Sarah's nostrils. She thought it was a dream, but her olfactory sense demanded she wake up and see what was going on. She emerged from the bivvy sac to see Shane, Susan, and Charlie sitting around the low fire with a camping grate supporting the pan.

"What time is it?" she asked.

Charlie got up and brought her a thermos lid full of coffee. "Almost eight. Leonard, Lori, and Aaron are on watch duty. Here's some campfire coffee. It's surprisingly good." Sarah noticed Susan throw a dirty look at Charlie for the backhanded comment. "And you can smell the bacon and eggs, I'm sure. You hungry?"

She didn't think she was, but her stomach growled in protest. "Yeah, I am."

"Food will be ready in a couple of minutes," Susan announced.

Sarah looked around. The kiva they were sitting in wasn't actually dug into the earth as she initially thought. The round structure was surrounded by a square of masonry walls, and the voids between the inner circle and outer walls had been filled in with soil, she assumed to provide stability and some insulation to the room.

All around the kiva were smaller square areas, walled off and separated by similar masonry walls, some of which were collapsing.

"It was an observatory for the ancient people," Shane said when he saw her looking around. "This kiva and the one to the west would have held ceremonies celebrating various lunar events. Every eighteen years the moon hits the end of its arc, and it rises between Chimney Rock and Companion Rock. You'd be able to see it from the kivas. It was a big deal to them. To some it still is."

"Yeah, Aaron told us about that last night," Sarah said. "It's amazing how much they knew so long ago."

Susan acknowledged the remark with a nod. "And today, people are lost without their phones. This current situation has woken up this generation to how much they relied on them." Her scold seemed aimed at Shane, but he took no notice of it.

"That hole," he continued, pointing at a square hole lined with more masonry, "would have housed the main support beam for the roof. The kivas would have been packed with people for the moonrise. There are only a few places like this in the world."

Sarah could sense his pride in the heritage of the area. She searched for something meaningful to say but was interrupted by Susan.

"Breakfast is ready!" she called out. She portioned out eggs and bacon for the four of them and passed plates to each of the group.

Sarah took a bite of the eggs. Seasoned with salt and pepper and cooked in the bacon grease, she could not remember scrambled eggs tasting this good.

"Oh my God, Susan, these eggs are fantastic!" Charlie said, echoing Sarah's thoughts.

Susan patted her ample belly. "If you can't tell, I do like to cook."

"These are the best eggs I've had in... well, I can't remember the last time I had eggs this good. Thank you," Sarah added. She took a bite of bacon and made an involuntary *mmmm* noise. "Even the bacon is perfect! Just the right crispness."

"Heritage breed pork," Susan explained. "It makes all the difference."

As they finished their breakfast, Shane told them more about the area's history, how many people used to live there, the ties to the Chaco Canyon communities, and the eventual abandonment of the site due to drought and changes in the climate in the twelfth century.

"It's incredible to think people were sitting where we are before anyone ever sailed from Europe," Charlie said.

"Centuries before. Europe was still fighting the

Crusades," Sarah added. "And the Chinese perfected gunpowder around the year one thousand. How different would things be if that invention had traveled East instead of West?"

"Well, it didn't," Shane said. "And our world was doomed to conquest."

Sarah and Charlie both realized, too late, that they'd offended Shane.

"I'm sorry," Sarah started to say, but Shane cut her off.

"No, it's okay. It's history, right? I mean, like it or not, things played out as they did, and we are where we are as a result. It's not like you personally did anything."

"Well, still, we didn't mean any offense. I was just trying to put the timeline in context of what I know of world history." Sarah gestured around them. "All of this is new to me. Thank you for teaching us about it."

Shane smiled, and his posture softened. "I'm sorry too. I get pretty worked up sometimes. I want to hold onto the Ute culture, and it gets harder all the time."

Charlie's radio crackled, and they heard a static-filled transmission. "That sounded like Leonard," he said as he picked up the handheld unit. "Repeat, we didn't copy."

"I said there's a car coming. A full-sized Blazer."

"Copy." Charlie turned to the others. "You guys sit tight, I'll go check it out."

He climbed up the wooden stairs that led out of the kiva and jogged up the trail to where Leonard and Lori were looking northwest. He was wheezing and out of breath when he reached them.

"Jesus," he gasped. "I used to live at nine thousand feet. A month in El Paso and I'm gassed at seven thousand."

"I know, I'm feeling it too," Leonard replied. He held a pair of binoculars out to Charlie and pointed. "They just passed the curve where Highway 160 turns east."

Charlie took the binoculars and looked through them. It took a few seconds of getting his breathing under control before he could hold them steady enough to see the vehicle. He recognized the oxidized blue paint and the red-and-primer-gray passenger door immediately. "Holy shit, we know them!"

Leonard was surprised. "Really? How small of a world is this?"

Lori asked the more important question. "Are they good people, or bad people?"

"Good, I think, or at least they were a month or so ago." Charlie handed the binoculars back to Leonard. "I'm going to get Sarah, and we're going down to meet them. Keep us posted on what they're doing, okay?"

"Yeah, for sure, Charlie. Be careful! Who knows what they've been through over the last month."

Charlie turned and trotted back to the kiva. Sarah was stuffing her bivvy sack in her backpack. She zipped it up and threw it over her shoulders, grabbed her rifle, and headed for the staircase. "Leonard radioed ahead," she explained.

Charlie nodded and descended the half dozen steps, retrieved his gear, and climbed back out. "Ready?"

Sarah nodded. "Yep, let's do this."

They double-timed it to their Mercedes SUV, covering the quarter mile in three minutes. Charlie was sweating as he started the vehicle and began winding down the three miles of turns and switchbacks to the get to the main road.

"They've turned onto Highway 151, headed south. You're going to have to hurry to cut them off."

"Thanks, Leonard," Sarah replied into the hand-held radio.

Charlie rounded one of the sharp, hairpin turns, and the back end of the SUV slid out for a second before he got it back in line for the next turn. He heard Sarah give an involuntary gasp. "Chimney Rock Drift!" he said, laughing at his play on the *Fast & Furious* movie title.

Leonard's voice interrupted Charlie's laughter. *"They've stopped to check out the bodies from last night. You've got a little more time."*

"Roger," Sarah replied into the radio. "Charlie, slow it down a little, please? I don't want to end up driving down the side of the mesa."

"We'll be fine," he replied. "We're almost there."

They rounded another hairpin turn, slower this time, and in a few seconds, they passed the visitors' center. From there, it was a straight shot to the monument entrance. Charlie put his foot down, and the powerful SUV shot up to seventy miles per hour, sending a plume of dust into the air behind them. He slowed down for the final curve and pulled onto the highway. The vehicle stopped in the middle of the two-lane road, angled, so the nose of the Mercedes pointed northeast. He held his hand out for the radio. Sarah passed it to him and checked her rifle, ensuring she had a full magazine in it.

"How are we looking, Leonard?" Charlie asked as he exited the SUV and checked his rifle, ensuring it was loaded. He flicked the safety off.

"Good, Charlie. They're moving again. Should be in your sight in a few seconds."

"Great, thanks."

Up the road, about a quarter of a mile away, the Blazer came into view as it rounded the curve. Sarah took a position behind the Mercedes with her rifle across the hood. "I'll cover you from here, Charlie, at least until we know it's really them. You do the talking."

He nodded without looking back, keeping his eyes on the approaching vehicle.

The Blazer slowed to a stop fifty feet from the Mercedes. The driver's side door opened, and a woman stepped out with her hands in the air. She turned so that her right hip was toward them and they could see the pistol she wore.

"I'm going to pull it out and put it on the hood," she called out. "Don't shoot."

She used two fingers to pull the pistol from its

holster, placed it on the hood, and stepped to the side, lacing her fingers behind her head. "I have two more people in the car with me. They'll get out one at a time and do the same thing."

Sarah kept the rifle aimed at the woman while the next person got out of the Blazer and put his pistol on the hood in the same fashion as the woman, and, like her, stepped to the side. The third person, also male, climbed out on the passenger side from the back seat. He put his pistol on the hood and stepped away from it.

"That's all of us," the woman said. "May I approach you?"

Charlie waved her forward. He looked back at Sarah and chuckled.

"My name is Robin Mitico," she continued. "I was a Pitkin County sheriff's deputy until the world went teats up. We've been holed up east of Aspen, trying to keep the infected pinned in town, but a horde showed up from... Grand Junction, or hell, Denver, maybe. Don't matter much; there were too many for us, so we got the hell out of Dodge. Figured we'd head down to that safe zone in El Paso. Now, I know why you're blocking the road, but I can assure you, we're no threat, and none of us is infected. You can check us over if you like."

"Get on your knees," Sarah ordered. Charlie gave her a look that said *What the fuck?*

"Well, now, that's not necessary..." Robin started to reply.

Sarah flicked her safety off.

"Okay, I heard you." Robin turned her head to the two men. "Boys, get to your knees."

Sarah walked around the front of the Mercedes and approached Robin but stopped a few feet short. Robin's face was a mask of calm.

"You don't recognize me, do you?" Sarah asked.

"No. Should I?"

Sarah smiled and repeated a line Robin used on her weeks ago. "Well, maybe if you take that edge outta your voice and focus, it might jog your memory a bit."

Robin's face registered genuine surprise. She looked at Sarah, taking in the fatigues and the rifle. The overall demeanor of the woman who a month ago had been on her knees at Robin's roadblock was much different. The woman in front of her wasn't afraid of her shadow, and her face was gaunter than it had been then, but she recognized her.

"Yeah," Robin said. "I do remember you. You were different then. Scared. Not like now." She looked at Charlie, then searched the area around them. "I recognize you, too, now. The beard threw me. Where's your third? Your husband? I think his name was Jack, unless I'm mistaken."

Sarah's voice tensed up. "He didn't make it."

Robin's face soured. "I'm sorry, honey. This new world is hard on us all. Can, uh, can we get up?"

Sarah laughed. "Yeah. Sorry about that. I just couldn't resist a little role reversal here."

"Dangerous game to play. These are desperate times, and people are apt to do desperate things."

"I would have stopped it before Marcus got the knife out of the back of his jacket or Sebastian got the LCP out of his. Clever, but we saw a little of everything in El Paso," Charlie said.

Robin was brushing the dirt from the road off her knees. "So you guys made it there? Are you enlisted, or what's with the getups?"

"We joined the civilian corps," Sarah said. "They gave us a choice on the way into town—FEMA camps or First Civilian Division. Charlie and I spent a month preparing defenses, doing security, cooking, you name it."

"But now you're here in southern Colorado. What happened, if you don't mind my asking?"

"It's a long story, but the short version is that the doctors..."

"*Some* doctors," Charlie corrected.

Sarah shot him a look before continuing. "*Some* doctors at the Army medical center were running experiments on people, Jack included. I had to leave after that."

"And there were more than a million infected coming at the city from the east," Charlie added. "So we don't know if Fort Bliss is even there anymore."

Sebastian scoffed. "So you're saying we should think twice about going."

"I would if I were you. Maybe wait for the offseason, beat the crowds."

Charlie's radio crackled.

"Charlie, Sarah, are you guys okay down there?"

Charlie keyed the talk button. "Yeah, we're good. This is who we thought it was."

"Good, good. Hey, the relief team isn't here yet. And I see what looks like a lot of smoke from Arboles. I think something's wrong."

Sarah looked concerned. "He's right. The day shift should be here by now. We should check it out."

Charlie nodded. "Leonard will want to come, I'm sure."

"They all will," Sarah added. "I don't think we can leave the road unattended though."

"We can help. What do you need us to do?" Robin volunteered. "Seeing as how our plans just fell through, we may as well make ourselves useful."

"Yeah, we can cover this road if you need it. Running a roadblock has recently moved to the top of our resumes," Marcus said.

Charlie's wheels were turning. "Okay, let's do this. If you guys are good watching this road, that will help. We're not really checking people here—there's a checkpoint closer to town—but we're trying to stop the infected from getting any farther south than this position." He turned to Sarah. "If they cover the road, we can get the others down here and head into Arboles together and see what's what."

"Sounds good to me. Call 'em down."

Charlie clicked the talk button. "Okay, Leonard, our friends here will watch the road and take care of any infected. You guys pack up and head down, and we'll head into town together, okay?"

He released the button. No response. He counted to ten. Still no answer.

"Leonard? Do you copy?" Another few seconds passed.

"Hi, Charlie. We're on the way down. Be there in a few."

"How far to this town?" Sebastian asked.

"About fifteen miles."

"Okay. Can you leave us one of those radios?"

Charlie stuck his hand out. "Take this one."

Sarah was back on the passenger side of the Mercedes, going through her pack. She retrieved extra magazines for her rifle and put them on the seat, then grabbed her duty vest from the back seat. She pulled it on and loaded the pouches with the magazines. Charlie went through a similar routine on his side of the vehicle.

"Here," he said to Marcus, holding his hand out. "You can block the road better with two vehicles." He dropped the key fob into Marcus's outstretched hand. "Just don't take off with it. I've grown fond of this thing."

Marcus nodded. "I'll take care of it."

They saw the rising dust cloud before Susan's vehicle came into view. There was no mistaking the massive rectangular chrome grille surrounded by a sea of white paint that was the 1972 International

Harvester Travelall. The three hundred forty-five cubic inch V8 engine roared when she hit the gas.

"I haven't seen one of those in thirty years," Robin said. "We used to have them for our duty vehicles in the PCSD."

"I think she got it from a police department," Sarah replied. "It has side-open doors on the back end. She said that was uncommon. Maybe it *is* one of your old ones."

Susan coasted to a stop next to the group and rolled the window down. "Are you coming, or what?"

"We're riding with you," Charlie said as he trotted to the rear door and pulled it open. "Make a hole, guys, let's go."

Sarah turned to Robin. "Thanks for helping. Sorry about before. I just couldn't help it."

"No worries, hon, I can appreciate the irony. I don't blame you, and in fact, I'd have probably done the same thing. Go on now, we'll be here holding down the fort."

Sarah trotted over to the white beast of a vehicle and climbed in the back. The door slammed shut with a loud *thud*, the engine roared to life, and they sped away to the south.

CHAPTER FIVE

ARBOLES, COLORADO. MAY 6

The approach to Arboles was blocked by a large, white school bus. Kamal could see no way around it. Three men stood in front of the bus, all holding rifles, and all of them had a pistol on their hip. To the right, thick scrub brush and a fence blocked any way around this roadblock. To the left was a dirt parking lot with a roadside shack that proclaimed *Deb's Good Eats* in front of a long, run-down building that bore no signage.

"Driver, please turn off your engine," the man in the middle shouted at them.

Kamal turned to his men. "Only Zand, Javad, and I talk to these men. Ario, you can say something in Spanish if pressed. You two, just pretend to be asleep."

The men all nodded their assent. Kamal turned off the engine and opened the door. As he stepped out of the cabin, the three men all pointed their rifles at the group of Iranians.

"Whoa, you can just stay there, mister!" the man in the middle shouted.

"My friend! I need to stretch my legs! We've been on the road for a long time now." Kamal smiled, his teeth gleaming bright white through the black of his massive beard. He stood to his full height, raising his arms over his head and faking a yawn, which turned into a real one before he was done.

The three men took in the massive form of Kamal. His arms, when fully extended, made his height from tip to toes almost two and a half meters. He weighed a hundred and thirty kilograms, and the beard made him look even more substantial. The effect on them was noticeable. They grew more nervous, the outer two men stepping to the side to put some distance between them, so they had more room to maneuver in case things went south.

In the car, Marduk laughed. "Look at them! Kamal is the size of two of them. They're going to piss themselves!"

"Quiet!" Javan admonished. "You're supposed to be asleep, remember?"

Kamal held his hands out to the side and spun in a circle. "You can see I am unarmed, my friends. We're just passing by, that's all."

"We have to make sure no one in your group is infected," Middleman said. "We don't want to risk bringing the disease into our town. I'm sure you understand."

"Yes, sure. There's no infection with us. You can

see." Kamal waved at the others to get out of the vehicle. Javad, Ario, and Zand climbed out, leaving Dariush and Marduk in the back. Kamal pointed to the approaching men. "You can see, they're healthy. No infection."

"Yeah, *my friend*, you're going to have to strip to your skivvies. I have to verify you've got no bites, scratches, or infected wounds." The man in the middle caressed the trigger guard on his rifle as he gave them instructions.

Kamal's smile faded. "My friend, it's not needed. We're in good health! You can see!"

"I can see you'd better start listening to us, *my friend*. We mean you no harm, but the longer you go without following instructions, the more I'm going to think something's not right about you. How about you toss me some ID?" He let the rifle hang from a sling and reached his hand out. His head rocked back, and a volley of gunshots peppered the three men standing guard. The three Iranians turned to see Dariush and Marduk hanging off of each side of the Toyota, smoke still rising from the mouths of the suppressors at the end of their rifle barrels.

"It was taking too long!" Marduk said. "We have a mission to complete, remember?"

A shot from the left hit the window on the door that Dariush hung on to. The window shattered, but the heavy tint held the pieces in place.

"There, on the roof!" Ario pointed to the dilapidated building behind Deb's Good Eats.

Dariush dropped from the door and ran to the rear of the SUV, getting some cover from the rear corner. A head peeked up from the building, and Marduk fired a shot, hitting the siding just next to the man.

"Dariush, cover me! I have an idea!" Marduk shouted. He tossed the rifle in the back of the SUV and sprinted to the school bus. Dariush fired a few shots, spacing them apart by a half second to keep the shooter pinned down.

The man on the roof sat up and fired several rapid shots in the vicinity of the Toyota, sending gravel into the air. Dariush heard one round strike the SUV.

Ahead, the bus's engine started. The air filled with the noise of grinding gears, and Dariush saw the shooter peek over the top of the roof. The Iranian fired a shot and was sure the man squealed. Hit or not, he dropped out of sight.

The bus started rolling backward, gaining speed as it moved through the dirt parking lot. Marduk kept his foot on the gas and rammed into the building right at the spot where the sniper had been shooting at them. Parts of the roof flew into the air, crashing back down in a rainstorm of debris. Gears ground again, and Marduk tried to pull forward, but the rear wheels were stuck inside the building. He let off the gas, and the bus rocked backward, crunching more wood and drywall in the process. He hit the gas, and the bus rocked forward, but again was stuck. He let it roll back again, and the moment it stopped he gassed it ahead. It pulled out of the structure this time, and the roof collapsed behind it.

The sniper fell with the wreckage of the building. He was still alive, but Dariush put two rounds into him, one in the chest and one in the head. Marduk trotted back to the group.

"That's how you take care of that," he declared, grinning broadly.

Kamal was unimpressed. "Do you think you could have made more noise? Do you even know the meaning of the word *discreet*? The whole town probably heard that. This is America, Marduk. Everyone has a gun. They're all on alert now."

Marduk scoffed. "Those four had guns. How did that work out for them?"

"Can we discuss this on the road? We're exposed out here," Ario said and climbed into the back of the Sequoia.

The rest of the group mounted the vehicle, and Kamal drove around the dead bodies on the road.

"Dariush, where to now?" he asked his navigator.

"It's just past the crossroad here. The next right. You'll see a run-down gas station. You'll turn right just before it and go left on the next road. It's a hundred and fifty meters on that road, then left and another two hundred meters. The house will be on the left."

"I got *right* at the gas station. Tell me the next turn when we get there."

Kamal followed the directions to the house. He drove past it, letting the group get a good look at it.

It was a one-story house built into a hillside, with a lower level walkout basement. An old orange pickup was parked on the side of the house nearest the road. A deck ran along the front of the house. A large propane tank sat behind it, almost in the thick pine trees that surrounded the structure on three sides.

"Did you all get a look?" Kamal asked. "I'm going to drive up this road a bit and turn around. I'll park back from the house a little. They won't be able to see us through these trees. We need a plan, quickly, before we run across more people."

"How do we know he's even in there?" Ario asked.

Marduk turned to Dariush. "Is there anything else in the information the tech team sent us? Anything that can be helpful?"

Dariush pulled out the tablet and turned it on. "His social media profile and mobile phone number... neither of those will do us any good. Oh—he has one vehicle registered to him. An orange pickup truck. That was at the house."

Marduk shook his head. "We last saw him in that Mercedes. And it's not here."

Behind them, a mud-covered Chevy S-10 pulled onto the narrow dirt road from an even tighter side road. Two middle-aged men sat inside the cab, and they turned to stare at the Toyota as they passed it.

The windows on the stolen Sequoia were tinted extra dark to block out the harsh Texas sun, so the men could not see inside, but they crept down the road with the passenger turning and staring back at them.

"Whatever we're going to do, we need to do it soon, or we lose the element of surprise," Kamal advised.

"We don't need every resident of this town trying to kill us. If we find the package, we still have to get out of here and get to a supply depot. Where's the closest one again?"

"Durango," Dariush said, checking his notes. "It's about... an hour from here. Unless we encounter trouble."

"I say we hit the house," Ario offered. "We're here, now. We don't have good intel, but we may not get another chance that will be this clean. We go in hard, front and rear entrances at the same time. Anyone that has a weapon, we drop them. If this Leonard kid isn't there, we grill anyone still alive to get his location and move on. In and out in five minutes."

Kamal nodded at Ario's plan. "Anyone object?" No one responded. "Okay, mic up, and let's go get this done."

CHAPTER SIX

ARBOLES, COLORADO. MAY 6

Susan slowed the big white SUV for the curve by Pinion Hills Motel Café, a local gas station, restaurant, and motel. Just past the café, they came across the first signs of trouble. She stopped and rolled her window down as they approached a trio of men standing off to the side of the road.

"Hey, Walter, what's happening? No one has been answering the radio," she said as she gestured at a tall, thin Indian man with a pair of long black braids hanging over his shoulders.

"Hiya, Susan. I'm not sure what's going on. The guys at the southern roadblock were killed, is one thing. Hollis radioed it in. He was rooftop snipin', said a pile of guys kilt Robert, Hollis Sr., and George. He quit responding. Turns out whoever kilt the first three kilt him too." He leaned over to see who else was in the SUV. "I don't know if they's connected, but some fellas busted up your house, Leonard. I'd be surprised if they wasn't linked. Your grandpa's hurt pretty bad. There's a pumper and medic up there now."

Susan pressed for more information, gesturing at the Chevy S-10 pickup lying on its side in the drainage ditch on the south side of the road. On the north, a Toyota Tercel was pushed off the road, almost into the trailer home. The driver's side corner of the hood was crunched in, and fluids were seeping into the dirt under the engine compartment. "What happened here?"

"Me and Carlos was heading to the marina to get some food when we saw a truck parked just up from the Naranjo, er, your place, Leonard. Texas plates, real dark, tinted windows. We was wondering what they's up to, and we came across Nelson over here. We told him what we seen, and he said it sounds fishy. Well, we decided to set up our own roadblock here, since unless they know their way around, they're coming out this way, and since they're from Texas, we figure they don't know their way around too well."

"Get to the punchline, Walter, we need to get up to see Dominic." Susan glanced at Leonard, who looked like he was about ready to jump out of the vehicle and run the half mile to his house.

"Oh, sure. So, we get the cars in position and get ready to interrogate these Texans, when there's a big explosion and fireball from back Naranjo's way. We debated what to do next, when we hear an engine roaring and that big black Toyota is barreling at us.

Even though we got the road stopped up, they ain't slowing down.

"Carlos fired a couple rounds from his Desert Eagle, and I got my rifle up and put a few rounds in the radiator and engine block, and through the windshield, but then they was on us, and we scattered. They hit the cars, sent 'em spinning, and kept right on driving.

"We cut over to the emergency channel and called in the pumper and the ambulance and ran on up to the Naranjos', er, Leonard's place and saw the fire. We got Dom out, but he's busted up pretty good. Now we're waiting on a wrecker to come flip the S-10 over so we can go get our food."

Susan put the Travelall in gear and hit the gas. "Thanks, Walter!" she called as they tore out and sped up the road.

After fishtailing around the right turn leading to Leonard's house, Susan slowed and pulled the SUV to the side to allow the fire truck to leave. Once it passed, she turned into the lower driveway. Everyone got out of the vehicle as quickly as possible, and Leonard sprinted to the ambulance, where his grandfather lay on a stretcher inside.

"How is he?" Leonard demanded. "What happened?"

A weak voice came from the stretcher. "Leonard?"

"Yeah, Grandpa?"

"Come up here."

Leonard looked at the EMT and received a nod, so he climbed in. "I'm right here, Grandpa."

Dominic Naranjo raised a bloodied hand and took Leonard's in his. His voice was raspier than usual, and the white sheet that covered him had blood soaking through in several places. "They were looking for you, Leonard. You have something they want. Whatever it is, they'll kill you to get it. Something you brought with you from El Paso. You need to hide, boy. They're going to be real pissed now. I got one and a half of them before they shot me down."

"Who were they, Grandpa? Were they from the Army?"

"No. Foreign men. They spoke to each other in a language I didn't know, but two of them spoke English to me." He stopped to cough, which racked him with pain throughout his wounded body.

"Take it easy, Grandpa. We'll figure out who this was, and we'll get them."

"NO!" The old man tried to shout. "Promise me you'll hide from them. You're not a soldier. Not like these men were."

"Son, we need to get him to surgery," the paramedic called out from the end of the ambulance.

Leonard nodded and stood to leave. "Grandpa, I'll come see you at the hospital! You keep fighting!" He climbed down, and grabbed the paramedic, lowering his voice to a whisper. "Is he going to make it?"

The medic pulled his arm free. "He's been shot. I don't think they hit anything vital, and we slowed most of the bleeding. He's tough and a fighter, and that makes a big difference, but ultimately it really depends on if the surgical hospital in Pagosa Springs is up and running. We can't take him to Durango because there's too many infected there. If Pagosa can take him, he's got a fighting chance. Now, we have to go. His odds get worse the longer we wait."

He climbed into the ambulance and shut the doors. A moment later, the driver pulled onto the road and turned right, back toward the main road.

Leonard barely had time to turn around before he was grabbed and wrapped in a bear hug. "Leonard, I'm so glad you're okay!" his dad said. "When I heard the call come in, I feared the worst. It was bad enough with Dad, but I couldn't stand to lose you too, not after you just got back from El Paso!"

Leonard hugged his dad back then wiggled free. "Dad, tell us what happened. Grandpa said these guys were looking for *me*?"

Cedric Naranjo looked at all the faces gathered around them. "I'll tell you what your Granddad told me. He was asleep in his easy chair, when the dog started barking and woke him up. He heard it yelp, so he got up to see what was going on. Before he got to the door, he saw shadows outside then the front and back doors were kicked in at the same time. Then—these are his words—a bunch of men that looked like Arabs rushed in at him. He swung his Bowie knife at one of them and cut off three of his fingers and part of his hand, and when that one fell down, he stuck the next one in the chest. He said they must have been wearing body armor because he didn't get any penetration. He got one more good swipe in, caught him across the neck. That one bled out in the doorway.

"After that, it was all them. The guys at the front door shot him a couple times, then they dragged him to the living room and started to question him." He turned and faced Leonard directly. "He said they asked about you, specifically, boy. By name. Said you took something from the medical center in El Paso. What are they talking about?"

"I don't know! I was there for weeks, but I don't know what they could want from me. I took some surgical masks...." He looked over at Lori. "I took a nurse. I don't know what else they could want."

"Well, whatever it was, it was worth trying to kill your grandfather, and killing Franklin and his dogs."

"What! Gramps didn't say anyone was killed!"

"Apparently Franklin saw these guys heading through the trees with their weapons, and he came over with his hunting dogs. Don't know if he got any of them. He's dead just inside the back door, and three of his dogs are dead."

"What about their bodies? Any clues on them? Identifying marks, name, rank?" Charlie asked with no shortage of sarcasm.

"They took their dead. Left nothing behind but blood, three fingers, and shell casings—5.56 mm and .40."

"And the fire?" This question came from Sarah.

"They blew the propane tank. Explosives, probably."

The group fell silent, the gravity of the situation settling in on them.

"Were they from the Army?" Sarah asked. "We did leave without telling anyone. Maybe they're looking for *us,* not something we took."

Charlie shook his head. "Nah. They're not going to waste the effort coming after a few civilians. And they wouldn't shoot up Leonard's house and murder people."

"Besides, Gramps said they spoke a different language to each other, but English to him. So, they may not even be from here."

"Maybe they're from Mexico?" Lori posited.

"No, Dad speaks Spanish," Cedric said. "This was something else. He said it sounded Middle Eastern, but other than hearing bad guys talk in movies, he wouldn't know."

"What would Middle Eastern people be doing in Colorado, during the world's worst disease outbreak, wanting something that Leonard took from the hospital?" Charlie asked, more to himself than anyone else.

Sarah's face changed, lighting up like she just thought of the cure for cancer. "This was terrorism."

It was Cedric's turn to ask a question. "What was? This attack?"

"No, the outbreak. Think about it. It hit major places all at once... Denver, Washington, Chicago... all at the same time. It's taken out our entire human infrastructure but has left the physical infrastructure alone."

"Not true. There have been riots and plane crashes, all manner of destructive things have happened," Cedric countered.

"Yeah, but that's all localized. It's not like what would happen if another country attacked us. No cities have been bombed. Think about it. This is just like what terrorists would do. Random killing of millions of people would really get them off."

"The logistical planning for something like that is beyond what any nation is capable of, with the possible exception of Russia, or maybe China. It's too big to be Al-Qaeda or even ISIS. And last I heard, this epidemic was global. Not just limited to our shores."

"Who cares if it kills everyone on the planet, as long as it kills us, right? Isn't that how they think? I once heard that the mullahs in Iran would trade ninety million dead Iranians if it meant wiping Israel off the map. Would it be such a stretch for them to do this? I mean, they wouldn't even need weapons, just a few sick people plopped in the middle of the right cities, right?" She thought about the planning, the science behind infecting a person and rendering them a mindless savage within twelve hours. Could someone pull that off without the governments of the West knowing about it? "I don't know, maybe you're right," she conceded. "The mention of foreigners just got me thinking."

"I'm sure we'd all like to have someone to point the finger at, but in this case, it's just nature. Someone came in contact with something in a rainforest somewhere, or from the tundra that melting glaciers exposed, something that humans haven't encountered for eons, and are no longer immune to. That's what smallpox did to the indigenous peoples of North and South America when the Spanish came over. With no natural immunity, it just burns through the population like a wildfire."

"What do we do now?" Charlie asked.

"We can't stay here, right?" Leonard said, more as a statement than a question.

"Not in this house, that's for sure," Cedric answered. "We need to bury Franklin's dogs and get his body someplace. Then I need to get to Pagosa Springs and check on Dad."

"I'm going to P. Springs too," Leonard asserted.

"No, son. Think. If these guys, whoever they are, were smart enough to track you down in Arboles all the way from El Paso, don't you think they'll check out the hospital?"

"How would they even know where he is?"

"I'm assuming they're monitoring the radio transmissions. Which reminds me, stay off the radios unless it's an emergency."

"Let's spend the night up on Chimney Rock again," Aaron suggested. "That's going to be as safe as anywhere, right? Unless they know where to look, they'll never see us up there, and we'll see them coming from a mile away."

"Okay, that's sounds good to me. We need a night watch up there anyway. But be careful—no lights after dark, low fires in the kivas only." Cedric sighed and looked toward the house.

"Cedric, why don't you let us take care of the dogs and your friend," Sarah offered. "We'll bury them at his place. Leonard will show us where it is. You can go check on your dad."

He considered it for a moment. "Okay, sure. But you guys get out of here and up to Chimney Rock before dark. I mean even before dusk. No headlights. You hear me?"

"Yeah, we hear you," Charlie said.

Cedric grabbed Leonard and gave him a fierce hug. He pointed at Susan, his subordinate officer on the SUPD. "You take care of them, Susan. You hear me? This situation is serious."

"Yes, sir."

He walked over to his black SUPD SUV and climbed in. He started the engine, looking at the group for a moment before putting it in gear and driving off to check on Dominic's condition.

"Well, we got graves to dig," Aaron said. "Fun times."

"Let's just get it done," Charlie said. "I'd like to get out of here before those guys regroup and come back."

With that thought in their heads, the group hustled about their work then piled into Susan's white Travelall and headed back toward Chimney Rock.

THEY REACHED the entrance to the monument and found Robin and her crew still blocking the road. A half dozen dead infected littered the roadway, anywhere from fifty to one hundred yards ahead of the vehicles.

"It's been pretty active here," Robin said. "They're probably coming from Durango, and now they're headed toward Pagosa Springs. We had an ambulance come through a little while ago, and a reservation cop a little while later, and we haven't seen any infected since then."

"That's good, I guess," Leonard responded. "Except it means they're following Grandpa and Dad into P. Springs."

"Your dad and grandpa?" Sebastian asked.

Leonard looked at Sebastian and was about to say something, but Sarah preempted him.

"Let's get back to the top of the mesa and set up for the night. We can make all the introductions up there."

They caravanned to the upper parking lot, with Susan leading the way in the old International, Charlie driving the Mercedes, and Robin behind the wheel of the big Chevy. Everyone took their packs and supplies and ferried them to the two kivas on the mesa. Susan assigned watch shifts, including Robin and her crew in the rotation. Susan volunteered for the first watch and took Sebastian and Shane with her. Robin and Marcus went back to the Chevy to get more supplies.

Down inside the kiva, Aaron got the fire going and put on a pot of water for coffee.

Around the fire, most of the group was going through their bags, taking the opportunity to reorganize things. Charlie got out a can of soup and partially opened the lid, then set it in the fire. The label burned off, and while the others pulled food from their packs, the smell of the soup heating up made them realize they were getting hungry.

Leonard was digging through his bag and paused. He looked around and saw Sarah. She glanced up, saw him looking at her, and gave him a smile. He nodded his head, indicating he wanted her to come over. She gave him the "one-minute" signal and zipped her bag shut.

Walking over to him, she said, "What is it, Leonard?"

He pulled a padded envelope from his pack.

"I think I know what those guys were after."

CHAPTER SEVEN

CHIMNEY ROCK, COLORADO. MAY 6

"What the fuck, Leonard? You're just now mentioning that you took this?" Sarah stared at him, incredulous.

"I forgot about it until they said something back at the house, and I didn't want to mention it to Dad. He'd be in more danger, and also he'd be pissed at me."

"Well, yeah, he'd be pissed. What's the deal? Why'd you grab it?"

"It was right after you stole my badge and sent me down to the first floor on the elevator at Beaumont. I couldn't get back to you without my identification, so I posted up in the corner of the lobby to wait for you.

"Like, maybe a minute later, Doctor Sanjay came down to the front desk and handed off this package to the guard at the desk. She stuck it in the bin he had set up for courier pickup. I thought it was weird that he would do that when everything was going to shit. Like, were couriers really still doing pickups?

"Then these guys from Homeland Security came in and got all over the guard—told her they were taking over, that she was relieved and should leave. It took her maybe two seconds to get her stuff and go. I figured they were going to throw me out, too, but they never even saw me. So, I waited until they were out of sight, and I went over to check it out.

"I was worried the Homeland guys were going to come back, and after what we learned about Sanjay, I wanted to know what he was up to. So, I left with the package. I got in the ambulance and was going to go back to the Fort when I saw Charlie and Lori in the Mercedes, and you know the rest."

"I remember that," Lori said. "I saw you put that envelope in your pack when we got in the trailer, but I forgot all about it."

"So, what's in it?" Sarah asked.

Leonard looked at the envelope for a second. "I don't know."

Charlie's voice startled them. "Well, it's important enough for someone to send a hit squad after it. Don't you think we should open it up and see what it is?"

"Jesus, Charlie, I didn't hear you walk over here!"

"Easy, Sarah. I wasn't trying to be sneaky or anything. And I'm serious, it must be significant for someone to go to all this trouble in the middle of all this."

"Well," Leonard said, "I guess there's only one way to find out." He turned the envelope over and found the little tab with the red ribbon attached to it, and he pulled it, ripping it open.

He reached inside the envelope and pulled out a stack of papers at least forty sheets thick. He flipped through them. The writing was in a language he didn't know. Several graphs were depicting chemical equations, a few pictures of bite wounds, both infected and non-infected, and tables with what looked like people's names. One section was under a header in English that read RAMMACHER and another that read WASHBURN.

"It looks like files about the disease," Leonard said. "But most of the writing is in some sort of code. I thought it was Chinese, but it's got all these other weird symbols."

Charlie held out his hand. "Let me see it."

Leonard handed it over to Charlie, who flipped through a few pages.

"It's Korean," he said.

Leonard looked at him with a dubious expression on his face. "*You* read Korean?"

"No, but see these ovals? That's unique to Korean. Japanese has more letters with curves in them, Chinese has neither."

"But you can't read it?" Sarah asked as she flipped through the pages.

"No, unfortunately, so that doesn't help us."

"Yeah, that's too bad," she replied, "Because I really want to know what the fuck this part says." She tapped on the section under the heading WASHBURN.

Charlie nodded. "Yeah, me too."

Leonard peeked inside the envelope. "Hey! There's something else in here!"

He stuck his hand in, reaching all the way to the bottom, and retrieved a small, rectangular object.

"What is that?" Aaron asked. This was the first time they realized that he had wandered over to their group.

Leonard held the small plastic case up in between two fingers. "It's an SD card."

Sarah made a sour face. "Again, that does us no good without something to read it with."

"Wait, I have a laptop in my other bag in the Mercedes," Lori said. She grabbed Leonard's hand. "Will you come with me to get it?"

"Of course!" Leonard turned to Charlie and Sarah. "We'll be right back."

The pair got up and climbed out of the kiva, then headed for the parking lot.

Aaron went to the fire and called out to the rest of the group. "Who wants coffee? Also, Mr. Washburn, your soup is boiling."

They all made their way to the fire.

"Coffee'd be nice, Aaron, thanks," Charlie said.

Sarah nodded. "Make that two."

Charlie used a pair of pliers to retrieve the can from the edge of the fire. He set it between his feet and pulled the lid the rest of the way off with the pliers, then used them to pour half of the "thick and hearty" broad-noodle soup into a tin cup he retrieved from his pack. He passed the cup and a camper's spork to Sarah.

With the upper half of the can empty, the temperature quickly dropped enough for Charlie to pick it up with his bare hands. He held it out, offering it to Aaron, who declined, so he pulled another spork out of his meal kit and began eating.

Aaron passed cups of coffee to the others, emptied the rest into a thermos, then put more water in the pot and set it back on the fire so he could prepare a package of dehydrated stew.

The trio had just finished their separate meals, when Leonard and Lori returned with her laptop. While she booted it, Aaron passed a cup of coffee to her.

"Okay, it's ready. Does someone else want to drive?" she asked, holding the laptop out.

"Sure," Sarah replied, taking it from the younger woman. "Memory card?" she said, holding out her hand. After Leonard passed the plastic case to her, she flipped the locking tab open and retrieved the small memory card. Then she popped it in the slot and clicked on the file explorer.

"Okay," she said. "There are some folders in here named with more of that Korean writing." She clicked and opened one, then opened a document. "More of the same. Dammit."

She closed the documents and folders. "Here's one labeled in English. 'Depots.' It's a PDF file," she said, and double clicked it.

The screen displayed a map of the United States, with dozens of dots of different colors all across the country. She zoomed in on the file and scrolled to their part of the country.

"Look at this. There's a blue dot in Durango."

"What does blue mean?" Lori asked.

"I don't know. Maybe there's a legend." Sarah scrolled down and found a key in the bottom left corner. "Here, there's a series of icons next to the dots. Blue has a Wi-Fi symbol, what looks like bullets, a hamburger with a glass, and a bed. What the fuck?"

"We know Sanjay was sending this to people who speak Korean," Leonard said. "Gramps told me the people who attacked him were big guys, a couple of them with huge thick beards. That doesn't sound like Koreans."

"So?" Sarah asked.

"So, if you have people from different countries, speaking different languages, you either have multiple translations, or you talk with pictures." He waved his hand, gesturing to the area around them. "People have done that for thousands of years. Petroglyphs are found worldwide. Emojis and icons are just modern forms of that."

"Okay, so in Durango they have Wi-Fi," Sarah started. "So did every burger joint and cheap motel before the outbreak. What's the big deal?"

"Maybe it's not just Wi-Fi; maybe it means Internet access in general," Aaron said. "Maybe they have their own connections or something. Ours are down."

"It might just mean communication in general.

And the bullets mean ammunition," Charlie offered. "That's obvious. The hamburger and glass mean food, the bed means... beds? What are some of the other icons?"

Sarah looked through the legend. "A fuel pump, a helicopter, and—Jesus—a fucking tank."

"These are supply depots," Charlie said. "Zoom out." Sarah zoomed the map out, and Charlie continued. "So it looks like all of them have ammo, beds, food... the red ones have fuel. Blue has Wi-Fi, or Internet, whatever, and vehicles. Green has everything, including helicopters and... what is that? Artillery? Armored vehicles?"

"Why would they have all of these places?" Sarah asked. "It doesn't make any sense to me! When we were talking to Leonard's dad before, I said this was terrorism, but now this seems far more complex than that. Sanjay was experimenting on Jack with this disease. He's sending information to people who read Korean—I think that narrows it down to the North Koreans, right?—with information about Jack and that guy Ram, and a file with a map to dozens of supply depots. Supplies for who?"

"Big bearded foreign guys who shoot up houses on the Ute Reservation," Leonard said.

"It doesn't make any sense," Sarah replied.

"It does if the outbreak was intentional," Lori added. "Go back to your assumption about this being terrorism and think about it from that perspective. The disease is released on purpose. It takes out most of the population, and those who are left, us, are scrambling for survival. Disorganized. The infrastructure is crumbling. I mean, around here, we're pretty isolated, right? So, you still have police, fire trucks, ambulances. El Paso has none of that anymore. It's abandoned, and the survivors are locked inside Fort Bliss. In the bigger cities, it's probably every man for himself."

"I'm still not connecting the dots," Sarah said. "This seems far too organized. Terrorism is stupid. They do pointless things with no purpose other than to hurt us."

"No, I think I see what she's getting at," Charlie jumped in. "Attacking America head-on would be suicide. Even if you sent a billion Chinamen here, we'd just stack the bodies. Americans have three hundred million guns and trillions of rounds of ammunition. We know the terrain. We have the best equipped and most well-trained military on the planet. But if you take out the bulk of the population, there's no one around to shoot those guns."

"Why wouldn't they just nuke us?" Sarah asked. "Why the complex conspiracy theory tactics?"

"Because we'd just nuke them back. They want the country, but if we kill all their people in the process, they gain nothing."

Lori nodded. "Right. And doing it this way, that well-trained military is scattered around the globe, also dealing with this infection among its ranks. The power grids are failing, so the fresh water supply is cut off. Starvation is going to be a problem, secondary diseases due to lack of sanitation will kick in. They've not only taken out most of the population, but they've also left everything else in disarray. It makes it a lot easier to invade."

"You think this is about an *invasion*?" Sarah asked, her tone belying her disbelief.

"Not just invasion. Colonization," Charlie said. "The more we talk about it, the more it makes sense that's what this is leading up to. Hell, there's parts of the country they could come into and take over without even firing a shot. Especially if they do it under the guise of international aid. The stores are empty, half the town, your family—your *kids*—are starving, and someone comes in with food? People would welcome them. And with these depots? They already have resupply in place. They don't have to deal with the logistics of bringing it here. If that's what this is, it has to have been in motion for a long time."

Charlie's words hung in the air.

Leonard finally broke the silence. "We might be in over our heads here."

Sarah turned the laptop screen around so everyone could see the map covered with dozens of different colored dots. "This certainly seems to have gotten a lot bigger than it was before we opened that package."

"That's a fact," Charlie said. "We need to figure out what our next steps are."

Sarah tapped the blue dot near Durango. "We're only an hour away, right? And the not-Korean-speaking hit squad is looking for us in Arboles, trying to find documents written in Korean and sent by... what was Sanjay? Indian? Pakistani? Fuck, everyone who hates us may have a hand in this thing. I say we check this depot out tomorrow, get away from the folks in this area. Keep them safe—well, safe-*ish*."

"It's risky. Lots of infected up that way." Charlie grimaced at the thought of fighting more of the unfortunate creatures.

"We'll have to deal with them sooner or later if we stick around here."

Leonard bristled at the comment. "*If* you stick around? Where are you going to go? I thought we were like, a team, or something."

"We are," Sarah reassured him, "but we can't hide out here forever." She shook the papers at everyone. "This stuff has changed the game. We have to translate this from Korean. If they have Internet access there, we can use that. Plus, if they have food, weapons... I bet it's secure too. Maybe we can get a decent night's sleep. I say we at least check it out."

"I'm in," Aaron said from the other side of the fire.

"Okay, that's two. Leonard?"

"Sure. Whatever."

"I'll go where Leonard goes," Lori said.

Sarah smiled. "That's four. Charlie?"

"Yeah, fuck it. Living is overrated these days, anyway."

"Oh, come on, it's not as bad as all that," a woman's voice said from behind them.

They all swiveled their heads to see Robin and

Marcus walking to the edge of the kiva, carrying a cooler between them.

"What?" Robin asked. "Are we interrupting something?"

Sarah gave them the condensed, ninety-second version of what they'd found in the package, and what their plans for the morning were.

"Sebastian is going to the medical center in Pagosa Springs with Susan tomorrow. He said he wants to help them secure the building." She looked at Marcus. "What do you think?"

Marcus quickly agreed. "Doing something with a purpose sounds so much better than staring at the road for hours at a checkpoint. I'm down."

"Count us both in," Robin said.

Sarah smiled. "That makes seven."

"Lucky number," Charlie remarked.

"You had to say something, didn't you?" Sarah said, with equal parts sarcasm and superstition.

Robin opened the cooler and started passing around cans of beer. "We packed 'em in snow from up in the real mountains," she said. "Might be the last cold beers we get for a while."

Marcus wrestled a plastic bag from the cooler. "Anyone want some venison? This is the last of a deer we harvested a couple of weeks ago."

"The last feast," Charlie said. "For tomorrow, we ride!"

CHAPTER EIGHT

Javad murmured in his groggy, semi-conscious state. The bandage was soaked with blood, and he was sweating, fighting off infection already.

"We need real medical help," Zand said to Kamal. "Half his hand is gone. He's got bones exposed. I think I've got the worst of the bleeding stopped, but I think it's getting infected, and we don't have the right antibiotics to fight it. Not here. Maybe in Albuquerque."

Kamal nodded. "Okay. Thank you, Zand. You've done your best with him."

He looked over the rest of the team. Dariush was cleaning his rifle. Marduk sat in front of a makeshift table, upon which a figure lay, shrouded in a blanket. Ario, his younger brother, rested under the improvised shroud, cold and pale after he bled to death because of that old Indian bastard.

That old man was quick with that knife, Kamal thought. As pissed as he was, he admired the old man's skill. He must have been a real warrior in a different time.

It was all such a waste. They lost Ario, Javad was out of commission, and they gained no information other than Leonard Naranjo wasn't there. Kamal cursed himself. The smart thing would have been to wait for better intel. He *knew better* than to go in blind like that. He was just in a rush to meet the team in Albuquerque and start to fight for real and be done with this clandestine nonsense.

He let out a heavy sigh. It was time to check in with Command. Kamal looked around the old barn for a spot where he could get some degree of privacy, but there really wasn't one.

They had spotted the rundown barn on the way into town. It looked like there had been a coat of paint on it at one time, but it had long since been burned away by the southern Colorado sun and decades of disuse. When things went sideways in town, Kamal had this barn in his mind as they fled. They veered off the road, and Dariush jumped out of the moving vehicle and used his tomahawk to whack a branch off the back of a pine tree. He used it to wipe out the tracks the Toyota had made on the dirt entrance to the barn. He did his best to reverse the bend of the grasses and weeds the truck drove over on its way into the barn.

The ruse had worked, at least for the time being. Several vehicles drove past them at high rates of speed, no doubt looking for them, but none of them seemed to pay the collapsing barn a second thought.

Kamal sighed again. He powered on the satellite phone and dialed the number for Command. It seemed like it took forever for the man on the other end to answer the call.

"Hamid."

"It's Kamal."

Hamid's tone lightened. *"Ah, Kamal! I need your good news."* His voice grew more hushed like he was trying to keep others from hearing him. *"Our NorKo brethren have been routed by Americans soldiers in Phoenix. We have to send in our ground troops earlier than we wanted. If you have the package, we need you to get to Phoenix and link up with Colonel Shah."*

"That's going to be a problem, sir. We haven't secured the package. The entire town here is armed, it seems. We had to engage with the locals. We've killed five, maybe six of them, but we lost Ario and Javad is wounded."

The silence that followed made Kamal's hair stand up on his neck. He *hated* dealing with these types of people. They were unstable, prone to violent mood swings, and often had people killed on a whim. He liked the anonymity of combat, the rush of the kill-or-be-killed situations. Politics and espionage were games he tried to stay away from.

Hamid finally spoke. *"Kamal, I cannot stress to you enough the importance of finding that package. If you let it get away, I will not be safe here. I do not want to end up like Nampoo Yi, with my head in a potted plant and my body dismembered and fed to Fearless Leader's dogs! If that happens, Kamal, my last act will be to sign your death warrant. Do you understand?"*

"Of course, Hamid. We will find the package, you have my word on that."

"So far, your word hasn't been worth much." Hamid paused, and his tone changed again. *"So, it's true what they say about the Americans? There's a rifle behind every blade of grass?"*

"Yes, sir. Well, at least from what we've seen. Their skill levels aren't that impressive, but they know the area and have the numbers. It's not going to be easy to take down the remaining population."

"You sound like you admire them."

Kamal thought about the old man at the house, his silver hair long and in braids on either side of his head, and the speed with which he drew that huge knife and took off half of Javad's hand in one motion, then stabbed at Ario and slashed his throat, all before Kamal could get a shot off. Not a movement was wasted. "It's not admiration, Hamid. I respect them. This is their land, and they're going to fight to keep it. We would do the same. If you don't respect that, you will underestimate them, and that, I think, would be dangerous." *I know it's dangerous,* he thought. *Ario and Javad know that now, too.*

"I suppose that's wise, Kamal. I will pass that on to Colonel Shah. Now, get the package, and then get to Phoenix. Next report same time tomorrow."

The call ended. Kamal powered the phone off then walked back to the Toyota and put it back in his pack.

"What did they say?" Marduk asked.

"Get the package, or they'll have us killed," Kamal answered.

"What did they say about Ario?"

"Nothing."

"But you told them he was dead, right?"

"Of course. Hamid did not address it other than to say if we fail, we're all dead."

"Selfish pricks."

Kamal studied Marduk's face. He didn't look sad or angry. He looked empty like there was nothing left of his human emotions. "Marduk, you know we're not going to be able to take Ario with us, right?"

"I know. We can bury him here. We'll come back for him and give him a proper burial in New Persia. But for now, we need to keep him safe from the wolves and lions that roam the American wilderness."

"Don't forget the bears," Dariush added.

Kamal huffed. "I think you two have watched too many movies. There are no wolves or lions or bears around here. That's Montana and Wyoming."

"I'd like to see a bear," Dariush said.

"Be careful what you wish for," Marduk said, gloom weighing heavy in his voice. "Let's get the hole dug against the back wall. Then we can go kill these Americans."

"We'll stay overnight here," Kamal advised. "We'll leave once it's light enough we don't need to use lights.

We all need the rest, and then, yes, we'll go kill the Americans."

THE TWILIGHT of morning began filtering through the wide cracks in the barn around six thirty. Zand started his small stove and began heating water for tea, and to hydrate their morning meals.

Marduk sat alone and silent in the rear of the barn, mourning before the mound that marked where his brother, Ario, was buried.

Dariush nodded toward Marduk. "You think he'll be okay for today?" he asked Kamal in a whisper. Zand's glance at him signaled he wasn't as quiet as he had thought.

"I'll be fine," Marduk said without turning around. "You worry about your job. I'll worry about mine."

Kamal checked on Javad. He was still unconscious, with blood seeping through the bandage on his hand, and his head was damp with sweat. The temperature had dropped into the negative overnight, so even with a mylar blanket over him, Javad shouldn't have been sweating that badly. This was confirmation the man was fighting an infection.

Zand passed around glasses of mint tea, and a few minutes later, a scramble consisting of reconstituted eggs and vegetables. After everyone had eaten their fill, Zand cleaned his cookware and buried the trash in a hole he had dug for the purpose.

Kamal ordered everyone to check their weapons and get their gear organized. Then with ten minutes until sunrise, the Toyota backed out of the barn and pulled onto the highway, aiming for Durango.

Thirty seconds after it disappeared, the black SUV that had been following the crew since their departure from El Paso emerged from a thicket of scrub brush and pulled onto the road, keeping its distance.

CHAPTER NINE

S arah stared at the keypad next to the door. Neither the entrance nor the garage door a few feet down had any visible lock they could try to pick, not that any of them knew how to pick a lock. The building was set into the hillside, so there was no back entrance to check.

Leonard was reviewing the documentation from the package for any sign of an access code to open the door but could not find one.

"There has to be a master code," Charlie groused. "If these are for an occupying force, they'd need something that any of them would know."

"What about the latitude and longitude? Each location on this map has those listed." Leonard turned the laptop around for Charlie to see.

"Maybe. Read them off to me. Let's try latitude first. And let's hurry. More of our friends are coming."

Leonard glanced up the road, toward the city of

Durango. A dozen of the infected lay scattered around, blood running toward the gutter from their fresh wounds. Leonard read the coordinates while Charlie entered them. Then the old man pressed the green button under the numeric keys. Nothing happened.

"Let's try longitude."

Again, Leonard read the numbers and Charlie punched them in. Nothing.

Sarah pulled her cell phone out of her bag. Charlie teased her about keeping it charged, but she wanted to have it available in case Internet service returned, or the cell networks came back online. Besides, she liked to have music in the car, and the radio stations had all gone silent. "Try 7-2-6-5-2-9."

Charlie raised an eyebrow at her.

"Just try it," she ordered.

Charlie punched in the six digits and pressed the green button. The lock clicked, the motor whirred, and he pulled the door open. "How did you sort that out?

She smiled. "It's 'Sanjay' on a phone's keypad. I figured if he's involved, he'd have a backdoor way to save his skin. I was right."

"Well, that was some good thinking! Let's check this place out."

Motion sensors turned on LED strips in the ceiling as they entered the building. The interior of the building was quiet, with no signs of life showing themselves. Past the entryway, a pair of hallways went left and right. Straight ahead, the main hall widened, and each side had long rows of big lockers with benches in front of them. Two more pairs of perpendicular halls were visible, with a third one in the distance just on the left side.

"We go by twos. Leonard with me, Robin with Sarah. The rest of you get our bags from the cars and watch the entry," Charlie directed. He turned to Robin and Sarah. "You two check the rooms to the left; we'll go right. Don't advance down the hall without us."

Charlie and Leonard went down the right hallway with their rifles at the low ready position. Ahead, they faced a door on both the left and right sides, and one straight ahead at the end of the hall, probably thirty feet ahead. They moved forward and found the side doors to be men's and women's bathrooms. A quick check revealed them both to be empty. The men's room was twice the size of the women's, but each had a full complement of what one would expect—toilet stalls, sinks, showers.

They returned to the hallway and moved to the door at the far end. Leonard turned the handle as Charlie readied his rifle to go in. The door flung wide, and Charlie burst in, the lights activating as he did so. Leonard was close behind him, dropping a water bottle to keep the door from closing all the way.

The room was a garage, with a massive gray van in the bay. The word SPORTMASTER was emblazoned on the side.

"We'll come back and check that thing out once we clear the rest of the depot," Charlie said.

They walked around the van to inspect the rest of

95

the garage. The far wall had a floor-to-ceiling array of cabinets stocked with parts. Hoses, belts, various engine components like alternators and fuel pumps, quarts of oil, antifreeze, wiper fluid, even tires, filled the spaces. In the rear corner sat a huge air compressor that could drive a lift under the van, as well as offering connections to hoses for a variety of air tools.

They walked around the rear of the van and returned to the side of the garage that had the door into the building. This side of the garage had a long workbench and cabinets on the wall. Charlie opened the first one and saw a range of air and electric tools. At the end of the workbench, near the door, was a massive rollaway tool chest. He pulled a few drawers open and saw screwdrivers, wrenches, ratchets, and sockets, everything arranged in neat rows. He whistled.

"They have a nice setup here. Enough to keep a vehicle running for a long time."

Leonard nodded. "It's like a mini service station. These guys really are well prepared."

They turned back to the building entrance and headed in to meet up with the two women checking the opposite side of the supply depot.

Sarah and Robin advanced down the left-hand hallway. It opened into a huge kitchen. A stove with eight burners, two grill tops, two ovens, and a prep station on either side lined one entire wall. Overhead cabinets were stocked with bowls and plates, with glasses on the side nearest the sink and refrigerator.

Other cabinets held mixing bowls, a large power mixer, a hand-held mixer, and other food prep supplies.

The center of the room housed three large tables with ten chairs at each one. More chairs were stacked in the corner, to the left of the entrance.

Robin walked over to the industrial-sized fridge and opened it. "Water bottles, sports drinks—ooh," she exclaimed and reached inside. She grabbed a couple cans and tossed one to Sarah. "I could have had a V8!" She cracked the can open and chugged the liquid inside. "Oh, man, is that good." She grabbed another and slid it into the pouch on the back of her vest.

Sarah broke the seal on her can and took a sip. She'd never been a fan of the blended vegetable juice, but Robin was right; it tasted like something sent from Heaven. Sarah gave in and downed the entire can. She grabbed her rifle from its slung position and gestured to a doorway in the middle of the right-hand wall. "Come on, let's check it out."

They proceeded cautiously into what turned out to be a huge pantry. Shelf after shelf was filled with canned foods, dehydrated meals, dried fruit, powdered milk and eggs, beans, rice... on and on for more than thirty feet. Robin whistled as she walked up and down the aisles of shelving units.

"Holy shit, this is enough food for..."

"For a small army?" Sarah interrupted.

"Yeah. Way to bring me back to reality."

The wall to the right of the entry housed another doorway. Sarah stepped toward it and looked out. She saw Charlie and Leonard peeking into the hallway leading to the kitchen. She gave them a whippoorwill's whistle, and the pair turned, looking her way, rifles coming up.

"Whoa, guys, it's us!"

"Dammit, Sarah, I said not to move on without us!" Charlie scolded as he moved toward her.

"Sorry, this room is attached to the kitchen."

"Kitchen?" Leonard asked.

"Yeah, and this is the pantry. We scored big time."

"Great," Charlie said. "Let's finish this search and get everything inside. Let's just stick together on the rest of these."

Across the hall was the women's dormitory. It held six bunk beds, a dozen footlockers, a row of makeup mirrors, and cabinets with towels, bedding, and pillows. Another cabinet held an assortment of generic women's clothing in various sizes. A pair of stackable washer/dryer combinations occupied a spot at the end of the storage.

Robin was digging through the clothes and held up a gray hooded sweatshirt to gauge the size. "Don't mind if I do! The one I have is getting a little ripe!"

"Come on," Charlie grumbled. "Clear the building now, shop later."

She put the sweatshirt down and followed the group out of the room.

The next doorway on the left led into an armory. A long rack held a few dozen rifles, mostly some variant of the AR platform, but a few scoped rifles and a few shotguns were mixed in. A pegboard above the long guns held dozens of handguns. Most were semi-automatic pistols, but there were also a few revolvers. A bank of cabinets on the back wall had a variety of slings and holsters, tactical vests and armor plates, and hundreds of magazines for both the rifles and pistols. A lower set of cabinets held thousands of rounds of ammunition. Along the top of the cabinets were cases holding an assortment of knives and tomahawks.

"I'm *definitely* coming back and shopping in this room," Robin said, excitement seeping from her voice.

"Yeah, no kidding!" Leonard seconded. "I see some stuff I can for sure use."

"Let's keep moving," Charlie prodded.

They crossed the hall and found the men's dormitory, equipped similar to the women's, except three times the size. In the rear corner, opposite the entryway, another door beckoned them. Behind this one, they found the depot's mechanical room, housing a pair of furnaces and two boilers to supply hot water.

"I wonder what the fuel is," Charlie mused.

"We can solve that later," Robin teased. "We have one more room to check."

This made Charlie smile. "By all means, lead the way."

The last doorway on the left led to a communications center. Several computer monitors sat on a long countertop at the back of the room. Adjacent to the door was a radio communications console. Charlie whistled at the different boards with their red and green lights, the dials on the two separate Motorola tuners, the screen in the center of the unit.

"Holy cow, this puts my radio setup to shame," he said.

"Hey, are we good?" Aaron shouted from the entryway.

"Yeah!" Charlie called back. "Bring everything back here!"

The foursome joined the rest of the group at the front of the depot, where everyone collected their bags and the boxes of meager supplies and brought them inside.

The mood of the group improved at the prospect of hot showers and clean clothes. Once they verified that the boilers were indeed putting out hot water, they set the order for showers. The guys all agreed to let the women go first, so Sarah, Lori, and Robin went to the women's room and got the showers steaming.

While the gals were showering, Marcus and Aaron set to work cooking up some food as Charlie, Leonard, and Shane started a couple loads of laundry.

After the women were done with their showers, they changed into clothes they got from the cabinets and started laundry of their own. The guys rotated into the showers and kept food going in the kitchen. After a couple hours, everyone was clean, fed, and dressed in fresh, dry clothes.

Charlie was in the communications room with Leonard, fiddling with the radio, when a light over the door turned from green to red. The change was enough to catch both of their eyes.

"I never noticed that before. What does that mean?" Leonard wondered aloud.

Screams from the front of the bunker told them it meant nothing good. They grabbed their rifles and ran into the hallway, where they found a giant bearded man in the entryway, a pistol placed against Shane's head.

"Drop your weapons or boy dies!" the man shouted, his voice thick with an accent.

Charlie and Leonard hesitated. The man pulled the trigger, a loud *pop!* filling the hallway as Shane's head rocked to the side, and his body crumpled to the ground.

The man called out in a foreign language, and another man shoved Sarah from the kitchen, into the hallway. The big man put the gun to her head. "Drop weapons or woman dies!" he commanded.

This time the pair dropped their rifles to the tile.

"Hands up and move forward!"

They raised their hands and began walking toward the front of the bunker.

"Where is Leonard? Where is package?" He shouted the questions, pronouncing Leonard in three syllables as LEO-nard.

"I'm Leonard," the young man said before Charlie could tell him not to.

"You stole package from hospital. Where is it? Give it to us or woman dies!" The big man pushed against Sarah's head with the barrel of the pistol for effect.

They had walked past the entrance to the men's dorm room, so Leonard pointed behind him to the doorway. "It's in my pack in that room."

The big man grabbed Sarah by the back of her neck and used the gun to gesture at Charlie. "You—old man—on your belly! Hands behind head! Move and die!" He gestured at Leonard. "You, stay like a good dog. Move and die." He turned toward the kitchen and spoke in the foreign language for a few seconds.

Robin moved from the kitchen, a third man pushing her roughly, causing her to stumble. "On the floor, now!" he shouted. His English gave away less of an accent than the big man's.

With Robin on the floor, hands clasped behind her head like Charlie's, the man turned toward Leonard. "You're Leonard?"

"Yes."

"I am Zand. Take me to the package. Don't do anything dumb, or you die, your friends die, everyone dies, and we *still* get the package. Understand?"

"Yes."

"Okay. Clasp your hands behind your head, and let's go."

Leonard turned and started walking back to the entry to the men's dorm. As he did so, something pounded on the front door. He began to turn, but Zand pushed him. "Eyes forward! Stop walking!"

The man who had brought Robin from the kitchen

looked at the six-inch video screen next to the door and said something in the foreign language. The giant bearded man replied and nodded at him.

The second man opened the entry door, and the next fifteen seconds sped by in a blur.

CHAPTER TEN

DURANGO, COLORADO. MAY 7

"There's no way we're that lucky! Allahu Akbar!" Dariush commented. Ahead of them, parked in front of the safe house prepared by Dr. Sanjay's contractors, was the Mercedes SUV they'd seen in the video at the hospital in El Paso.

"It's not luck," Marduk interjected. "It's justice. Today they pay for my brother's death."

Kamal locked eyes with him. "Listen to me! You are not going to start exacting revenge from anyone until we have the package in our hands. Once we've achieved the objective, you can carve them up and rape their corpses for all I care. But you do not get to kill anyone until I say so. Understood?"

Marduk's jaw clenched. "Yes, Kamal. I understand."

While they watched, several people came out and retrieved supplies from the Mercedes and the large, older vehicle parked a few meters away.

"I counted five," Zand said. "Three men, two women."

Dariush nodded. "That's the same count I got."

"How did they get in?" Marduk asked.

Kamal grunted. "Obvious. They have Sanjay's notes and memory card. It must have contained information about the safe houses and supply depots. It's proof they have it, which is good. They also didn't notice us, so their situational awareness is horrible. We have a good advantage. Everyone recheck your gear. Zand and I go in first. We'll control the people we encounter. Dariush, Marduk, you two come in second. Remember the objective is to identify Leonard, get the package, transmit the contents to Hamid in Pyongyang, and join the main fight. Everyone on the same page?"

They all confirmed they were in sync. Dariush nodded at the unconscious Javad. "What do we do with him?"

"We leave him for now. Control the situation inside, then come and get him when it's over. We can hope the place is stocked with antibiotics, and we can start to treat his infection."

Dariush nodded.

"Anything else?" Kamal asked. No one said anything. "Okay, then. Let's go."

THE OPERATION HAD GONE SMOOTHLY. Dariush inputted the access code and the group

105

entered the building without anyone spotting them. Kamal and Marduk went to the right and found the Indian boy in the bathroom.

"Quiet or die, boy!" Kamal said in English, his pistol aimed at Shane's head. "You are Leonard? Nod for yes."

The boy shook his head.

"Come, boy. Come now." Kamal led the young man into the hallway and back toward the entryway. Across the hall, he saw Dariush and Zand had corralled the two women into the kitchen.

"Where are the other two men?" Kamal asked the women. He put the gun to the boy's head. "Answer, or he dies."

The women looked confused.

"Three seconds. Answer. One. Two."

"All right!" the younger one screamed. "They're in the computer room."

Kamal turned to face the main corridor, when two men with rifles came from the farthest doorway.

"Drop your weapons or boy dies!" Kamal shouted at them. The men stood their ground.

What makes these Americans so slow to do what they're told? he wondered to himself. He pushed the barrel flush against the boy's head and pulled the trigger. The young man's head rocked to the side, and his body collapsed as all the muscles went slack. Blood sprayed back onto Kamal, and the air smelled of spent gunpowder and burned hair.

Kamal addressed Dariush and Zand in the kitchen.

"Bring the woman!" he commanded, gesturing at the younger of the two.

Dariush pushed Sarah into the hall, and Kamal pressed the gun to her head. "Drop weapons or woman dies!"

This time they complied. "Hands up and move forward!" The pair raised their hands and began walking toward Kamal. "Where is Leonard? Where is package?"

The younger man spoke up. "I'm Leonard."

The older man cringed and shook his head. He apparently didn't want the boy to answer. Kamal would remember that. For now, he continued with his questions.

"You stole package from hospital. Where is it? Give it to us or woman dies." He pressed the barrel against her head for effect like he had just done with Shane. The woman squealed, making Kamal smile at the thought of how scared she must be. Maybe they will let the women live long enough to wish they were dead.

Leonard pointed to a doorway three meters behind him. "It's in my pack in that room."

Kamal grabbed Sarah by her neck and moved her in front of him, just in case any of this crew tried to shoot at him. "You—old man—on your belly! Hands behind head! Move and die!" He pointed at Leonard with his pistol. "You, stay like a good dog. Move and die."

He turned to the kitchen where Marduk had

joined Zand. He spoke in Farsi to them. "Zand, bring the old woman out here and put her on her belly, then take the boy and get the package. Once you verify it, kill him. Marduk—once Zand confirms we're green, you can kill whoever you want to."

Marduk's stern face broke into a wide grin.

Zand pushed the older woman into the hallway. "On the floor, now!" She lay down and clasped her hands behind her head like the old man had done. Zand advanced down the hall.

Zand hadn't been able to see the boy when he announced his name, so he wanted to be sure. "You're Leonard?"

The boy nodded. "Yes."

"I am Zand. Don't do anything dumb, or you die, your friends die, everyone dies, and we *still* get the package. Understand?"

"Yes."

"Okay. Clasp your hands behind your head, and let's go."

The young man turned and started walking toward the room with the package, when there was a loud pounding at the door. Zand instructed the boy to stop and keep facing away from him, and he turned to see what was happening at the entrance. They had undoubtedly attracted the attention of the infected when they drove through the southeast corner of Durango. It was probably just them trying to get in.

Dariush looked at the small video monitor. "It's Javad! He's up and wants in!"

Kamal's brow furrowed. "You're certain?"

"Yes, look!" Dariush stepped to the side to show the video monitor with Javad's sweaty face filling most of the screen.

Kamal nodded. "Let him in, quickly. The infected are probably close."

Dariush pulled the door open to let Javad in.

Javad stumbled inside the doorway, as though he had been pushed. Too late, Dariush realized that he *had* been pushed. He dropped to the floor as the first shot from the stranger's rifle grazed his neck and struck the wall in the hallway, sending chips of paint and chunks of drywall into the air.

Zand raised his rifle to shoot at the silhouette in the doorway. Before he could pull the trigger, a searing pain ripped through his chest. He looked down and saw an arrow shaft protruding from the right side, the metal broadhead dripping blood. Thinking Leonard had somehow shoved an arrow through him, he turned around but. Instead, there was a different young Indian boy just inside the doorway across from the room Leonard was taking him to, pulling back a second arrow in a compound bow.

We miscounted their numbers! Zand thought as the boy released the arrow. This one struck above the left collarbone, severing his carotid artery and the jugular vein before clipping the spine and protruding from the back his neck. His legs went slack, and he saw a spray of blood spurt onto the wall, almost hitting the ceiling. *Is that coming from me?* he wondered. All he could do then was stare at the ceiling while gunfire and the sounds of battle raged all around him. His vision went gray, the focal point fading to a small circle in the center of his view. The noise around him seemed to drift far away. Then it was gone.

In the entryway, the younger woman went limp. Kamal wasn't expecting her to go deadweight, and she slipped from his grasp. The man in the doorway was still firing his rifle. Kamal dove to the right, into the hallway toward the bathrooms. Dariush belly crawled into the kitchen on the opposite side, where Marduk grabbed him and pulled him to safety. The old woman was gone, and just as Marduk drew a bead on the younger woman, a hand reached in from the entry and pulled her away. Marduk's shot hit the tile floor, sending chips and shrapnel flying from the point of impact. A few seconds later, the first infected came barreling through the doorway.

CHAPTER ELEVEN

The man yanked Sarah out of the entryway just as a bullet from someone smacked the tile right where her head had been. She caught some pieces of tile, maybe even some fragments of the round that hit it, on the side of her face. Her eye clamped shut involuntarily, and she felt warm, wet liquid running down her cheek.

"Move it, Sarah!"

A familiar voice pushed her to move ahead. Who was it?

"Go! Run, woman! There's a horde of infected coming down on us!! That's it, that way. Go!"

She put one foot in front of the other, trying to clear the cobwebs from her mind as she followed the person through a doorway. Kamal's massive hand had wrapped two-thirds of the way around her throat and choked off her oxygen supply. One second, she was wiggling, trying ineffectively to break free, and the next she was being dragged from the building by someone she thought she knew but could not place.

With one eye shut, her depth perception was lacking, and she stumbled, falling to the gravel that covered the edge of the road. The pain woke her up somewhat. She heard two sources of gunfire—one from behind her, inside the safehouse, and the other from the man who was giving her directions. She scrambled to her feet and turned to see a blurry figure rushing at her.

"Come on, Sarah. I bought us a few seconds, but you have to *move!*"

He ran with her for a few strides, turned and fired a few rounds, then caught up with her again.

"How are you doing? Did you get hit? Are you shot?"

So many questions.

"Can't tell," she gasped, already getting winded from this all-out flight from danger. "Don't think so."

"Good, because I left my trauma kit in the car. Here, go that way!" He pushed her to the left, onto a dirt road that rose away from the street and wrapped around a hillside.

Again, he stopped and fired several rounds from his rifle. He caught up with her, and she recognized the sounds of a magazine being changed out.

"We have to go back," Sarah said between gasps.

"No way, too many Ikes."

"Ikes?"

"Ikes. Infected. Just keep going."

"Where? Where are we going?"

"Away from the Ikes!"

As if on cue, the screams of the infected ripped through the air. Sarah knew that sound all too well from the encounters she'd had in El Paso and on the trip back to Colorado. It meant they were hunting.

They kept running up the road. It wound around the hill and opened to a big, flat area covered with construction equipment. Scattered across the hilltop were earth movers and backhoes and front loaders, all heavy equipment intended to work on building a new road into a new subdivision. Long sections of pre-formed concrete pipe segments were lined up, ready to be put in place by construction workers who weren't ever coming back to build a storm sewer line that would never be used.

The man spotted a big concrete cone, five feet wide at the base, narrowing for two feet to a thirty-inch column, which extended vertically two more feet. The column had a twenty-four-inch opening in the top, designed for a manhole.

"Over there," he shouted, guiding Sarah to the four-foot-tall structure. "Get in!" he directed, and he half helped her, half threw her through the opening. He climbed up and pulled his arms in tight. "Watch out below," he said and dropped inside.

He was winded from what was probably at most a half-mile sprint. *Fucking altitude,* he thought. He tried controlling his gasps for air as the sounds of the pursuing infected grew louder. The oblong shape of the cone allowed them to squeeze back, away from the opening overhead. He hoped the infected wouldn't find them in here. If he had to fire the rifle, it would deafen both of them. *Well, for about thirty seconds, then we'll be dead.*

The scuffling of feet on gravel and dirt grew louder, and he could tell they were running right past their position. None of them stopped. He thought he counted fifty but had no way to be sure. In any case, it was too many for them to take on by themselves.

With the infected fading into the distance, he turned his attention back to Sarah.

"Here, let me see you," he said.

His voice clicked in her head.

"Sergeant Duckett!" she exclaimed.

"Shhh! Keep it down!"

"Sorry. What the fuck are you doing here?"

"Saving you from an Iranian hit squad."

She understood the words, but they didn't make sense to her. "Iranian? Duckett, what is happening?"

He put a finger to his lips as more shuffling feet scuffed their way past them. In a whisper, he said, "We'll be here for a while. Plenty of time for me to tell you my story. First, let's check out that eye."

"SOMEONE JUST GRABBED SARAH!" Leonard shouted to anyone who would listen.

"We got bigger problems, Leonard," Charlie said as he changed magazines. "The whole infected population of Durango is coming down on us. Get your gun going!"

Charlie had been on the firing line a few times when the First Civilian Division was putting up the perimeter defenses, so he was used to shooting the infected. Leonard did not have as much experience with that part of the operation in El Paso.

Robin reached out to Leonard. "Give me that gun, son. Get in the armory and load magazines with Aaron." She took a position next to Charlie on the right side of the hallway and started shooting.

"Center mass is fine," Charlie directed. "No need for headshots. Stop their heart, and they go down just fine."

"I'd wager I've killed more of these things than you, Charlie. The buzzards are eating pretty good up towards Aspen."

Marcus joined the pair in the hallway, kneeling between them, and soon the three of them fell into a rhythm... shooting, grabbing a fresh magazine from Aaron or Leonard, and reloading so that at least one person was always firing. In a few minutes, they had a pile of bodies stacked up in the entryway, blocking eighty percent of the opening.

Charlie raised a hand. "Hold your fire."

Through the gaps in the pile, they could see some of the infected outside passing the bunker, headed north. Screams from the outside signaled they were in pursuit of prey.

Robin read Charlie's thoughts. "I hope that's not for Sarah and the mystery man."

"Who else would it be for? At least it means they're still on the run. Probably."

"Um, guys? We still have a crew of murderous foreigners up front to deal with."

Charlie and Robin looked down at Marcus, realizing he was right.

As if on cue, a hand grenade flew from the left side of the hall, hit the wall, and bounced onto the tile, rolling toward them. A hand popped out from the kitchen on the right side of the hallway and lobbed a second grenade, this one traveling straight at the trio.

Robin dove into the armory, landing hard on the tile and hitting her head on the edge of a shelving unit. She went still, blood draining from the head wound.

Charlie and Marcus dove into the men's dorm room. Charlie executed a pretty decent shoulder roll, but Marcus's foot slipped in the foreigner's blood that now covered the floor as well as the walls. His leg shot out from under him just as two successive blasts shook the hallway. Pieces of shrapnel blew through the thin drywall. Smoke detectors started blaring.

Charlie rolled over and did a quick damage assessment. No wounds, no blood. Ears ringing, but they were already doing that from the noise of the rifles in the hallway. He remembered the foreigners at the front of the building and raised his gun up, aiming it at a point on the wall where he estimated the bullet would travel through to the entryway. He fired a few rounds just to try to keep their heads down. He heard cursing —at least, he assumed it to be cursing—and smiled.

"Psst! Charlie!"

He looked across the hall at Leonard. The kid held up a pair of hand grenades, and Charlie's smile grew bigger. He motioned for Leonard to toss one to him.

"Hey!" he shouted. "Why don't you assholes take off? Cut your losses and live to fight another day?"

"Maybe you fuck your mother and die. Give us package. We'll kill you quick."

"Come and get it, sugar puss." Charlie pulled the pin on his grenade. He motioned to Leonard to get ready but wait a minute before throwing his.

He lobbed his grenade down the hall at an angle. It hit the floor just past a dead infected and rolled to a stop right in the entry of the kitchen. Charlie stepped back and felt the building shake from the explosion. He nodded to Leonard, who leaned out and threw his grenade. He threw it a little too hard, though, and it landed in the pile of infected. This explosion was more muffled, and when Charlie peeked around the corner, bits of flesh were scattered around the hallway.

He heard more cursing from the front, and another grenade bounced down the hallway. Charlie looked up at Leonard, a surprised look on his face, and dropped back into the room, landing hard on his butt. Another explosion shook the building.

KAMAL'S EARS RANG. Once again, they had underestimated the Americans, but even with the hidden archer killing Zand, they were in good shape. It was the arrival of the man outside who used Javad as a ruse to gain entry to the building that had really screwed things up for them. Zand going down, Javad collapsing in the doorway, and the arrival of the infected was too much happening at once. Now the Americans had their guns back, and apparently a supply of grenades. That made sense since this was a supply facility as well as a safe house. He did the mental math. The old man, the old woman, Leonard, and the one with the arrows—there were at least four people back there with access to the armory. Plus, the other woman and the mystery man could be lurking outside. It would be a hard fight to get the package, and harder still to get clear of the building if there were people posted outside. For now, the infected would have them on the run, but he could not count on that to be the case for long.

He looked over at Marduk and Dariush. Dariush looked okay, but Marduk had blood running down his face, and his pupils were the size of coins. He had a concussion. That decided it.

He motioned at Dariush and mimed pulling the pins on two more grenades and tossing them down the hall. Then he held up a smoke grenade, gestured to himself, then pointed at Dariush and Marduk, and jerked a thumb toward the exit. Dariush nodded.

They got up and gathered their things, getting

ready to make their escape. Dariush whispered in Marduk's ear, and he nodded in response and gave a thumbs up.

Kamal counted down from three and tossed his grenade. Dariush did the same. The two explosions shook the building enough that part of the ceiling in the hallway collapsed. Kamal threw the smoker down the hall, and when it popped, Dariush pushed Marduk toward the pile of bodies, shoving him through the opening on the right side. Kamal turned his back to the stack of dead infected and fired his rifle down the hallway, spraying rounds with abandon back and forth, high and low. When the magazine was empty, he climbed through the roadblock of flesh and joined the remains of his team outside.

CHAPTER TWELVE

DURANGO, COLORADO. MAY 7

Duckett dug into his inside jacket pocket and pulled out a flat bag of water. He unscrewed the cap and gave it a squeeze, gulping down a couple of mouthfuls, then he turned to Sarah.

"Lean your head to the side," he instructed. "I'm going to flush some water over that eye, try to wash it out. You need to force it open, okay?"

She nodded, and he let water trickle over the eye. She blinked rapidly, her eye fighting to close, but she managed to keep it pried open. He stopped and passed her a handkerchief.

"Here, pat it off, but don't rub it. See if you can open it now."

She blotted her face with the cloth and forced her eye to open. She blinked several times, but it stayed open. "Okay, everything's blurry, but at least I can see. My eye isn't ruined, thank God."

She went to hand the cloth back to Duckett but

startled herself when she saw the blood on it. "What the shit? Is that from my eye?"

"No, here, let me see that." Duckett took the rag and splashed some water on it, then wiped her face clean. A trickle of fresh blood ran in a small rivulet from her temple down her cheek. He wiped it away, then folded the handkerchief into a triangle and wrapped it around her head. He tied it off in the back, making sure the small wound was bound, and tucked the third corner under the knot in the back. "There. That should take care of it until we can get a better look. It's just a small cut, but head wounds bleed a lot. Makes it look worse than it is."

She motioned for the water bag, and he passed it over to her. She took a long draught from it, then offered it back to him. He took another swig and passed it back. "Kill it," he said.

She drained the rest of the water and wiped her mouth with the back of her hand. "Duckett," she started to say, but he put a finger to his lips.

"Shh. Just chill for a few minutes. Let's make sure the Ikes are gone, then you can ask me whatever you want, okay?"

She bristled for a second, then nodded her head. It made sense. She leaned back, trying to get comfortable, but the conical shape of the concrete structure made that impossible. Duckett lay down with his knees bent. Sarah leaned back against his legs, letting the weight of her torso settle against him. She closed her eyes and listened to the world outside their concrete hideout.

Far off, she could hear the renewed sounds of gunfire and explosions. One big one, and another. A couple of minutes passed, and she heard another explosion, and a second, and a third.

"What is that?" she whispered.

"Grenades, most likely."

"Are you serious? We have to get back there and help them!"

"As long as we keep hearing that, your guys are alive. And there's nothing we can do, Sarah—whatever's happened has happened. We're lucky to escape that horde."

She was going to protest, but the sounds of returning infected told her that they were going to be stuck for a while.

"They're drawn back by all that noise," Duckett said. "Hopefully they got that door shut."

Fifteen minutes passed by. They heard a couple more explosions, more gunfire, and more infected passing them by. The gunshots were louder, sharper.

"It sounds like someone is outside now. The Iranians are leaving, most likely. That's good, they should draw a lot of the infected after them."

Sarah turned her head so she could see Duckett's face, surprised at how comfortable she had been lying against him. "Iranians?" She sat up and turned to face him. "And did you see the size of that motherfucker that had me by the neck? That was one of the biggest humans I've ever seen. Jesus, that bastard scared me.

What the fuck is happening, Duckett? Why don't you fill me in on everything?"

He sighed and sat up too, though his shoulders were hunched over against the angled concrete. "I liked it better when you were lying on me."

"I bet you did. Details. Give them."

"I meant it was more comfortable." She just stared daggers into him. "Okay. What all do you want to know? Everything that happened since I last saw you?"

"That's a good place to start."

"Including what happened to your husband?"

That caught her off guard, and she paused for a long few seconds. "Yes."

"All right. Let's see... last I saw you, you were pointing a gun at me and forcing me to open the containment lab. You disappeared, but before you did, you asked me to release Ram. Sound familiar?"

"Yeah, Duckett, I was there, remember?"

"Well, I went down to release Ram, and I found his partner, Jesse, with some butch-looking lady—no offense—breaking him out. The new lady, she was hard, mean looking. She and Jesse seemed to be fast friends, and we had a real tense moment. Since I was cutting him loose anyway, I showed my belly and let them take off.

"About that time a bunch of shitheads from Homeland showed up and told me they were taking control of the facility. Alarms were going off all over the place, infected were in the hallways, some paramilitary group was breaking Ram out of isolation—and, as it turned out, killing Dr. Sanjay—and I was there by myself. So, it took me about two seconds to say *fuck it* and let Homeland take over. I knew they were in over their heads."

"I ran into a couple of those guys as I was leaving."

"You did?"

"Yeah, they were coming up in the elevator as I was going to go down."

"Well, they didn't last long. When I left you, I had no idea what your plans were, but I figured you were going to off your husband and then yourself. Imagine my surprise when I got to the security office and saw you on camera leaving through the front entrance. I pulled up the feed from the containment wing, and there was Jack, covered in blood, lab coats and Homeland dying all around him.

"I figured out that you had cut him loose—why, I don't know—and he must have released the other infected. He never fully gave in, you know."

Sarah gasped. "What do you mean?"

"I mean, after he and his cadre of ghouls took out the doctors and the Homeland pussies, he took out the ghouls. Didn't want them to kill more people, I guess. Innocent people, I mean. He ripped their necks open with his bare hands. It was gruesome as shit. Anyway, he tried using the Homeland guy's MP5 to off himself, but he couldn't figure it out. It was like that part of his mind was fried. I felt bad for him."

"Did you..."

"Yes. When I found him, he recognized me. I

expected him to charge at me and have a go, but he just looked sad. He tapped his chest, right where the heart would be, and held his arms to the side. I *think* he said, 'Do it,' but he wasn't able to speak clearly, you know? But he kept after me, tapping his chest and holding his arms out. I raised my pistol and said, 'Is this what you want?' He nodded his head, so I shot him."

Sarah let out a sob, louder than she had intended. She saw Duckett's face register alarm, and he looked up at the opening like he expected an infected to drop in on them. She used her right arm to pull her left elbow tight to her face and sobbed silently.

"I'm sorry, Sarah, but if you had been there, you would have done it too. He didn't want to exist like that."

She didn't know if she was more upset that Duckett had killed her husband, or that she *wasn't* there to do it. His last request to her was to turn him loose so he could get revenge on the doctors for experimenting on him, and she had honored that. But then she'd left, abandoning him to his fate.

Duckett was smart and didn't say anything. Sarah had her sobs under control, and nothing he could say would help her right now. He reached out and rubbed her arm in a show of compassion, but let her sorrow run its course.

After a few minutes, she finally spoke. "Sorry. I hadn't really processed everything that happened. Jack asked me to untie him and get out of the hospital. I granted what I thought was his dying wish. It turns out his last wish was to die, and I wasn't there for him." She lost her voice in another round of sobbing.

This time, Duckett pulled her close, wrapping his arms around her. She grabbed him back, burying her face in his chest, and cried for a good, long time.

CHAPTER THIRTEEN

DURANGO, COLORADO. MAY 7

The arrow snapped the infected's head back, and it crumpled to the ground outside the door.

Inside, Aaron stood guard, waiting for the next creature to try to claw its way into the building. After the foreigners fled, the masses that had been outside thinned out, following the Mercedes as it sped away.

Charlie was pissed at himself about that one. He had gotten into the habit of leaving the key fob in the console so anyone in their group who needed it could take it without searching for the keys. It could be life or death if they were being chased by infected, and he didn't think they had to worry about thieves in this new world.

Once they killed the smoke alarms, the infected stopped coming as frequently, but they could not turn their backs on the door. Aaron had bow hunted with his father for years, so he was the natural choice to cover the door and make quiet kills that wouldn't draw more infected.

Lori had been hiding against the wall in the women's dorm during the battle. It would have been the last place the foreigners would have looked had they walked in there, but it was also close to the grenade blasts. Shrapnel had ripped through the drywall and clipped her ear and shoulder. She did some self-triage then tended to the more severe wounds suffered by Robin and Marcus.

She cleaned Robin's head wound and closed it with butterfly bandages and super glue. Robin wasn't happy with how much hair she shaved off to close it up, but it was done.

She had tried to save Marcus, but his wounds were too extensive. When he slipped in the hallway, his legs took the brunt of a grenade blast. The femoral artery in his left leg had been nicked, and he lost too much blood. He hung on long enough to say goodbye to Robin, but once he knew she was all right, his will to fight left him, and he died.

Rounding out their losses was Shane, whose body was buried under a heap of the infected just inside the front door.

The hallway was covered with blood. The foreigner Aaron shot with the arrow bled out, Marcus bled out, and the thirty or so infected in the doorway must have drained ten gallons onto the tile.

"All of that is a bio-hazard," Charlie admonished

the crew. "Be extra careful walking through there, especially if you have any open wounds."

Once she was done treating everyone else, Lori needed attention. Leonard removed the piece of shrapnel from her shoulder and, following her directions, stitched up the wound. She had taped up her own ear, covering the missing bit with gauze that was now bright red. The pair cautiously weaved down the hall to the kitchen, finding more blood just inside the doorway. She made coffee and heated up some soup while Leonard found a mop and some bleach and set about cleaning the hallway.

Charlie and Robin found a sheet and wrapped Marcus's body in it, then wrapped a heavy wool blanket around that.

"It doesn't seem real," Robin mused. "After all the shit we went through together, the fight to get clear of Aspen, the hiding and fighting in the forest, Marcus and Sebastian seemed invincible. You know, when we first left Aspen, before we saw you at the roadblock, we had a larger crew."

Charlie shook his head. "No, I didn't know that. I know very little about you, actually."

"Well, we had gotten maybe a thousand people out of town, headed south, but five times that number chasing them. We knew we had to stop the infected from coming out of town. Fifteen people were willing to stay and fight. We knew we'd never kill them all, but we blocked the road as best we could. We took out a bridge and dynamited a rock overhang, brought it down on the highway. By the time we got clear, we were down to ten people, and three of them were wounded, either bitten or scratched. Not that it made a difference which. We all knew what that meant. A wound from the infected was like a bullet to the head, only slower.

"Anyway, those three stayed behind to keep any infected occupied and stop them from following us. Of the remaining seven, four left in the following days. Some were upfront about it, some snuck off in the night. After that, it was just me, Marcus, and Sebastian."

"I'm sorry, Robin. I liked him, and Lori tried to save him, but..."

"Don't. She did what she could. We're lucky any of us are alive. Who knows how much time any of us have? We just need to make what time we have count."

MARDUK WIGGLED through the gap between the dead infected and the doorframe, tumbling to the ground on the other side. He landed in a puddle of blood, soaking the back of his shirt and pants with it.

"Move!" Dariush shouted as he came through behind him. Marduk moved, still groggy from the grenade blast. Daruish landed with a little more grace than Marduk, and he managed to avoid the pool of blood.

They heard the pop of the smoker and the sound of

Kamal emptying his gun into the hallway to keep the Americans' heads down. A second later, he emerged like a massive, bearded Goliath being birthed from a mountain of dead flesh.

They started toward the Toyota but stopped after a few steps. Although it had survived the collision with the cars as they fled Leonard's house yesterday, someone took it upon themselves to flatten all four tires.

Kamal scowled. "The mystery man. Marduk! You're the transportation expert. We need a vehicle."

"Hey!" Dariush called out from the side of the Mercedes SUV. "I think fortune smiles on us! Allahu Akbar! They left the fob in this one!" He climbed in and pressed the start button, and the engine roared to life. He put the car in gear and sped over to the Sequoia, where they hastily transferred their bags and equipment to the Mercedes.

Shrieks sounded behind them, and Kamal turned and fired at approaching infected, knocking a half dozen to the ground, but scores more were advancing from the hill a half kilometer away. They started shrieking as well, and more sounded off from the area in front of them.

"Kamal, we're ready! Let's go!"

Kamal nodded to Dariush, climbed in the passenger side of the vehicle, and Dariush sped away from the scene.

In the back seat, Marduk was a mess. Kamal could not tell what was Marduk's blood, and what was transferred from the pile of the infected. His head lolled side to side, and he was fighting to stay awake. Kamal reached back and took the rifle away from him, lest he accidentally shoot it inside the car.

"Hand me your pistol, Marduk," Kamal ordered.

"What? Why?"

"You're shell-shocked. I don't want any accidental discharges."

Marduk ejected the magazine from the gun and the round from the chamber and handed them over to Kamal. He also passed him a grenade and a knife with a nine-inch fixed blade. "There you go, boss."

Dariush looked at Kamal and smirked.

"What is it?" Kamal asked.

"Nothing. It's just—I know he's not right in the head. If he were, he would have told you what to do with that request. I've never seen him give in like that."

"Just find us a spot to rest and clean up. We need to figure out our next move and let Command know the status."

"Are you going to tell them about Zand and Javad?"

"Yes. They'll find out at some point anyway, and if I lie, they'll have me killed. After this failure, they might anyway."

From the back seat, Marduk started snoring. Kamal gave a wry chuckle. "He might be the lucky one in all this."

"OKAY, I haven't seen any infected for ten minutes," Aaron said. "Can we do this and get it over with?"

"Yeah," Charlie replied. He, Aaron, and Leonard were dressed in Tyvek coveralls and long rubber gloves. They found the gear in the cleaning closet where Leonard got the mop and bucket.

They exited the building from the big garage door and walked to the main entrance. Robin followed them with her rifle, scanning for any signs of infected.

The three men began pulling bodies from the pile, dragging them to the side of the entrance, and dropping them.

"What's the over/under?" Aaron asked.

"Twenty-five, including the foreigners, and… and Shane," Leonard said, the last part draining the mood.

"I'm glad I didn't see it," Aaron replied. "I don't know how you can handle that, man. I think it would eat me up having that in my head."

"It was fucked up, for sure. I guess I'm just numb. When it happened, I just… I don't know. I froze up inside."

"I get it, I really do. Sorry."

They finished clearing the bodies away from the door, then dragged out the ones inside the entry.

"Twenty-six, not counting Shane," Charlie said. "Never count your own amongst the enemy. He deserves more respect than that. We'll wrap him up and put him with Marcus until we decide what to do with them."

Lori brought a couple of sheets and one of the

heavy wool blankets, and they wrapped Shane in them. Robin found a hose and connected it to the sink in the kitchen then used it to wash the remaining blood and gore out the door, off the entryway and into the gutter. Then, she closed the door.

The men were all in the garage, stripping out of their protective gear before coming inside the building. Robin stopped them at the door.

"I know you guys are tired, but I think we should get as much of this gear as we can into that van out there. That's our new party wagon. And, I'd like to see if we can get my Blazer inside too, load it up. Then we're not putting all our eggs in one basket. What do you think?"

"Sounds good, Robin," Charlie said, giving her a wink. "You and I will jockey the vehicles around; you guys start getting things ready. Let's get food first, then ammo, then some of those weapons."

Thirty minutes later, both vehicles were loaded with supplies. The group was tired, sweaty, and filthy from head to toe. Everyone wanted a hot shower more than anything, so they agreed to have two people shower at a time with three on guard duty in case the foreigners came back. Charlie and Robin went first, eliciting whistles and catcalls from the younger members of the group.

Once everyone was clean, they fixed some food, boiling up more soup because it was easy. Leonard was the one to broach the subject of the missing team member.

"What are we going to do about Sarah?"

Charlie sighed and put his spoon in the soup bowl. "I don't know, Leonard. I would say we should go look for her, but we don't have the manpower to leave this place undefended."

Robin nodded her head. "I agree. She knows where we are. If she's still safe, not bit, or whoever snatched her hasn't done her harm, our best bet is to stay put and wait for her."

"For how long?" Leonard persisted. "We can't stay here, can we? Those guys will be back soon. We need to get somewhere safe, where they don't know where we're going to be."

"How *did* they know we would be here?" Aaron asked.

"I don't know," Charlie said. "I bet they have the same map we do, and this was the closest resupply station. Or maybe we tripped an alarm when we opened the door. Who knows? Either way, it was our bad luck."

Aaron blinked at Charlie for a few seconds. "I hate this new world. Shane was a good friend. I don't think 'our bad luck' covers it."

"Sorry," Charlie offered. "I guess I've been dealing with this for a lot longer than you. The day it came to my area was the day I learned my son was infected, and I had to start making peace with losing him. And he and Sarah had to kill their way to my place, so Sarah's been dealing with this nastiness for a long time too. At least, it seems like a long time. It's only been six weeks since it started, but the world is forever changed."

"Dude, depressed much? If that was supposed to make me feel better, it didn't."

A humming noise sounded off from the entryway, and the green light above the kitchen entry turned red.

"Shit, get ready," Robin called out. "They're back!"

CHAPTER FOURTEEN

DURANGO, COLORADO. MAY 7

The pile of dead bodies in front of the supply depot reeked of perforated body cavities and feces and the coppery smell of spilled blood. Sarah was looking amongst the collection for signs of her friends but didn't see them.

"Someone cleaned up," Duckett observed. "And left beardy Joe there for the buzzards. I bet it wasn't the Iranians left him out like that."

"How do you know it's one of them?"

"I saw them at the hospital in El Paso. He's one of them, all right. He had two hands back then, though, not one and a half."

"That was courtesy of Leonard's grandfather," Sarah told him. "I suppose there's nothing for it but to go in, yeah?"

Duckett waved his arm in an *after you* motion. Sarah walked past him and up to the keypad. She punched in the numeric sequence for SANJAY. The door hummed then the latch released.

She pushed the door open, and a cacophony of smells hit her. Gunpowder, bleach... and stew? Her stomach gnawed at her the second she recognized the smell of food.

A glance up the hallway gave her a burst of panic-driven adrenaline. The walls were shredded and scored, the floor and ceiling bore the scars of battle. Even though the smell of bleach gave away the fact that someone tried to clean up, there was evidence of blood all the way up the hallway.

She raised her pistol to the low ready position and called out, "Hello? Anyone home?"

She heard Leonard exclaim, "Sarah!" A second later he ran out of the kitchen, dropping his rifle to its sling, and gave her a big hug. "I'm so glad you're okay! Holy shit, and Duckett! What the hell are you doing here?"

"Let's get inside and get the door shut, huh? I feel exposed out here, kid."

Leonard stepped back and let them both in and shut the door behind them.

He turned around and saw Charlie hugging Sarah, followed by Lori, Robin, and Aaron.

"Where's Marcus?" Sarah asked.

"He, uh, he didn't make it," Robin answered, the pain evident in her voice.

"Oh, no, Robin, I'm so sorry."

"Thanks. He was a good guy."

Charlie was looking Duckett up and down. "I've not been introduced to you. I'm Charlie." He held his hand out. "I guess we have you to thank for saving Sarah?"

Duckett shook Charlie's hand with a firm grip. "I was just in the right place at the right time. She didn't need much saving."

"Yeah, about that. How *did* you end up in the right place at the right time?"

"You want to hear the whole thing?"

Around the room, heads nodded.

"Okay. Well, I think you all know the events that led up to your exodus from El Paso, so I won't go back that far. You got out before things got really bad. Millions of Ikes came to town a couple days after you left. The Air Force bombed the shit out of them all the way across Texas, but there were still so many that made it through. The defenses held, though, and Bliss is still intact. Or, was when I left a couple days ago. They're doing shifts up on the walls, and man, it's just non-stop. Mowing down Ikes, and when the piles get too high, they soak 'em with fuel and burn 'em down to bones. The next wave of Ikes tramples those bones into dust as they come marching in. You know the movie *Starship Troopers*?"

"Yeah, of course," Leonard answered for everyone.

"Well, it felt a lot like the big battle at the outpost on Planet P. Anyway, the bulk of the Ikes..."

"I'm sorry," Aaron interrupted. "Ikes?"

"Infected," Sarah answered for Duckett.

139

"Gotcha."

Duckett continued. "Anyway, a few days into it, we've got wounded piling up, civilians hurt..."

"How many civilians made it in?" Charlie interjects.

"Not sure. Three million. Maybe more."

"Holy shit. That's going to get messy."

Duckett nodded. "I expect so. But the alternative is being dead, so pick your poison, you know? Anyhow, we've got injuries mounting, and we're running out of some of the basics—ibuprofen, antibiotics... shit, even Band-Aids. The brass had decided not to extend the border walls all the way to Beaumont since the building was overrun with infected and whole floors had become biohazard zones. But since I had worked at Beaumont and knew my way around the place, they sent me on a mission to get meds.

"Well, me and two other guys. We got out of Bliss and over to the medical center and filled duffels—I mean dozens of them—with all the meds, supplies, bandages, IV bags. Whatever we could fit in the truck, we did. We were on the way back when I saw black ops guys coming in hot to the medical center. I would have missed them, but one of them overshot and flared up when I happened to be looking up. I hopped out of the truck and sent the other two guys back to Bliss. I hope they made it.

"I was maybe a mile from Beaumont and had to haul ass back there. The truck had drawn the loose infected in the area, but you don't want to be exposed for too long out there if you can help it, you know what I mean? Anyway, I figured these guys had infilled" — he looked at Aaron— "that's *infiltrated* the building by the time I got back there. I went in through the front door, probably not the best idea from a stealth perspective, but I didn't have a lot of time to figure out what was going on.

"I went into the ground floor security office and pulled up some of the cams. I saw six guys in Sanjay's office, a couple of them beardy as fuck, especially the big guy. I got ears on them from the cam in the hall outside Sanjay's office. They were speaking Farsi. At least, I'm eighty-five percent sure that's what they were speaking. In Vegas, eighty-five percent is one hundred percent, you know what I mean?"

Everyone nodded, and Leonard said, "Yeah," even though he did not know what that meant.

Duckett continued. "Anyway, these guys are Iranian as fuck and on some sort of secret mission that had them jumping into Beaumont Medical Center and rummaging through Sanjay's office. I thought I might get caught when they sent a couple of them to the front desk, looking for something, but they passed right by the office I was in.

"They made a move into the master security office upstairs, the one with all-access that *should* require military clearance to get into. They got in easy enough. What they didn't know, is that from either security room you can ghost any terminal in the hospital."

Duckett could tell no one knew what he was

talking about, so he explained. "You can access the terminal someone is using and see everything they're doing. They reviewed several recorded segments of cam footage. They watched Lenny here steal a package from ol' Doc Sanjay. They watched a band of mercs interrogate and kill ol' Doc Sanjay." He turned to Sarah. "One of the mercenaries was the scary-looking woman who was helping bust Ram out when I went to let him go, by the way. Anyway, the last thing they accessed was Lenny's personnel file."

Leonard blushed at this, embarrassed enough to not bother correcting Duckett for calling him Lenny.

"So," Duckett continued, "when they went to sleep, I snuck out and commandeered an unused Homeland vehicle. The next morning, *they* commandeered an SUV from the parking lot and headed north. Looking for Leonard, I assumed. I had your address from watching their search, so I figured I knew what general direction they would go. The hard part was staying back far enough not to let a glint of light off the windshield or anything stupid like that give me away, yet staying close enough so I didn't lose them. I *did* lose them a couple of times, but knowing their general destination helped me find them again. It was riskier than it sounds—if they suspected me of following them, I'd be as good as dead."

Leonard bristled at the news. "So, you mean you *knew* they were headed to Arboles, and you didn't warn *anybody*?"

"How could I? I told you, I was a ways behind

them. I needed—*need*—to gather intel and get it back to someone who knows bigger picture stuff than I do."

"My gramps might be dead because of your *intel*. We almost died because you didn't warn us."

Charlie put a hand on Leonard's shoulder. "Leonard, he didn't know we were here. Think about it."

"I didn't—not until I saw that Mercedes parked out front. They had watched canned footage of you leaving with that thing pulling your trailer, so I recognized it right away. I had to improvise a plan real quick. I heard a gunshot and knew I didn't have much time, so I grabbed that wounded fella—the one your gramps put a big hurt on, Leonard—and used him as bait to get them to open the door with their guard down. How I'd keep from getting shot by them, or you, I had no idea. But I knew I had to go in, no matter the outcome. I couldn't just let them kill you."

"Well, you showed up just shy of too late," Charlie said. "And I'm real grateful that you got Sarah out. I thought for sure she'd been shot."

Sarah lifted the bandana to expose the scratches where tile chips or bullet fragments had opened bloody trenches next to her eye and into her hairline. "It was closer than you know," she said.

Duckett continued. "So that's how I got from there to here. We know what these guys are after, and we know they're not going to stop until they get it. Question is, what's our next move?"

"We have several sheets of information from Dr.

Sanjay, but it's written in Korean," Charlie said. "I was going to try to use their comms system to access the Internet so we could translate it, but I haven't figured out how to get that thing to work. It's way more complicated than my civilian rig was."

"I know someone who might be able to help," Robin offered. Everyone turned to her.

"Don't hold back on us," Charlie prodded.

"Well, it would mean taking a road trip."

CHAPTER FIFTEEN

"Aren't you going to call Command?"

Kamal looked at Dariush and let the question hang in the air before answering. "No. Nothing good will come of that, brother."

Dariush was stunned but quickly hid it behind a mask. Kamal, however, noticed his reaction.

"You're surprised?"

"I am, Kamal. You've always been the one focused on processes and procedures. This is not like you."

"It's not like me to lose half of my team to a pack of amateurs. I've played this too soft."

"Dead men can't answer questions, Kamal. We had to know they had it."

"We were sloppy. *I* was sloppy. Miscounting the people in the safe house cost us Zand. And whoever was outside cost us Javad. If I were Command, I'd have me removed from this operation."

"And replaced with who? You know there's no one

to spare. Honestly, I'm surprised they freed us up for this thing. And Javad was off op anyway. I liked him, I did, but he was a liability with his injuries."

Kamal gave Dariush a look that withered the smaller man. "I was responsible for him. Like I am for you. Shall I cast you aside the moment you get injured?"

"I didn't mean to be callous, but we all know the risks of this operation, Kamal. No extraction is one of those risks. We had no way to treat his wounds, his infection. I hate it that he's dead, but there are three of us left and a mission to complete."

The knots in Kamal's clenched jaw pushed his beard out, making his massive head appear even larger than it already was. He relaxed his jaw, a sign that put Dariush at ease.

"You're right. We know they have the package now. We need to get Marduk back on his feet, and then we go back in there heavy. No questions, no talking. We take them out, secure the package and get out of here."

"Good. We can kill them and move on to killing other Americans. New Persia will be glorious." Dariush knew that referencing Kamal's vision for a new Persian empire, one free of the influence of the Mullahs, would keep the big man's spirits high. It appeared to have worked.

"Yes, Dariush, we can remake this land into a great empire. There is so much space here, surely the early heroes of this great conflict will be rewarded with land.

And if not, we'll take it anyway. But that's for later. First, we need to complete this mission, and I need to make a call."

Kamal left Dariush to watch over the sleeping Marduk and moved into the office of the auto repair shop they had commandeered for the moment. He shut the door and powered on the satellite phone. In a moment he was connected with Hamid Sari.

"Kamal, tell me the good news. The rest of the Command staff are getting nervous."

"My news is mixed, sir. We've located the package and confirmed the targets have it in their possession. However, we were unable to secure it due to an assault by a large number of infected. We had no choice but to retreat. Now that we know where the package is, we have a plan to mount a final assault and recover it."

"Kamal, I cannot tell you how disappointing this is. Do you expect me to go back in there and tell them that you have failed again? *They'll send another team to have you killed."*

"Hamid, you cannot sit in a room half a world away and pretend that you know anything about what it is like here. The Americans who are still alive have survived because they can fight, and they are facing extinction. You know an animal is the most dangerous when it's backed into a corner. Add hordes of the infected, and this is not a straightforward op.

"We had to move slowly and confirm the location of the package, and we've done that. Now we can get in, kill everyone, and get out. You want to have us eliminated and send in a new team? Do it. Your head will be on a spike next to Nampoo Yi's by the end of the day. If I were a betting man, I would place money on that."

Hamid considered Kamal's indignant attitude. It was the fire he wanted to see, that much was sure, but he didn't care for the threat at the end, even though it was probably accurate.

"Okay, Kamal, you have another day. I will tell the Command staff that you're still in pursuit of the package and expect to have it in your possession imminently. Do not let me down again, Kamal, or your head will be on that spike long before mine."

Kamal opened his mouth to speak again, but the call ended.

He returned to the lounge where people waiting for their cars to be serviced would wait, back in a time when there were people worried about getting their cars serviced. Now it was nothing more than a rest stop for people on the run. The empty food cans and the disgusting state of the restroom told Kamal they were far from the first people to hide here.

"Any signs of life from Marduk?"

Dariush shook his head. "No. He's the same. How was the call?"

"It went as expected. Get the package or die."

"I know the people in Command are a means to an end, but do they really find such talk motivating?"

"I don't think they care. Hamid is afraid for his life. The NorKos are ruthless and cruel, but they lack a noble purpose. An enemy with a purpose is easy to figure out. This group of people is chaotic and unpredictable. In my opinion, the sooner we cut ties with them, the better. But until we have a cure in hand and no longer need them, we have to play things their way. And that means Hamid is at their whim. He's desperate and lashing out at us. That much I understand."

"What's our next move?"

"Rest and eat. Once it's dark, we go back to the safe house and kill everyone, reclaim the package, and get on with our master plans."

"Excellent." Dariush broke out a broad smile, leaned back in the vinyl seat, and closed his eyes.

"YOU'RE SURE YOU'RE CLEAR?"

Marduk responded right away, which Kamal viewed as a good sign. "Yes, Kamal. The cobwebs are gone. I was stunned, that's all. A grenade went off near my head. Even you, with your massive skull, would have been shaken by that blast."

Dariush laughed. Making fun of Kamal's head was a sign that Marduk was indeed back in his right mind.

Kamal likewise smiled. "Okay then, it's been fifteen minutes, and no signs of life. They may have someone on guard, or they may be asleep. Either way, you see someone, kill them."

Marduk's grin turned malevolent. "With pleasure."

The trio approached the entrance to the safe house on silent feet. It felt good to Kamal to be moving and going in with a clean-sweep mission. It should be easy.

The men adjusted their night vision and prepared to enter. Dariush entered the access code and swung the door inward.

Marduk swept in from the right side, moving to the left, while Kamal went left to right. Dariush followed, softly closing the door. He covered the main hallway while the other two men checked the rooms to either side. They returned a few moments later, signaling *all clear*, and advanced down the hall.

Marduk had already cleared the pantry, so the team moved into the women's dorm. Kamal signaled two people were in beds to the left and one to the right. With their suppressed pistols raised, they put three rounds into each form on the cots.

Kamal was surprised when his rounds struck the wall behind the bunk. He reached down and pulled the covers back to reveal pillows instead of a person. The other men whipped the sheets from their targets and found the same decoys.

"Trap!" Kamal whispered. The three men assumed defensive positions, expecting an attack from the Americans, but there was no movement, no noise. Kamal moved to the doorway, approaching from the left side. He saw no threat, no signs of life at all.

He motioned to the other two men to move behind him. He crossed the hall into the armory with Marduk on his tail. Dariush covered the hallway.

The shelves in the armory were picked over, with only a handful of pistols and rifles left. The ammunition cabinets were bare.

"I have a feeling the birds have flown the nest," Marduk observed.

Kamal cursed. "Come on, let's check the last room."

They found the men's dorm was set up with the same decoys in the bunks.

Kamal removed his night vision and reached for the light switch, waiting for the other two to get theirs off before clicking it.

In the light, they could see the room, aside from the decoy bunks, had hardly been used. Dariush went to the comms room. Other than some collateral damage to the cabinets from the battle, everything appeared to be undisturbed.

"Let me check something out," Dariush said. He ran down the main hallway toward the front of the safe house and turned left, into the first hall off to the side. Kamal and Marduk moved forward as well.

Dariush came in from the door at the end of the side hall. "They took the vehicle that was here."

Kamal scoffed. "We stole theirs, so they stole ours. What of it?"

"We can track it. Every one of our vehicles has a GPS device in it. We can follow their movements and go straight to them. The information I need should be in the site documentation. It's going to be on the computer."

Kamal smiled. "Get to it then."

Dariush took off to the comms room.

"Kamal, what is this supposed to be?"

Kamal went to Marduk, who was pointing at a sheet of paper on one of the tables. It contained a drawing of a hand with the middle finger extended, but the middle finger was a circumcised penis that appeared to be ejaculating. The letter "U" was underneath it, and below that, it said, "Iranian pieces of shit."

Kamal chuckled.

"What does it say?" Marduk asked again.

"It says that when we find them, they're going to die painfully. Allahu Akbar!"

CHAPTER SIXTEEN

TINCUP, COLORADO. MAY 8

The huge 4x4 van was surprisingly light and agile. They'd used far less gas than they expected to burn through and had to stop once on the way to siphon gas for Robin's Blazer. The van was configured for transport rather than camping, so it had three rows of seats, allowing the group to spread out a bit.

The drive would usually take four and a half hours, but they had to deal with roads blocked by abandoned and wrecked cars, along with pockets of infected hordes, and wound up using a lot of back roads. The van's 4x4 capability came in handy quite a few times.

Robin slowed down at the last curve on County Road 765. They passed a pair of people on opposite sides of the road, both of them sitting on their tailgates, one truck pointed north, the other aimed south. Robin waved at the man on the northbound side of the road. He waved back and said something into a walkie-talkie.

Charlie waved as they passed the man, and again he returned the wave.

"Real friendly up here," Duckett said from the passenger seat.

Charlie nodded and pointed at a sign made of rough-hewn timbers, formed into a square. Five slats hung from the middle of those timbers with alternating rows of red and black lettering.

WELCOME TO
TIN CUP, COLORADO
THIS IS GOD'S COUNTRY
PLEASE DON'T DRIVE THROUGH IT
LIKE HELL

DUCKETT CHUCKLED. "That's different. Doesn't get much more homespun than that."

"You say that like it's a bad thing. I love these places. Hobb's Valley was like this. Everyone knows everyone else, looks out for each other, but they don't get all involved in your shit, you know?"

"No, man, I don't know. I grew up in Kansas City. Never saw a mountain until I joined the Army, let alone a mountain town."

"Well, they're friendly, but they're going to look at us like we're Martians. At least, at first. Mountain folk are strange. First, you have to realize they live far away from people on purpose. They're friendly, they appreciate manners, but they don't trust outsiders."

Partway through the tiny town, Robin pulled over into the dirt parking lot of the Tin Cup Store. "Store" was a stretch; it was a little red building with an American flag hanging from the front. Above one of the windows, a wooden sign read *Elv. 10,157 ft.*

Charlie pulled in behind Robin, drove past her and turned around, then backed up and parked with the front end of the van pointed toward the street.

Robin got out of the Blazer, followed by Leonard and Lori. She walked around to the van's side doors, which Aaron had just pushed open.

"Okay, guys listen up. We're here to see a guy named Frank James. I know Frank from way back. He spends most of his days here, so I suspect that hasn't changed—assuming he's still alive."

"You mean we spent seven hours in the car, and the guy might not even be alive?"

Robin looked at Duckett. "Do you speak Korean?" He shook his head. "Know anyone who does?" He shook his head again. "Well, no one else had any bright ideas, so here we are. Frank was friends with my dad. They served together in Korea, and Frank brought a mama-San home with him. He's fluent—speaking, reading, writing—the real deal. His wife passed some time ago, and he's been holed up here in Tin Cup ever since. He's not a mountain man, per se, not in the Jeremiah Johnson sense, but he's uncouth and probably smells bad. He's also going to talk shit to us. That's just his way. Don't take anything personally. Don't take his crap, but don't get too aggressive talking shit back to him. Got it?"

Around the group, they all said they understood.

"Okay, just me, Charlie, and Duckett go for now. Frenchy's isn't that big of a place, and I don't want to bring a crowd. You guys can hang out here, and we'll wave you over if we need you."

Leonard started to protest, but Sarah put a hand on his shoulder. "It's fine, Leonard. Let them go."

Charlie grabbed the backpack from the van and the trio headed across the dirt Main Street to a bridge that crossed over a pond. They climbed a ten-foot staircase that ended at a wrap-around deck in front of a log cabin. The window displayed a sign that said *Frenchy's Café*. Another sign, to the right of the entrance, announced the elevation as 10,167 feet.

Confused, Duckett pointed at the sign, but Robin cut him off. "Yeah, I know, the stairs raise the elevation by ten feet from the store. It's a running joke."

Charlie pulled the door open, allowing Robin and Duckett to walk through, then he followed them inside.

The interior was an open space under a vaulted ceiling. The supports and joists were massive logs, while planks formed the ceiling and floor. A cow skull adorned one of the supports. Everything about Frenchy's was rustic and authentic, down to the people who occupied the space. A dozen people sat at the half dozen tables that filled the open room, and they were all staring at the trio of strangers who had just walked in. Every one of them had their hands on a pistol or rifle, except an old man with wild white hair and a bushy beard that had more than a little food spilled on it.

"All that's missing is a record scratching as the needle gets yanked off it," Duckett muttered under his breath so only Charlie could hear it. Charlie chuckled but didn't reply.

Robin walked over to a table facing out a side window and sat next to the white-haired man. "No gun for you, Frank?"

He scoffed. "You see all the others in here? I got no need for one."

"Not even with the infected?"

"You see any infected in here? No? It's because everyone has a gun! When the sickies show up, if they get past the others, I'll get my gun."

"It's good to see you, Frank. I'm glad you're still above ground."

He turned to look at her for the first time, chewing on a long strip of bacon that was half in, half out of his mouth. "You've gotten old, Robin. Your face has more wrinkles than a Chinaman's ass."

"Chinamen have wrinkly asses?"

"You ever see one?"

"No. Don't think so."

"Well, they're smooth as the day they was born. And your face ain't." He turned back to his plate and shoveled some egg and some corned beef hash into his mouth.

"Frank, we need your help."

"Who's *we*? You got a turd in your pocket?"

She nodded at Charlie and Duckett. "The people I came here with."

"Well, bring them over," he said. Then he raised his voice to a shout. "I ain't gonna shout across the room at them!"

The two men hustled across the room, ignoring the laughs and comments from the rest of the patrons, who relaxed and left their weapons where they were.

"Set down there," Frank said as he gestured at the other two chairs. He looked them over while they situated themselves. "What have we got here?" He pointed at Charlie and said, "You're old, can't decide if you're crotchety or grizzled. I lean toward grizzled. And you, Army. I got no truck with you. You wear the uniform, you get a pass." He turned back toward Robin. "What's up with the Injuns and the women across the street? You think I'd scare 'em off?" He shoveled another forkful of food into his mouth.

"You can be a real prick, but no, we didn't want to crowd the room."

"Pity. I like the Injuns. The women I don't trust, but the Injuns are all right." He could see he wasn't going to get a rise from the trio, so he pressed on. "What is it you need? You must be pretty desperate, to drive to this ass-crack of a town looking for an old coot like me."

"Hey! Watch what you call this town, Dirty Frank, or we'll toss you in the pond and give you a bath!"

Frank turned to the local at the nearest table. "Only if you'll wash my back, Roger." He winked at Robin. "The back of my sack!" He laughed at his own joke hard enough that he started coughing, spitting chewed bits of egg on the table and into his beard.

A waitress approached the table. "If you all haven't lost your appetites, can I get you anything?"

Charlie nodded. "Coffee'd be great."

"Same," Duckett added.

Robin smiled at her. "Make it three."

Frank finished the last of his breakfast and pushed the plate to the far side of the table. "So, what is it ol' Frank James can do for you?"

Robin nodded at Charlie, who unzipped the backpack. "We've come across some information that may be very important. The only problem is, it's written in Korean, and we're fresh out of people who can translate it."

"Shit, it's been years since I've used that language. Not since Jeong's family stopped writing after she died. Clinton was still calling the shots then. I can't help you."

"I bet it will come back to you if you take a look," Duckett said.

"Oh, you bet it will, do you? What the fuck do you know? Maybe I don't *want* it to come back, Junior. Maybe it brings back shit I'd rather not think of. Besides," he turned his head toward Robin, "don't you have your Googles and whatnot to answer this shit for you?"

"Not since the Net went down," Charlie said. "My son died for this information, Frank. I know you don't owe us anything, but some nasty folks have tried killing us for these papers, too. Killed one of Robin's good friends, got one of Leonard's friends."

"Who's Leonard?"

"He's one of the Indians outside. They put his grandfather in the hospital. Whatever is on here, they're willing to kill anyone who gets in their way to get it back."

"Get it back? You mean you stole it from someone?" the local at the nearest table exclaimed. Every head in the place was looking their way.

A man with long red hair and a red beard, full, but well kept, chimed in. "They tried killing you, and you came here? Bringing trouble to our doorstep? I think maybe you all should get moving."

"What the fuck kind of Viking are you, Lars? You ain't getting into Valhalla with that attitude," Frank shot back at him.

"I'd rather not go to Valhalla, period, Frank. I'm in no hurry to die, especially for some out-of-towners' problems."

Charlie cleared his throat. "Listen, this illness that's taken out most of the country was not just a pandemic. It was a deliberate attack. The people who did it were working with a doctor in El Paso who tortured my son, Jack. He was infected but never turned. We assumed they were trying to figure out why he wasn't losing his mind like everyone else who was infected, but they weren't. They were dosing him with whatever this thing is, and it eventually overtook his immune system and killed him."

Murmurs of disbelief rippled through the group, with *I told you!* coming from a couple people.

"It's true," Duckett added. "I worked at the place where it happened. We—the Army—had no idea what this doctor was doing. He's dead now, but his last act was to put this stuff into an envelope and leave it for... well, we don't know who. The documents are in Korean, but the people chasing us are Iranian."

Another man wearing a camouflage vest and ball cap scoffed. "Figures, those sneaky fuckers. We shoulda nuked both countries when we had the chance. Turned that desert shithole into a sheet of glass and taken the oil underneath it."

"And to think we gave them hundreds of millions of dollars. Paid them to kill us off," chimed in another man.

"*We* didn't pay them, *Obama* did," a woman proclaimed.

"He was the President, like it or not," Camouflage vest said. "So yes, *we* paid them. Tried to buy friend-ship, like Chamberlain in Munich in 'thirty-eight with Hitler. Appeasement never works."

Others in the room nodded.

"MacArthur wanted to nuke the Norks in 'fifty-one, but Truman wouldn't let him," Duckett said. "At least that's what my gramps said. He hated that place."

"Your gramps fought in Korea?" Frank asked.

"Yeah. Fought in the islands in the Second World War and went back over in 'fifty. My grams said he was never the same when he came home the first time. Said war was the only thing that made sense to him. When he came home from Korea, he said he'd done enough killing, finally had his fill of war."

"Hell, boy, they had multiple scenarios for nuking the Norks and China. Truman wasn't askeered of using them bombs. They even made practice runs in 'fifty-one, using dummy bombs. It was the French who convinced Truman not to do it. They were askeered of Russia taking over more of Europe while we was nukin' it out with China. Besides, when you get right down to it, what was there to nuke? Buncha huts and shanties? The Norks was so spread out I don't think it woulda done much, and as it was, we leveled that whole damned country with conventional bombs. All it did was drive them buggers underground."

The man in the camo vest said, "Figures the French would cry foul. They're the ones got us pulled into Vietnam."

The people at the other tables veered off into a half dozen conversations of historical and more recent geopolitics.

"Kelly!" Frank called out.

The waitress came over with three coffees and set the pot on the table. "Yeah, Frank?"

"Seven specials, please. These folks are hungry, I'm sure. And I'll need more of *my* coffee." He turned to Robin and tapped the stack of papers. "Get the rest of your people up here and get 'em fed. This is going to take me a while."

"THEY'VE NOT MOVED for two hours," Dariush said. He accessed the tracking software, using the satellite Internet dome they had affixed to the roof of the Mercedes. With it, they could access their secure network, send text updates to their superiors, get updates on events, and, as they were doing now, track their tagged vehicles.

"Or the van hasn't moved. We can't assume they haven't changed vehicles." Kamal wasn't optimistic they were going to catch up to the group. The mountain roads were impossible to get any sort of speed going. Every time he got a bit of open road where he could put the gas pedal down, a sharp curve made him slow to a crawl, barely above fifteen kilometers per hour.

"Any other news?" Kamal asked Dariush.

"Yes. The base in New Mexico was breached by the Americans."

"Where?"

"New Mexico."

"Where in New Mexico?"

"Alberkeeurkee," Dariush struggled with the pronunciation.

Kamal laughed. He loved making Dariush say that. No matter how many times he was corrected, his tongue just couldn't wrap itself around *Albuquerque*. Kamal grew serious again. "What happened at the base?"

"American paramilitary units got in. They had one of the codes."

"That's bad. We have a lot of equipment in Albuquerque." He stole a glance at Dariush, who returned a sarcastic smile. "What are you grinning about?"

"They're sending in artillery, T-14s, to dig them out."

"What? They'll destroy the helicopters and other mechanized units there! And why are they exposing the T14s already? The Americans aren't supposed to know this is an invasion. We haven't accounted for all their military assets yet. These fools are going to tip our hand too soon."

Dariush checked his watch. "Well, it's too late. The battle has already started."

Kamal clenched his jaw, his beard jutting out an additional inch on each side of his face.

"This air is so thin!" Marduk complained. "How do these Americans live at this altitude?"

Kamal stared at Marduk in the mirror for a moment, his glare shrinking the man. "You've been to the top of Mount Damavand with no oxygen. You're part of the *niruhaye vizheh*. Act like it. Dariush, how much longer to get there?"

Marduk mumbled under his breath that he knew damn well he was part of the Iranian Special Forces but didn't say it loud enough for Kamal to hear. He leaned to the side and watched the scenery go by as he absently scratched at his scalp.

In the front seat, Dariush consulted the GPS unit. "GPS says three hours."

"Send an update to Command. Let them know we're on the move and will have an update in three and a half hours."

CHAPTER SEVENTEEN

TIN CUP, COLORADO. MAY 8

"Here's *your* coffee, Frank?" Kelly said as she set the mug next to him on her way to clear off another table

Leonard looked at the dark liquid. "What makes it *your* coffee? Is it like, a special blend or something?"

Kelly passed by with an armload of dirty dishes. "It's only coffee in the loosest sense of the word," she sniped as she disappeared into the kitchen.

Leonard looked after her for a second before it clicked. "Oh, you put whiskey in it!"

Frank took a long drink from the mug and winked at Leonard. "It's one of my secrets to a long life, boy. That, and not doing stupid shit."

Leonard chuckled. "How old are you?"

"I was born in Missoura in nineteen hundred and thirty-one, smack in the great depression. Can you imagine that? People who could barely put two beans together to feed themselves bringing a kid into the world?"

"It happens all the time on the reservation."

Frank considered the comment for a moment. "Aye, I guess it happens all over. I suppose if you've got no money, you've got limited options for entertainment, and fuckin's free. Add that to my list of things that lead to a long life. Fucking whenever you can. One day you'll wake up, and you'll find there's no lead in the pencil. Use it while you can, son."

Leonard looked across the room at Lori and blushed.

Robin and Sarah walked in the front entrance. They'd grabbed spare jackets, hats, and gloves.

"The temperature is down twenty degrees in the last two hours," Robin said. "That wind is bringing some arctic air down on us. Feels like a spring snowstorm's coming."

Sarah passed a lined jacket and a wool hat to Leonard, and Robin handed off the same items to Lori. She joined Sarah at the woodburning stove where they warmed their hands. "Oh man, does this feel good."

"Have some of my coffee," Frank offered. "It'll warm you up real nice. Kelly'll fix you a cup." He gave Leonard a wink.

Robin sat down at the end of the table. "How's the translating coming, Frank?"

"I'm about half done. My hand was cramping, so I'm taking a break. I have old fingers, Mitiko. Old fingers and a slow mind for Korean. It's coming back," he raised a hand and tapped his temple, "but the file clerk in my head didn't put everything in the right place, if you know what I mean."

"Just do your best. It's all we can ask for."

Sarah sat at the opposite end of the table. "Can I see the pages you've done so far?"

Frank slid the stack of paper over to her. "Hope you can read my writing. If not, tough shit 'cuz that's as good as it gets."

She smiled at his comment, then focused on the first page.

Esteemed council, the electronic copies of these documents have failed to send. I fear the global networks may be failing. While they may yet reach you in electronic format, I am sending these hard copies, along with a memory card, as a backup.

The news is not good, I'm afraid. The disease is highly effective, infecting an estimated ninety-five percent of the population. A cure, or at least a halt to the progression, is proving elusive.

The two cases we had were interesting. Of the two, Washburn proved to be useless. While he was initially not affected by the disease, he did carry it in his blood. We tried different vector loads and ultimately, we were able to overcome his immune system, and this morning he turned. Interesting, but not very useful.

The other man, Rammacher, is different. Not only has he proven resistant to all our methods of infection, but each blood test also comes back clean. His immune system actually cleans all signs of the disease. Rammacher may be the key to putting Pandora back in her box.

SARAH LOOKED up from the papers, her eyes rimmed with tears. Reading what they had done to her husband, it was all she could do to hold herself together. She spotted Duckett sitting at a table on the other side of the stove, cleaning his weapons.

"Duckett, do you know what happened to Ram?"

"I expect those mercs have him. They left in a hurry after I let him go. Why?"

"Well, according to this, he may be the last hope for mankind. It might be good if we knew where he was."

"I know he was desperate to get back to his family. They're in California, but I have no idea where. If I had to guess, that's where I'd say he was headed."

"Frank, let me see that pen for a minute please."

He handed the pen to Sarah. She scribbled some notes in the margin and drew an arrow to Ram's name.

RAM ESCAPED custody before Beaumont Medical Center fell to the infected. Last seen with a para-military/mercenary force. His family is in California; believed to be his objective.

LIGHT SNOW BEGAN FALLING as the tempera-ture dipped below thirty degrees. Kelly brought out plates of steak and mashed potatoes for the denizens of Frenchy's.

"It's venison steak. Hope that's okay with you folks."

Duckett perked up. "Why wouldn't that be okay? It sounds amazing!"

"Well, some folks don't like it. Say it tastes gamey."

"Those people are ungrateful snobs. This looks great. Thank you, again, for taking such good care of us."

"It's my pleasure. We appreciate what you all are doing for us." Kelly smiled at Duckett and headed back into the kitchen.

Aaron started cutting his steak. "I appreciate the

food, but what is it, exactly we're doing? It feels like we're just hanging out."

Duckett took a sip of *Frank's coffee*. "Once Frank is done translating this thing, we're going to figure out how to get the information into the hands of someone in the government who can take action on it. Depending what it says, of course."

"Yeah, kid," Frank said through a mouthful of venison, some of the juice dribbling into his beard as he spoke. "We're saving the world! One day they'll write songs about us and shower us with riches!"

The door swung open, and Charlie and Robin came in, each carrying a box filled with food from the van. Charlie stomped his feet to get the snow off his boots before advancing into the room, and Robin did the same. They took the boxes to the counter.

"Where do you want these, Kelly?" Charlie asked.

She nodded to a spot off to the side. "Just set them over there. Thanks again; that's awfully nice of you folks. Grab a seat, I'll bring you some dinner."

The man in the camouflage vest sat at a table by the big tree trunk support pole. He thrust a Dixie cup out to both Robin and Charlie.

"Here," he offered. "This will warm you up!"

They both looked in their respective cups, saw the dark fluid inside, and tilted them back.

"Smooth, ain't it?" the man asked.

Charlie had one eye closed, letting the heat from the liquor finish its journey down to his feet and back. "Shit, friend, what is that?"

"Moonshine, Charlie! Didn't you get that over in Hobb's Valley?" Robin teased him. She looked the man in the eye. "I didn't catch your name before."

"Name's Carl. And you're right, it's from my own distillery. I've got a cabin with a rig up toward Jones Mountain. I make about five barrels a year. I'll give you a couple of bottles for that food y'all gave us."

"Thanks, Carl, but it's our pleasure. You all have put us up all day, fed us, made us feel welcome. It's the least we could do," Robin said.

"Still, I'd like to give you a couple," he persisted.

Charlie had both eyes open again. "Tell you what, Carl, you help me get another couple boxes, and we'll make it a trade. Sound good?"

"Aye, let's do it!"

The two men strode back out into the snow, headed across the street to the van.

"That's it!" Frank exclaimed. "Your translation is done!"

Duckett kicked Sarah's foot under the table, and she lifted her head, startled out of her nap.

"Huh? What? Duckett? What's happening?" She reached for the pistol on her hip, thinking they were under attack again.

"Relax, Sarah. Frank finished the translation."

"Oh, okay. Shit, I was out cold." She yawned and stretched her arms over her head in a big "Y" shape. "Thank you, Frank. You're a Godsend!"

"Now, I don't know about that. I'm glad I could be

useful, but you all have to figure out what to do with this stuff."

She surprised him with a big hug, braving the funk of his body odor and the food in his beard. She gave it a playful tug. "You should clean that out. You're going to get ants."

Frank laughed. "Wouldn't be the first time! Now, where is that bottle of Carl's?" He walked over to the tables bunched up in the middle of the room and filled a paper cup with the moonshine.

On the table, near the bottle, a walkie-talkie crackled.

"Carl, we're switching out. It's fucking freezing out here. Tell Kelly to get some coffee ready if she hasn't already."

Sarah and Frank stared at the radio, neither one making a move to pick it up. Sarah glanced out the window and saw Charlie and Carl crossing the street, headed back to the café. She picked up the radio.

"Hi. You don't know me, but Carl just ran outside for a minute and left the radio here in the café. I'll give him your message, and Kelly has coffee ready."

There was a pause, then the voice spoke again.

"Okay, appreciate it. Also, tell him we haven't seen the hipsters in the Mercedes again. I don't think they're going to come back through town."

Sarah's blood froze in her veins. "What Mercedes?"

"Some bearded hipster-looking guys drove through in

a Mercedes SUV about an hour ago. Figured they were headed to the café. Lars said they went real slow, almost stopped at the store but headed on north out of town."

"You said this was an SUV?"

"Yeah, one of the boxy ones with the flat windshield. I don't know the model, so don't ask."

"Was it silver?"

"Yeah. You know 'em?"

Sarah jumped as the door opened and Charlie and Carl walked in with two more boxes of food. Charlie saw the look on Sarah's face. It reminded him of the look he saw back at his cabin when Rollie woke up infected, and Sarah had realized that the only way he could have gotten infected was from exposure to her husband's blood; and therefore, Jack had to be infected too. It was a look of panic.

"Sarah!" he said, dropping the box to the floor and kicking it toward the kitchen. "I know that look. What's the matter?"

"They're here."

"Who?"

"*Them.* The Iranians," she said with a trembling voice. "We need to leave. Now."

CHAPTER EIGHTEEN

K amal slowed for the last curve heading into the tiny town. A pair of men on either side of the road had spotted them. One of them picked up a radio and said something.

"So much for the element of surprise," Dariush said.

The man on the northbound side of the road waved, and Dariush waved back, smiling.

"What are you doing?" Kamal asked.

"Blending in. Someone waves, you wave back, right? And you say," he switched to English for one of the only phrases he knew in the infidels' language, "Howdy, partner!"

"Yeah, you blend in well with that accent. How close are we?"

"According to this, it's ahead on the left."

Kamal slowed down. "Get our rifles ready, but

don't hold them so anyone can see them. But be ready to go if it starts." He glanced in the rearview mirror. "Marduk, do you hear me?"

Marduk's sunken eyes looked back at him. He looked exhausted, and he was sweating despite the cool temperature in the vehicle. *The blow to his head must have been worse than we suspected,* Kamal thought.

"I'm ready, Kamal. Death to America." Marduk's right hand was on the rifle, but his left reflexively went to his head and scratched it.

A small red building sat on the left side of the road, and a cabin was on the opposite side. A narrow foot-bridge crossed over a pond, and a flight of stairs rose to meet a deck that surrounded the front and side of the building. A dozen men and women were outside. Each one of them had a rifle, either over a shoulder with the barrel pointing straight up, or slung military style. Several of the men were smoking cigars.

"Does every American have a gun?" Dariush asked.

"Behind every blade of grass..." Kamal answered, even though he knew the question was rhetorical.

"There!" Dariush exclaimed, pointing to the left at the van parked on the lee side of the small red building.

Kamal slowed almost to a stop. The van and the large SUV next to it were both empty; at least, there was no one visible inside either vehicle. Aware that the group on the deck were watching them, Kamal acceler-ated, continuing north and drove out of town, passing another pair of people on either side of the road. Again, one of the men waved, and Dariush returned the gesture.

"Kamal, where are we going?"

"We're going to be smart for once on this mission, Dariush. We're going to find a spot to hide out and wait for a time when the odds are in our favor. Since it was the only place that looked occupied, I'm making an assumption the Americans were in that cabin across the pond. We're three men. I'm not going to underestimate their abilities again. We wait for the van to move, and we track it and ambush them on the road."

"They saw us. They'll be ready for that."

"No, I don't think they connected the dots. There was no reaction from the people outside that cabin, and the sentries at the edge of town said 'Howdy partner' as we passed. We bide our time, and we'll get them."

"HOW LONG AGO DID THEY drive through?"

Lars looked at his watch. "Probably ninety minutes ago. Look, I'm sorry. I didn't know we were supposed to be looking for that car."

Charlie was looking through Carl's night vision rifle scope. "It was just a failure of communication. We should have stressed that a bunch of Iranian madmen were probably on their way here. I'm sure you would have let us stay, right?"

Carl chuckled. "Yeah, we would have sent you packing, that's for sure." He reached for his rifle. "In fact, now that you mention it, shouldn't you be going?"

Charlie passed the rifle back. "Yes, we should. Thanks again for the help, Frank, and please thank Kelly for the hospitality and food. If we get out of this thing alive..."

"Don't," Carl interrupted. "Even if you get out of this, please, just forget about us. We're doing fine. If we need anything, we'll look for help."

Charlie stuck his hand out. Carl grabbed it and shook it. "Fair enough, Carl. Good luck to you guys."

"You too, Charlie."

The group moved to the door and carefully descended the stairs to the bridge, trying not to slip in the snow. As they approached the street, they scouted up and down the road to ensure no one was coming. Charlie's scan with the night vision scope hadn't revealed anyone lurking around their vehicles. Satisfied the way was clear, they skittered across the road and split up into the two different rides—Charlie, Aaron, Leonard, and Lori in the van, and Robin, Sarah, and Duckett in the Blazer. Charlie rolled down his window and motioned for Duckett, sitting in the front passenger seat of the Chevy, to do the same.

"Okay, we're clear on the route, right? And if we get separated, you know the meetup points, correct?"

Duckett nodded. "We take 267 east. First meetup south end of Mirror Lake, second meetup Pagosa Springs, third is Chimney Rock. Got it."

"And you have the copy of the package? Double check."

Duckett turned to Sarah and asked her. A few seconds later he turned back around. "Yeah, Sarah has it."

"All right, let's roll."

"THEY'RE MOVING."

Kamal sat up and raised the seat back. "Which way? Surely Allah will smile on us for once, and they're headed north."

"Allah is not smiling. They're going south."

"We're going to make this trip in two steps. Remember the sentries at the edge of town?"

"Of course."

"When we get to the last bend in the road, you and Marduk get out. I'll give you three minutes to get into position, and I'll approach them slowly. When they show themselves, you take them out. Then we head through town. Clear?"

"Clear," Dariush confirmed.

"Marduk?"

"Yeah, clear."

"Okay," Kamal started the engine. "Off we go." He pulled the Mercedes back onto the main road, turning left to point them south, back into town. He was worried about the snow, but the all-wheel drive vehicle was stable and had no issues with the few inches of accumulation.

THE APPROACHING HEADLIGHTS SLOWED, then stopped.

"Vehicle coming from the north."

"Is it the Mercedes?" Carl asked into the walkie-talkie.

"Can't tell. They have the brights on."

"Don't let them pass. One of you pull your truck across the road. If they move forward, the other one shoots the driver."

Carl waited for a response.

"Okay. Eddie's going to pull across the road and—"

Carl stared at the walkie, waiting for the rest of the sentence. Nothing. "Mike? You there? Do you copy?"

A few more ticks of his watch. No response.

"Mike? Eddie?"

No response.

"Carl, we got movement out here," Lars shouted through the window.

Carl jumped up and ran out to the deck. Lars had his rifle on the railing, tracking a vehicle moving down the main street. He pulled his own gun to his shoulder and got the scope centered on the car.

It was the square-bodied Mercedes.

"It's them. Light it up," he said. He pulled the trigger and worked the bolt to load another round.

"NICE WORK, you two. Now be ready for contact. We're going back through town. Expect an ambush, especially from the cabin above the pond."

He'd have to drive slower than he wanted to due to the snow on the road, and that made them more vulnerable to attack.

They hit the edge of town, and Kamal turned off the headlights. The combination of the snow and the quarter moon made the night light enough that he could navigate without the lights.

"We'll need to turn left in point-five kilometers," Dariush counseled.

Before Kamal could reply, the rear window exploded inward, showering Marduk with glass. Kamal swerved to the right, then the left, pressing the accelerator to speed up.

"Marduk! Get some fire up there!"

Dariush was opening the sunroof. Another round hit the side of the vehicle, and another hit the front fender. Dariush, now standing in the seat, swung his rifle to bear on the cabin. He fired several quick shots, not knowing if he was close, just wanting to get the Americans to duck their heads. His next salvo was concentrated on the dark shapes he saw behind the railing. He saw the big tempered window dropping large chunks of glass.

Gunfire from below him let him know that

Marduk was finally engaged in the fight. He dropped back inside the cabin and checked the GPS.

"Turn left at the next street!" he shouted, louder than he needed to, but adrenaline was coursing through his body.

Kamal slammed on the brakes. The antilock system kicked in, rattling the vehicle so much that, at first, he thought they were taking machine gun fire. The car slowed enough to make the turn, and he had his foot back on the gas. Dariush shut the sunroof, and the center of Tin Cup grew smaller in the rearview.

CARL LOOKED through the scope at the disappearing Mercedes. Between him and Lars, he knew they hit the thing at least a half dozen times. Hopefully, they got one or more of the Iranians. His shots went wild when they fired back, but at least neither he nor Lars had been hit.

He turned and looked at the shattered window. Where it used to say *Frenchy's Café*, it now read *chy's Café*.

Kelly'd be pissed about that. Where would they get someone to come and replace the window and re-do the sign in *this* world? He had a feeling he'd be the one doing the work. That was all right; he didn't mind.

He walked inside and heard a groan. They'd turned off the lights to hide their positions better, so he flipped the switch. It took a minute for his eyes to adjust to the light, and when they did, he saw Kelly lying on the floor, covered in blood.

"Aw, hell! Lars!! I need help in here!" He rushed to Kelly's side to do what he could to help her.

CHAPTER NINETEEN

"Thank God for four-wheel drive in this thing," Charlie said. "I can't imagine taking on these roads in this weather in a rear wheel drive van."

"Can't we go any faster?" Aaron asked.

"Not if you want to stay on the road. Four-wheel drive gives you better traction to go, but it doesn't stop any faster."

"I know, I just meant, I mean..."

"I know, Aaron. We can't get enough distance between them and us. I'll go as fast as I can."

"Look up there," Lori said, pointing to the left. A pair of headlights bounced along, on an almost parallel path to theirs. "You think it's them?"

Charlie thought for a second before answering. "It would be a big coincidence if it wasn't, wouldn't it? But how would they know these roads well enough to be up there? I mean, I've lived in these mountains most of my life, and I've never driven on this road. It's not exactly a major road, and that one has to be tiny compared to this one."

Ahead, the tail lights of the Blazer lit up as Robin hit the brakes. They fishtailed back and forth, the headlights flashing up into the canopy of pines, then down into the snow on the ground. The big SUV stopped in the middle of the road, turned slightly askew, one headlight pointing straight up into the trees.

Charlie hit the brakes, and the van started to skid, so he let them off and let the wheels turn again, then he began pumping the brake pedal as fast as he could. He wasn't going to stop in time. He saw an opening in the trees to the left and steered toward it, still pumping the brakes and turning into the skid.

It was a driveway. The post with the mailbox made a loud *pop* as the van hit it, the black USPS box flying one way and the red box for the newspaper going another. The van slid past the Blazer, missing it by two feet, and came to a rest with the front end pointed into the driveway and the back end in the ditch on the far side of the entry.

"Everyone okay?" Charlie asked.

They all answered in the affirmative. He hopped out to check on the Blazer and found the front driver's side corner smashed in, the headlight askew. A big deer, a buck with a good-sized rack of antlers, was lying on the hood, one foreleg jammed through the windshield, the other pawing weakly at the glass. The rear legs weren't moving, so Charlie assumed the spine had been broken. The creature wheezed, frothy blood spilling from its mouth and nostrils.

Lori ran to the Blazer to check on the occupants. Robin was okay. Sarah, sitting in the back, was fine. But Duckett was covered in blood. The deer's hoof had smashed through the windshield and split his forehead open.

While she was tending to Duckett, Charlie went back to the van to see how bad it was stuck. He started the engine and got it moving forward. The back end kept sliding sideways until the ditch shallowed, and he got it back on the driveway. He was going to execute a three-point turn and get it pointed back at the main road, but the drive was a horseshoe, so he followed it around the bend and back to the road a couple hundred feet in front of the Blazer.

After putting it in park, he turned to Aaron and Leonard. "You two stay here. If I don't come back, you take the van and get the hell out of here, you understand? Don't look back, just go."

"We're not leaving you," Leonard said.

"Don't argue. Someone has to make it. Promise me."

"We promise," Aaron said. Leonard shot him a look.

Charlie got out and started walking back toward the Blazer. He could just make out the shape of the deer on the hood, when gunfire erupted in front of him.

"Shit!" he said aloud. He ducked down and moved

to the south side of the road and ran in a crouch toward the sounds of battle.

"THEY'VE STOPPED."

Kamal took his foot off the gas. "What do you think? Ambush?"

Dariush considered it. "Maybe. They know that we're here, clearly, since they had the townspeople shooting at us. But why would they make a stand against us now? They think they've gotten away from us."

Kamal turned off the lights and slowed to a crawl. "Tell me when we're a half kilometer away. We'll stop and go on foot, surprise them, get the package and go."

A few minutes later, they stopped. Kamal opened the rear of the Mercedes and grabbed his pack. He pulled a mylar-lined jacket out of a pouch on the side, shook it out, and slipped it on then slid a tactical vest over it. He put extra magazines for his rifle in the pockets then shouldered the pack.

Dariush was likewise preparing to go. Marduk was struggling with his vest.

"Marduk, come on, we need to go. Do you need help with your vest?" Kamal offered.

"I... yes, I could use some help. I am not myself since the concussion."

Kamal studied Marduk for a moment. He indeed was not himself. The bravado and over-the-top alpha male was gone, and an unsure mouse had replaced him. Kamal helped pull the vest over Marduk's head. His hand brushed over something slick and wet, and he realized Marduk's head was bleeding.

"Marduk, you're bleeding!" He began checking the man over for wounds. "Were you hit back in town?"

"No, I don't think so. I got glass all over me. Maybe cut me?"

The concussion must have been far worse than Kamal had thought. This was a risk to the mission. "Marduk, I need a truthful assessment. Are you fit for this op?"

"Yes, Kamal. Kill Americans." He managed a sneer, but it was less intimidating than it was feral.

"Just do your job, Marduk. We're almost done here. We kill these Americans, we get the package, and we'll be in Phoenix in the morning. Then we'll get you the medical treatment you need, okay? But I need you to do your job. Can you do that?"

Marduk straightened his vest and started loading magazines into the pockets. "Yes, Kamal. I can do job."

Kamal turned to Dariush. "Are you ready?"

He nodded. "Let's get this done."

They set out at a slow jog, knowing the van was only four hundred meters ahead. They adjusted their night vision. Ahead, they could see tail lights from a vehicle sitting diagonally across the road. As they drew closer, they saw three figures inside. The driver had the door open.

"I'll take the driver. Marduk, back seat. Dariush, front seat."

"Where are the others? There are four more. We should account for them before we engage with these three."

Of course, Dariush was right. They'd rushed into previous encounters and paid heavy prices by underestimating the Americans.

The snow cushioned their steps, making their approach quieter than they could have hoped. They moved slowly, veering off to the left, into the woods along the road, taking an elevated position. Dariush leaned in close to Kamal.

"That is not the van. It's the other large SUV we saw back in town. I see tracks ahead. I'll go see what I can find out. You wait here with Marduk."

"Make it fast. Coms channel three."

With the snowfall growing heavier, Dariush disappeared from sight in just a few steps. Wind whipped through the woods, sending snow cascading down from the tops of the pine trees, causing a momentary white out. Kamal's fingers were feeling the pinpricks of pain from exposure to the cold. He glanced at Marduk and saw steam rising from the man's head, almost like the cuts from the glass were letting his internal heat escape.

"The van is a hundred meters ahead of your position," Dariush said over the walkie-talkie. *"I only see two people in the van through the infrared. I can take*

them out now, or come back and help you with the larger group. You make the call."

Kamal considered the course of action. "Take them out. We'll work these four." He turned to Marduk. "Okay, we're going to approach the vehicle from two angles. I'll come from the front, you from the rear. We put everyone on the ground, we recover the package, and we get out of here. You good to go?"

Marduk looked back at him with a strange expression. "Good."

Kamal started to say something, but Marduk's eyes drifted to the left. He raised his rifle, the suppressed barrel aimed just to the right of Kamal's head. The flash from the muzzle blinded him for a minute. He dropped to his left, out of the path of Marduk's fire. He rolled to a kneeling position, rifle raised, looking for whatever had caused Marduk to start shooting. Several deer scampered through the woods as Marduk kept pulling the trigger.

Even suppressed, the shots made enough noise that Kamal was confident the Americans had heard them. He grabbed the other man by the shoulders. "Marduk! Stop! Give me your weapon!" He jerked the rifle away from him and tossed it away into the woods. He should have known better than to bring him on the operation. He was obviously not fit to be in combat.

Before he could turn his attention back to the vehicle on the road, gunfire erupted from below, rounds slapping the ground and splintering wood from nearby trees. He saw shapes moving around the SUV and fired at them, using a quick line of sight to get rounds close to them, giving him time to find better cover.

"Kamal, what's happening? I heard shots."

Kamal keyed the talk button. "Stay on mission. I've got this."

He turned his attention back to the road. One of the people was prone on the ground, but he couldn't tell if they were wounded, dead, or just using the position to stabilize a shot at him.

He found a spot behind a large pine tree butted against an eighteen-inch high rock to hide behind. He took a second to breathe and calm his nerves, lowering his heart rate. He could tell, scanning the area, that none of the Americans knew where he was. He had a good bead on one of the Americans, and he squeezed the trigger.

CHAPTER TWENTY

EAST OF TIN CUP, COLORADO. MAY 8

Charlie ran to the side of the Blazer. He found Duckett leaning over the hood with his rifle pointed into the woods north of the vehicle. Lori was squatting behind the front tire. "What's happening?"

"We heard shots from the woods up there," Duckett said, pointing into the woods. "Suppressed, I think. When we returned fire, we spotted some figures running around, but several deer came out on the driveway over there, so I can't be sure how many were people versus animal."

"I can't see the Mercedes. Do you know where they came from?"

"Probably saw us stopped and came on foot."

"We should get everyone moving to the van and get out of Dodge. We're sitting ducks out here."

"Agreed," Duckett responded.

Sarah pushed the passenger seat forward and

crawled out of the back seat. "Robin was hit when they returned fire. I don't know how badly."

"Got my leg," Robin's disembodied voice drifted under the Blazer.

A round thumped into Charlie's chest, sending him to the ground. Lori scuttled over to him while Duckett fired a few shots into the woods. He heard another shot and felt the buzz of the bullet as it passed inches from his head. He ducked and ran to the rear of the Blazer. "Sarah, when I say *now*, I need you to fire into the woods. Concentrate on the area about ten yards from the driveway, fifty or so yards back. Empty your magazine. Okay?"

"Yeah, okay." She flopped out of the vehicle and took Duckett's spot by the front tire. "I'm ready."

"Now."

She stood and spun around, quickly getting her bearings and firing the rifle, shooting two or three shots in one area, moving her point of aim a few feet, firing a few more shots, until her magazine was empty. She dropped down behind the fender just as a volley of shots pinged off of the hood and thumped into the body of the deer.

Robin's rifle started barking from the other side of the Blazer. Sarah stole a look at the rear of the SUV; Duckett was gone.

AARON AND LEONARD sat in the van with the side

doors open. They watched Charlie through the snow until he disappeared.

"Man, we were so close to getting the frick out of town," Aaron lamented. "I just want to get back home and sleep in my bed for like a week. I hate this shit."

A series of thumps reached their ears.

"Was that gunfire?"

"I don't know," Leonard replied. "It seemed far away if it was."

A few seconds later, the sounds of a volley of unsuppressed shots washed over them.

"Now *that's* gunfire," Leonard said. He grabbed his rifle and flipped the safety off. Aaron took the cue and did the same. "I feel like a rat in a cage here, Aaron. I think we should take positions in the woods above the van."

"If you think so, okay. I'll follow your lead."

Leonard stood to get out of the van when a round from a rifle hit him in the chest and knocked him back. Before Aaron could react, another shot caught him right over his heart, and he collapsed to the floor of the van.

Seconds later, a figure emerged from the snow, advancing on the van. The bearded man slung his rifle behind his back and jumped into the vehicle. He used a small flashlight with a red filter to look around the rear cabin and spotted a black backpack. He grabbed it, unzipped it, and saw a series of papers inside, printed with Korean lettering. He checked the smaller pouch and found a memory card inside a small plastic case.

"Subhanallah!" he said aloud. He slipped his own pack off and stuffed the contents of the black bag into his, then he shouldered his bag once more and stepped out of the van. As he prepared to run back into the woods, he heard a groan behind him. He spun around and found one of the young dark-skinned boys moving. He raised the rifle, aiming at the young man's head.

DUCKETT HOPPED into the woods on the south side of the road. When he'd moved far enough downhill to be hidden from the shooters on the other side, he sprinted a couple hundred yards west. He was about to cross back and circle around behind the shooter, when something caught his eye. It was the shape of a vehicle, obscured by the snow. He ran a little farther and saw that it was the Mercedes. He ran over to it and checked inside. No one was home.

Inside the cab, he saw the key fob in the console. He smiled, started the engine, and pulled it forward, around the last bend in the road before the Blazer. He slowed down and opened the door, aimed the front end to the left of where he thought the Blazer sat, and hopped out, leaving it in gear. He watched for a second to ensure it was moving forward with the engine idling, then he ran up the hillside.

When he had gone farther up the hill than he estimated the shooters were, he turned back to the east. He slowed his pace, trying to get control of his breathing.

As he moved ahead, he saw a figure crouched behind a rock. The man was focused on the idling Mercedes that had run off the side of the road and wedged itself against the hillside.

Duckett brought his rifle up and took aim. Just as he started to squeeze the trigger, something to his right growled.

He turned his head and was surprised to see one of the bearded Iranians just a few feet from him. Duckett stood and took a step back. The man snarled and snapped at the air, then renewed his focus on Duckett.

"Oh, shit!" Duckett exclaimed. He knew an infected when he saw one.

The Iranian threw his head back and let loose with a screech that echoed in the snowy night air. A hundred yards away, near the house at the top of the drive, deer that hadn't been spooked by the gunfire began to flee. The Iranian's head snapped back to focus on Duckett, locking eyes with him for a second, and then he charged.

KAMAL HEARD the muffled shots coming from the direction of the van and knew Dariush had taken care of the objective and killed the two people. He would wait and get confirmation from Dariush on the status of the package. If he recovered it from the van, they would simply go back to the Mercedes and get the hell out of this place. He had lost track of Marduk but had a good position with excellent cover. He'd be able to pick off the Americans with minimal risk of exposure to himself. If the package wasn't in the van, then once Dariush joined him, they'd have the Americans trapped and could end this in just a few minutes.

He had taken fire from the person on the ground in front of the big SUV, but before he could end them, they'd crawled under the vehicle and out of sight. He thought he could see a blood trail in the snow so he may not have to worry about them for much longer.

A noise from below and to his right caught his focus. He strained to see through the snow as a dark shape moved down the road. Another few seconds passed, and he recognized the Mercedes.

Marduk! What do you think you're doing?

The German SUV rolled forward, the driver's side tires edging off the road to the shallow drainage trough, then running against the edge of the hill, providing enough resistance to stop the idling vehicle. Kamal tried to see into the cab, but too many trees were between him and the road. He did not see any activity or sign of Marduk. If he didn't know better, he'd think it was a...

Trap.

As the word entered his mind, a blood-curdling screech erupted behind him. He knew this sound well from his interactions with the infected. It was one of them, but he thought it odd to hear one this far into the wilderness.

He spun around and looked up the hillside. He

saw one figure running toward another one. The one charging at the other had a heavy beard. It looked like Marduk.

Suddenly all of Marduk's symptoms came crashing into Kamal's mind. He'd been wrong about everything. He attributed everything to the concussion Marduk had sustained during the battle at the safe house, but in reality, few of them were related to that. Everything else was due to infection. The scratching. The problems with speech. The sweating. All of it.

Up the hill, the man Marduk charged toward lowered his center of gravity, and when they collided, the man dropped backward and used his feet to pitch Marduk over his head and behind him.

Marduk was airborne for a few seconds as he dropped down the hill, hitting hard and tumbling several more meters. The snow helped cushion his fall, but Kamal was positive there were broken bones in that infected body.

If it felt pain from the fall, it didn't acknowledge it. It immediately rose to its feet, looking for the prey it had just been chasing. Instead, it locked its eyes on Kamal and charged, closing the distance remarkably fast.

LORI FOUND Charlie on the ground, a hole in his chest spurting blood into the snow. She put her hand over the wound, applying pressure, but she felt blood pulsing between her fingers with every heartbeat. Based on the location of the injury, she suspected the bullet cut through one of the complexes of arteries above the heart, maybe even the aortic arch. That only meant one thing.

He was going to die. She didn't have the equipment or facilities to save him here. Even as she thought this, the pressure of the blood pumping started to lessen; the heartbeat wasn't as steady.

Charlie reached a hand up to her, and Lori grabbed it with one of her blood-covered hands. "It's okay, Charlie. You're going to be all right." She lied to him. She didn't know what else to say. He gasped for air, his hand clawing at her. "I'm here, Charlie. You're okay. It's okay now."

His hand relaxed, and his arm fell to his side. He was gone.

She wiped her bloody hands on her jacket and low-walked back to the SUV, looking for Robin. "Robin," she whispered.

"Under here," Robin called back.

"How's your leg?"

"Hurts like hell."

"How's the bleeding?"

"Not bad. I don't think I need a tourniquet."

"Shhh!" Sarah admonished them. "Something's coming."

Up the road, from the west, they heard the low rumbling of an engine.

"Shit, they're flanking us. Lori, get Charlie's rifle.

Robin, be ready to shoot feet and legs, or whatever you can see."

"Maybe it's Duckett," Lori offered.

"Maybe. Be ready just the same."

"Hey, Sarah, um, it's about Charlie..."

"I know, Lori. You were ten feet away. I'll deal with it later. If we don't pay attention, we all might be joining him."

Sarah's head turned momentarily when she heard a pair of suppressed shots coming from the east, toward where the van was parked.

No, not Leonard and Aaron!

The engine continued rumbling toward them from the west, and as it came closer, Sarah could see it was the familiar Mercedes. It drifted off the road and stopped against the embankment. It appeared that no one was inside the vehicle. There was no movement, no signs of life other than the idling motor.

Above them, on the hillside, something screamed into the night air.

"Infected?" Lori asked. "What the hell would they be doing way out here?"

Something crashed in the brush, and they saw movement close to where Duckett had told Sarah to concentrate her fire. The infected screeched again, and they could see a struggle between two people, but Sarah could not tell if one of them was Duckett.

An unsuppressed gunshot rang through the air, again from the direction of the van. A second one followed.

More crashing and rustling in the underbrush drew their attention back up the hill. A third figure had joined the fracas. One of the three people broke loose from the rest and ran down the mountain toward them.

"Sarah!" Duckett screamed from the hillside. "He's coming right at you! Shoot him!"

DARIUSH DREW a bead on the young man who was groaning. He must have been wearing body armor. That won't help him *this* time.

Something screamed, the sound piercing through the night. It was the sound of the infected, and it was coming from the direction of the other vehicle. Dariush turned toward the west, debating for a second about killing the Americans or rushing back to help Kamal and Marduk. He saw a hint of movement from his right, but before he could do anything, a gun roared at him. He felt the bullet hit his right shoulder, just below the collarbone. His right arm went slack, dropping the rifle into its sling. He toppled off balance and fell backward, landing on his pack. He tried to reach his pistol with his left hand but found himself staring into the face of an old, grizzled American with white hair and a crazy white beard.

"Go fuck your mother," Dariush said to the man, but he realized he'd spoken in Farsi.

"No comprendo, Ahab." The white-haired man pointed the pistol at Dariush's face. "You know what?

This here Army-issue 1911 kilt twenty-three North Koreans and six Chinese. They'da kilt me, but Bette here had other ideas. Now I get to add one Iranian to that list."

"Go fuck your mother," Dariush said again, this time in his best English. It was one of a handful of phrases—most of them curses—he knew in the infidel's language.

The old man pulled the trigger, hitting Dariush in the left eye, the self-defense round opening up on impact and blowing out the side of his head.

"You'll see her before me, shitbird, and she'll be kicking your ass for eternity."

KAMAL HEARD the gunshots from the direction where Dariush had gone. The spacing between them told him Dariush wouldn't be coming to help, and that posed a problem. He was able to handle Marduk, despite his flailing arms and snapping teeth, but when the American advanced on him, he knew he could fight one or the other, but not both. He spun around to keep Marduk between himself and the American, then put a foot up on Marduk's chest and kicked him as hard as he could, sending him sprawling, and knocking the American off balance.

He made a quick decision. Rather than shoot the pair of them and expose his location to the group below, he decided to make a run for it. He could use the cover of the trees to get to the Mercedes and make his escape back toward the small town.

"Sarah! He's coming right at you! Shoot him!"

Son of a whore!

He heard the woman's rifle start barking below him and to his left. It forced him to alter his course. There was no way he'd make it to the Mercedes. It was too close to the group on the road, and the American on the hillside had the high ground.

He chose to head back up, away from both of them. A pair of shots directly behind him told him that Marduk's short second life was over. He kept going, lungs burning, legs aching, but he knew if he stopped, they would kill him. He had to escape and evade.

The snowstorm made for excellent concealment. Visibility was less than twenty meters. After a solid two minutes running as fast as he could go, he slowed down and ducked behind a rock formation. He held his breath for a moment, straining to hear if he was being pursued. His heart was beating so hard, it was all he could hear. He gasped and drew a few heavy, deep breaths, then held them in.

He only heard the wind in the pines.

CHAPTER TWENTY-ONE

Hamid typed in all caps: "STATUS!" He hit enter harder than he needed to, but his frustration was showing through. The last message he had received from Kamal's team was that they were in pursuit of the van. They had their beacon locked and were closing in on them. That was forty-five minutes ago.

Kasra Amol walked into the room and sat down, two attendants in tow. They stood on either side of her, scanning the faces, looking for threats. The other people in the room stopped their activities and watched the powerful woman. She was feline in her movements and acted like she was playing with her prey whenever she talked with people. She ruled the program without mercy.

"Well, Hamid? What is the status?" she purred.

"They're in pursuit of the van. It is as good as in our hands."

"That's what we thought yesterday, isn't it? And the day before that? Are you sure you're not overcommitting, Hamid?"

"I am just relaying their last communication, Kasra."

"Do you know what happened to the last person who let me down, Hamid?"

"Yes, Kasra. His head is on a spike."

Hamid knew the real reason she killed Nampoo Yi was the way he treated the wife and daughter of Dr. Sanjay, but he dared not correct Kasra while she was making a point. She was rubbing his nose in it in front of the rest of the program staff, and he had no choice but to take it.

His system beeped. "The vehicles are moving again." He had the map of Colorado on his screen. There were two dots on the display; a red one, the van with the GPS beacon in it, and a blue one, the purloined vehicle with the satellite communication bubble attached to the roof. They were moving at a moderate speed, not like one group trying to outrun another.

"Put them on the big screen," Kasra ordered.

Hamid tapped a few icons on his screen, and the big sixty-inch monitor at the front of the room mirrored his. According to the map, the vehicles were passing the southern tip of Mirror Lake.

Hamid pulled up the encrypted messaging application. Again, he typed "STATUS REPORT" and hit enter. Everyone in the room watched and waited. For several minutes, nothing happened other than the vehicles continued southern progress on the map.

"Hamid, it's obvious. The American fat asses have killed your vaunted *niruhaye vizheh*. We've wasted days—and a supposed special forces team—trying to pussyfoot around with these people. You have one more chance to reclaim the package. Pull some of the aircraft from the operation in Albuquerque and take these pieces of shit out. If you don't have that package in friendly hands before the next status meeting, *your* head will be decorating a pole in my yard alongside Nampoo Yi."

"Yes, Kasra. It will be done."

"Shut up! You've said that for days. Stop *saying* you'll do it and *do it*."

The satellite phone next to Hamid's laptop rang. He had a new appreciation for the cliché *saved by the bell*.

"Kamal? What is your status? I see. Yes. We can see that on screen. Yes, we were discussing that very thing. I will make it happen. And Kamal? This is your final chance."

"Well? Don't keep me in suspense, Hamid," Kasra was purring again.

"Kamal is alive. The rest of the team is dead. They were engaged in battle with the Americans, and one of Kamal's team had apparently been infected. He succumbed at a crucial point of the battle and Kamal had to disengage. The Americans are on the move, and Kamal asked for retrieval at his location. He wants a helicopter so they can take out the Americans once and for all. And he said this time, either they're going to die, or he is."

"And you share his fate, Hamid. Don't forget that. I can't spend my time wiping your ass. Our next status meeting is in twenty-four hours. We will have the package then or..." —she picked up a sour plum candy from a tray and jammed it onto the end of a pencil— "this is your head." She smiled at him as she put the pencil in her mouth and removed the candy with her bright white teeth. She pushed the sour candy into her cheek and smiled again. "Your hourglass is emptying, Hamid."

She stood without saying anything else and stalked out of the room, her two attendants trailing behind her.

KAMAL DISCONNECTED the call but left the satellite phone on and the antenna extended so Hamid could collect his location and pass it on to whoever would be coming to get him.

He had circled back to the location of the battle, coming in from the top of the ridge. He saw an old, beat up truck driving away from the scene on a smaller road higher up on the mountain. It was headed back toward Tim Cup.

While his pack was on the ground, he fished through it and found an emergency blanket with a brown-and-gray camouflage pattern on one side and reflective Mylar on the other side. He shouldered his pack again and wrapped the blanket around him to conserve his body heat. The temperature had dropped into the negative, and he wasn't dressed for that kind of cold.

He found Dariush's body. The Americans had rifled through his pack, no doubt recovering the package after Dariush had taken it from them. They shot him in the face, which angered Kamal. He'd enter the next world without that eye. He vowed when he killed the Americans, he'd take all of their eyes, so they'd be blind in the next world.

He remembered that there was a house at the apex of the horseshoe driveway. Bracing himself against the cold and the snow, he marched to the structure and kicked in the door. Inside he found a lovely, well-kept home. Most importantly, it was vacant, and the next most important thing was that it had a wood burning stove. In a few minutes, he had a fire going, and heat began to radiate throughout the house.

His satellite phone rang, and he scrambled to get it out of the side pouch on the backpack.

"Kamal," he said.

"It's Hamid. The pilots have your coordinates, Kamal, as well as your number. They'll contact you when they're inbound."

"Excellent. I will bathe in the Americans' blood, Hamid. It will be a baptism."

"Just get it done. Both of our lives depend on it."

CHAPTER TWENTY-TWO

PAGOSA SPRINGS, COLORADO. MAY 9

Leonard and Duckett turned their lights off, as directed, and coasted into the parking lot for the Pagosa Springs Medical Center.

The officer at the edge of town put duct tape over their brake lights, leaving a silver-dollar-sized hole so the lag vehicle would not be totally unaware when they hit the brakes. Leonard and Sarah looked at each other with *why didn't we think of that?* expressions on their faces.

"These things don't see real well," the cop explained. "Especially at night, and in a snowstorm. They'll follow my overheads, and you can slip into the parking lot. Follow the path between the storage containers. You'll all get an exam, or you don't go inside. That's just standard nowadays."

The flashing red-and-blue lights faded, and sure enough, ninety percent of the infected that were following them continued straight and pursued the police cruiser. That left a dozen still following their two vehicles.

Halfway into the parking lot, they came across parallel rows of steel cargo containers. Most were green, but the ones at the end were red. White arrows were painted on them, each one pointing to the lane between the containers. The reflective paint made them stand out in sharp contrast to the red doors.

They followed the instructions and drove down the center of the ten-foot-wide lane. At the end of the red containers, steel guides welded to them on both sides held a massive steel plate in place. A tall steel arch spanned the traffic lane. A thick cable was attached to the plate, holding it in the air. The cable ran from the plate through a pulley mounted to the arch, and down to an emergency vehicle with a winch. As soon as the van cleared the plate, a man reversed the winch and the plate dropped down, sealing the entryway from the pursuing infected. In a second, they started pounding at the steel, leaving bloody streaks on the unyielding surface.

Forty feet ahead, a second winch-cable-pulley-arch-steel-plate setup blocked their entrance. Beside Leonard's window a piece of the cargo container, shaped like a massive plus symbol, swung inward and a man appeared in the center of it. He motioned for Leonard to roll the window down.

"Hi there. Sergeant Moody radioed over y'all were coming. Anyone in your group bit, scratched, or otherwise infected?"

"No," Leonard replied.

"You all will have to get screened to enter the facility. No screening, no entry. Understood?"

"Yeah, got it."

"All weapons must have safeties engaged inside the facility. Failure to comply will result in expulsion from the facility. Resist and get shot. Understood?"

"Yes."

"Will there be any problems?"

"No."

The man closed the portal, and a second later, the big steel plate rose in its guides. A man with a light baton directed the vehicle forward. Leonard pulled through the emergency entrance and parked on the far side of the glass doors. Then Duckett pulled the van ahead and parked behind him.

Emergency room attendants emerged from behind blackout curtains and came out with a pair of gurneys.

"Sergeant Moody radioed that you have wounded who need to be treated? Who's in worse shape?"

The van's side doors opened, and Robin hopped out onto one foot. Her other leg dragged out like a noodle. The pants were blood-soaked, a tourniquet holding back further loss of the precious fluid.

Duckett waved the second gurney over to the side of the van and pointed at the unconscious Aaron lying on the rear seat. "He was shot high in the chest. The bullet struck a plate, but he's been in and out since then."

They used a backboard to slide him out of the van and onto the gurney, then wheeled him inside.

Another man in scrubs approached the group. He looked at Duckett's bandaged head. "Do you need to be looked at?"

"Hell, doc, we probably all do. Leonard's been shot, I was kicked by a deer. We've all seen some shit."

"Okay. We don't have a lot of resources, so let's let the emergency cases get taken care of, and since you're all vertical we can screen you and get you inside." He pointed at two of the midsized twenty-foot long containers. "Left, ladies. Right, men."

Sarah and Lori entered the container on the left while Duckett and Leonard went to the right. Both had side-access doors that swung out. There were two women inside the lefthand container. One end had a few chairs lined up next to a small woodburning stove. The smokestack exited through a hole cut in the outside wall, but the smell of woodsmoke was prevalent in the enclosed space. The fire in the stove had burned down to embers, but the heat coming from it still had the interior plenty warm.

"One of you can have a seat near the fire while we inspect the other one. Who wants to go first?"

"I'll go," Sarah volunteered. "You can warm up, Lori."

The procedure was very similar to the one she went through back when she was first admitted to El Paso. These women were efficient, and she was done in no time.

Lori had not been through the process before, but she was a nurse, so she was comfortable getting undressed and examined by the women, especially after seeing Sarah go through it with no qualms.

"Okay, ladies, thank you. You're cleared to go in."

They thanked the women and left the container.

"Fuck, it's freezing out here," Sarah blurted out. "Let's get inside!"

A man at the first set of sliding doors pulled them open. "Sorry, they're not automatic. We're trying to save power. Wait inside the curtain for a minute," he said.

They parted the overlapping blackout curtains and walked into the airlock entry. The man made sure the curtains had entirely closed before he slid the next set of doors open, and Sarah noticed for the first time that in addition to the curtains over the doors, the glass was painted black.

Only half the lights were on in the lobby, leaving it feeling abandoned and a little sinister. A lone attendant behind the desk offered them seats where they could wait for the guys to come in from their inspections.

Sarah sat heavily in the chair and leaned her head back. She was exhausted, and it was starting to hit her hard. She had just drifted off when the noise of the doors being pulled open woke her up. Duckett and Leonard walked in smiling.

"Nothing like a little poke-n-prod to let you know someone cares," Leonard said. "How was yours?"

"Peachy," Lori replied. She went to Leonard's side and put a hand on his back, guiding him over to the chairs, but he shook her off and went to the desk.

"Is Dominic Naranjo here?"

She smiled. "Yes. He's our favorite patient."

Leonard looked like he grew three inches from all the weight lifted from his shoulders. "That's my grandpa! Can I see him?"

"You must be Leonard! He talks about you all the time. Let me show you where he is. Your father's still here, too. I'm sure he'll be glad to see you!"

Leonard held out his hand to Lori. "You want to come with?"

She smiled and grabbed his hand.

"Hey, you got anything like coffee in here?" Duckett asked the attendant.

She pointed down the hall. "Break room, third door, right side. It's pretty good, considering. Let me know if it's empty, and when I get back, I'll make some more."

Duckett nodded toward the break room. "Come on, Washburn. Let's give the kids some time alone with family."

"Sarah, you're not coming?" Leonard asked.

"We'll go later. You take your time."

The desk attendant led Leonard and Lori down the hall, turning left at the first intersection. Duckett held the break room door open for Sarah, and she scooted past him.

He made for the coffee pot right away, filled one of

the Styrofoam cups, and extended it to Sarah. She thought for a half a second, then took it. He poured a second one for himself and moved to the couch that filled most of one wall. Sarah sat down next to him and laid her head back, sighing as she sank into the cushions in all the right places.

"Mmmm. This is really comfortable."

"Yeah, it is," he replied. "I wonder how many doctors have crashed out here after long shifts."

"Better not to think about it. According to TV, which, surprisingly, I do *not* miss, they've probably been having sexy time on it too."

There was a long, awkward pause before Duckett said, "Yeah, probably best not to think about that."

He shut his eyes, the events of the last two long days replaying in his mind. Within minutes, he was dreaming of infected hordes chasing him and mad Iranians tracking him down. In the dream, he hid in a dumpster, but the Iranians knew right where he was and opened the lid. He jumped out, into the alley, and ran away to a railyard. He hid inside a boxcar, and they slid the door open seconds later. He ran past them again and dove into a lake.

In the fashion that only happens in dreams, he was able to breathe underwater. He swam to a sunken boat, maneuvered his way inside, and opened a bench seat. All the life jackets popped out and floated away, and just as he was going to hide, the radar screen beeped. He swam to the boat's bridge and watched the radar screen; with every sweep, the dots got closer until he could see the Iranians right outside the boat.

It's like they can track me! he thought in his sleep. *I need to get rid of the tracker. But where is it?*

He searched his pockets but came up empty. He took off his jacket, in case the tracker was sewn in. He swam out the rear of the cabin and hid behind a rock, but the Iranians were still coming after him. He stripped out of the rest of his clothes and swam naked into a cave. He didn't see the Iranians any longer, but a glow began to illuminate the cave. He turned around and saw Sarah. She was naked too.

"They can't track you if you strip down," she said, somehow able to speak under water. She swam over and wrapped him in an embrace, kissing him on the mouth. She was warm and soft, and she ran her hands all over his body. Then the light disappeared from the cave, and he was alone in the dark.

"Sarah!" he called out. There was no answer.

It took a second to realize he was awake in the break room. Sarah was gone, but Leonard and Lori were sitting at a nearby table, laughing.

"Dude, you crushing on Sarah, or what?" Leonard asked.

"What?"

"You were moaning and calling her name, bro. We were about to leave you alone to, you know, finish your dream, or whatever."

Duckett was embarrassed for a half a second, then

regained his composure. "Shut it, Naranjo. It wasn't like that."

"So, what *was* it like," Lori prodded.

"Haha, gang up on me. Where is she? I have an idea about the van and why they were able to track us down."

"Get in line. My dad's already figured it out."

CHAPTER TWENTY-THREE

K amal had unpacked and re-packed his gear, cleaned his weapons, and cleaned his suppressors. The pilot of the Blackhawk that Hamid had arranged for him called the sat phone and told him he was getting ready to come to pick him up.

"I don't just need a pickup," he said. "I need a team. Preferably nine or ten men, but I'll take what I can get."

"That will take some extra time. The operation in Albuquerque isn't going well. They need all their resources."

"If we don't get this information, none of this matters. Do you understand? Do I need to get Hamid on the line?"

"No, sir, you don't. I'll work it out. It will add time though, probably double the time to four hours."

Kamal clenched his jaw. "Make it happen faster

than that. And one more thing. I want an Apache escort."

"Yes, sir. I'll call back with status."

Kamal put another dry piece of wood in the stove. He had no idea how long the house had been empty, but the timber stacked inside was dry and burned quickly. He only added more whenever he felt the temperature start to drop. He didn't want to risk the locals coming to investigate if they wandered too close.

He found ample canned food in the cabinets, well within the expiration dates, so he ate his fill.

He decided to call Hamid to give him an update. When he answered, Kamal could feel the tension through the phone.

"Kamal, you should be on a helicopter. What is happening?"

"The helo will be here in three hours," he lied. "Then I complete the mission. But I need their coordinates."

"One moment. Let me pull that up."

Kamal waited while he heard Hamid cursing on the other end. After a few moments, Hamid said, *"Okay, here we go."* He read off the GPS coordinates and didn't ask if Kamal needed them repeated. *"I've been watching them, and both vehicles are together. They've been stopped for the past couple of hours at a medical center. If they move, I will let you know. Now I must go; I have things to tend to."*

The connection dropped. Kamal was getting irritated with Hamid. It was probably good for them both that they were a half world apart.

He retrieved his duty vest. He had his knife mounted on the left side, upside down, for easy access for his right hand. He slid the knife out of the sheath. From tip to pommel, it was twelve and a quarter inches, but the blade was seven and a quarter inches of that length, from tip to guard. Kamal imagined driving it all the way into the heart of each of the Americans and watching the horror on their faces as they felt it sever their blood vessels, felt their life force drain away, never to return to their bisected hearts. Of course, he'd more likely shoot them or slice their throats, but the images still made him smile.

Even though he could use the knife to shave hair from his arm, he got out his whetstone and honed it once more. The process always calmed his nerves, helped him find his center. Soon, he would avenge his teammates, complete the mission, and receive the accolades of a hero in his homeland. It would be hollow for him. The accolades belonged to his team as much as to him. He would ensure their place in history was documented.

HAMID HUNG up the phone and returned to his task. He knew his time was limited, no matter the outcome of today's mission. He should be more nervous than he was, knowing that fifteen of his twenty-four hours had elapsed, and the helicopter hadn't even picked Kamal up yet.

The operation in Albuquerque had not gone as planned and was made even worse by him pulling not one, but two helicopters from them. The pilot should have picked Kamal up before now, and Kamal just said it would be another three hours. That probably meant four or five, and then they still had to get to the vehicles and hope the Americans were still there. A lot had to go right for him to keep his head. But even that was not certain.

Kasra Amol was psychotic—brilliant, but psychotic. Hamid knew two things. First, he assumed that she had already decided she was going to remove his head irrespective of the mission's success. Since he liked his head, he didn't plan on being here when she came looking. Getting out of North Korea was not an easy task, but he had prepared for the possibility.

Immediately after the status call, he sent an encrypted message to his contact, who messaged back that everything was still in place and waiting for him to give the word. He messaged them that he was activating the emergency plan.

The second thing Hamid knew was that Kasra Amol expected him to try to escape. She did not think Hamid was intelligent, so this ham-handed plan would capture the eye of her spies, and she'd believe she had the mouse in a trap. Several people were now working on an escape plan that was set up to fail. But what she *didn't* know—at least, Hamid prayed to Allah she didn't—was that when she sprung her trap, he would already be in the South.

He sent a second encrypted message to a different contact. This message simply read *It's time.*

He hoped Kamal was successful in his mission, but even if he was, Hamid would not be here to celebrate.

CHAPTER TWENTY-FOUR

Sarah smiled at Duckett when he walked into the lobby. "Hey, Duckett. You feeling rested?"

"Yeah." He looked at his watch and *holy shit!* he'd been out for six hours. "Why didn't you wake me up? We're burning daylight here. Leonard tells me his dad has thoughts on how they found us in Tin Cup."

"You were snoring so hard I didn't have the heart to wake you."

"Impossible. I don't snore."

Sarah burst out laughing. "I think that deer kicked you harder than you thought. You were shaking the entire couch, my friend. Come on, let's go talk to Cedric."

Duckett looked at her like a confused puppy.

"Leonard's dad."

His face lit up. "Ah, okay, gotcha!"

They walked to the front entrance. A different kid than the night before pulled the door open for them, then opened the outer doors as well. When they got outside, the temperature had risen to thirty degrees, but in the shadow of the covered entryway, they could see their breath. It had continued snowing through the night, leaving eight inches on the ground and about half that on their vehicles.

"Where's Cedric?" Sarah asked the man outside.

This was also not the same man as the one last night. He wore scrubs under a heavy denim jacket with a sheepskin lining. "He was over there last I saw him," the man said, pointing to the right.

They walked around to the far side of the emergency entrance and found a forklift with one of the small ten-foot storage containers raised into the air.

"Cedric?" Sarah called out.

He leaned out of the raised storage container. "Hey! Come up, you need to see this!" He raised a walkie-talkie and pressed the button. "Bring it down so these two can see what's happening."

The man running the forklift brought the storage container down, waited for the signal from Cedric, and raised it back up.

"I found the GPS tracker in the van. We use something similar in the SUPD vehicles. I took it out, but I figured if they were tracking it, they'd know we did something to it, and they'd send their people to the last known place it pinged to look for you. So, I wired it to a six-volt battery, taped it all together, and put it in a little duffel bag. Then, and you're going to love this part, I put the bag over an infected's head. Officer Sterling is leading a little horde away from us." He handed a small pair of binoculars to Sarah. "It's the one in the gray jacket with the light blue duffel bag."

She turned the focus ring until she could see the police SUV leading a half-dozen infected away to the east. One of the infected had a blue duffel hanging around his neck that jostled around as he pursued the cop.

She passed the binoculars to Duckett, who peered through them and started laughing. "That was a brilliant idea. Anything that can buy us time is a good thing."

"You sound like Martha Stewart," Cedric said. "Anyway, I think we should move someplace else. If they have been tracking your position, like you said, this will buy us some time. But once they discover the ruse, they're going to look for you here since this is where your vehicles have been all night. It puts everyone here in danger."

"I've thought the same thing," Duckett said. He nodded toward the infected GPS decoy. "This stunt will keep them occupied for a couple of minutes, but I agree they'll come back here once they figure it out. We need to give them someplace else to go."

"Where would that be?" Sarah asked.

"I think they have another way of tracking us." He pointed at the satellite communication dome the Iranians had mounted to the roof of the Mercedes. "That bubble is a satellite Internet connection. The Homeland vehicle I borrowed in El Paso has one too. I know they can track that connection. It triangulates a signal from multiple satellites and locks in on the strongest one, switching to the next strongest as the car moves, or the satellites go out of range. It's how it keeps its signal while you drive. From a tracking perspective, it might as well be a GPS unit. I was thinking we take the Mercedes back to the supply hut in Durango and grab that Homeland vehicle I left there and meet up later."

Cedric nodded. "That could work. They'll catch on to the GPS trick but assume that you don't know they're tracking the Mercedes. From their viewpoint, you guys going back to a secure location would make total sense."

"Right, and when they find out we're not there, they'll have no idea where we are. Which, by the way, where will we be?"

"Chimney Rock," Sarah said. "It gives us great visibility, right? And we'd hold the high ground. That's important, right?"

"It is. Cedric, your thoughts?"

The older man looked thoughtful for a minute then said, "Yes, that's probably as good a place as any. It's isolated from any collateral targets, and we'll see them coming from miles away. I like it." He pressed the button on the walkie. "Bring us down, Sebastian."

The forklift operator lowered the storage unit to the ground.

"Sebastian?" Sarah exclaimed. She hopped out of

the container and trotted back to the lift. "It *is* you! Have you been in to see Robin yet?"

"Wow! Hi, Sarah! When they said more people came in last night, I didn't get any names. What happened to Robin? Is Marcus here too?"

"Oh, Sebastian so much has happened. Marcus was killed in a gunfight with Iranian commandos in Durango."

His face registered disbelief. *"Iranians?* That doesn't even make sense."

"It's true," Duckett interjected. "And they're probably tracking us here, so we should get moving."

"Wait, so what happened to Robin?"

"We went to Tin Cup to see one of Robin's old friends, and the same people followed us. They attacked us again outside of town and she got shot in the leg, but she's fine. Why don't we go check on her, and then we can get the gang ready to go," Sarah suggested.

"I'll be right there," Sebastian said.

ROBIN WAS SITTING up in her hospital bed, slurping spoonfuls of chicken broth. She grinned when Duckett and Sarah appeared in her doorway.

Duckett rapped on her doorframe. "Hey Robin, you taking visitors?"

"Oh, hell yeah. Only if you tell them I would like

some real food. This chicken water ain't going to cut it."

"We'll do that," Sarah said. "We heard the surgery went well."

"Yeah, that's what they told me. I'll keep the leg, anyway. May not be dancing any time soon, though, not that I did that much before. The doc said the bullet fragmented, and the pieces tore some different paths around my thigh, and they aren't one hundred percent that they got all of them, but he said, overall, I was fortunate." Her face turned sour, and tears welled up in her eyes. "I wish I could say the same about Charlie. That haunts me."

Sarah reached out and put her hand on Robin's arm, her eyes tearing up, as well. "I know. It was horrible. They brought his... body inside last night and put him in their morgue. Said they'll hold him until we can do a proper burial."

"That's good. So, what are the next moves? What do we do with the info on the disease?"

"*We* don't do anything. *You* heal that leg. The rest of us will figure out the next steps."

"Oh, come on! You're going to leave me here alone? I may not be able to run, but I can shoot. You need all the guns you can get. And if you think I don't want in on avenging Charlie's death, you have another thing coming."

Duckett nodded his head in agreement with her. "I know, we all want to get these SOBs. But the fact is, you're not mobile, and that will be a liability if they come back after us. And second, they have this location from their tracking device. There's a good chance they'll come here looking for us and kill everyone they find. You can help protect the staff and patients."

"I know you're just trying to make me feel useful. But you're right, I couldn't do much out there. I hate not being able to help!"

"I am trying to make you feel better, but I'm also serious. The people here need protection."

A knock at the door interrupted them.

"Sebastian!" Robin called out, wiping the tears from her eyes.

He walked over to her bed and handed her a stuffed bear holding a small balloon that read *Get well soon*.

"Sorry, the gift selection is kinda sparse."

She held her arms out wide and gave him a big hug. "Oh, Sebastian, it's great. It's good to see you. You heard about Marcus?"

"Yeah." He lowered his head. "That sucks. I should have gone with you guys."

"And maybe you'd be dead too. Don't second-guess things. I'm running out of people I like."

"Or that like you!"

She laughed. "Touché."

"We're going to gather the gang and get moving before the Iranians show up and kill everyone in the hospital," Duckett interjected. "You two carry on as you were."

"Duckett," Robin said, halting him in mid-turn

toward the door. "Where are my guns? In case they *do* show up, I want more than a stuffed bear to throw at them."

"I'll make sure they bring them to you."

"Oh, and Duckett?"

"Yeah?" He turned back to her a second time, his voice heavy with frustration.

"Remember to tell someone I need more than chicken broth. This stuff is getting old."

"I'll take care of it," Sebastian said. He took a few steps toward the door. "And take me to her guns and stuff. I'll bring them back to her."

CHAPTER TWENTY-FIVE

EAST OF TIN CUP, COLORADO. MAY 9

Kamal pulled the bandage off of his arm, wincing as the tape pulled hair with it. He chuckled to himself that he could take a punch to the face and not be bothered by the pain but ripping out a few hairs on his arm made him wince like a woman.

That's a woman's noise. That was a line from one of the few American movies he liked; *The 13th Warrior*. He enjoyed it because the main character was Muslim and the people who made the film didn't make him the bad guy or mock Islam. He was tough and heroic, facing a menace who no one could stand up to, and he was the one who figured out how to beat the enemy. The rest of the characters were Vikings, which, while objectionable, were not as bad as if they were Americans, and they respected the main character and his religion.

He shook his head, clearing the thoughts of the movie from his mind, and pulled the knife from the sheath on his vest. Holding the blade at the right angle, he shaved the hair from the area around the wound so he could get the clean bandage to stick better.

Wound. It wasn't really a *wound* so much as it was a time bomb. He sighed as he looked at the two half circles of puncture wounds that, in a forensic exam, would match perfectly to Marduk's teeth.

He didn't even realize the bite had punctured his skin until earlier in the afternoon when it started to itch. He'd cleaned and bandaged it, then sat and worried about what the ramifications were. He tried to count off the time from when he thought Marduk was exposed to the disease. It had to be when he fell in the puddle of blood at the safe house. He'd started showing symptoms—sweating, lethargy, and the scratching, which Kamal had noticed but didn't assign the proper importance to—about fifteen hours after exposure. It was twenty-six or twenty-seven hours before he gave over to it. Kamal's clock was ticking.

The edges around the bite were red and angry, despite the antiseptic balm he'd put on it earlier. He boiled some water on the wood stove and used the antibacterial soap he found in the kitchen to scrub it clean again and smeared more of the balm on it, before placing a gauze pad over it and taping the edges.

Maybe he'd be all right. He was bitten fourteen hours ago, and he hadn't started sweating. There were no feverish chills and no urge to scratch at himself. It was possible he wasn't infected, or maybe he was immune.

The satellite phone rang, so he hustled over to the table and grabbed it. "Kamal here."

"Confirming pick up. We're leaving the Durango airport. Had to stop for fuel. One hour out."

"Good. You got a team pulled together?"

"Yes, but it wasn't easy."

"And have an Apache with you?"

"Yes."

"Perfect. I'll be waiting."

He ended the call and placed another. He didn't wait for a greeting but started talking as soon as the line connected.

"Hamid, I need the current location of the van. Is it still at the medical center?"

"No, it's moving. It's a couple of kilometers northeast of Pagosa Springs. They seem to be having trouble. It's not moving very quickly."

Kamal remembered the clogged roads they traversed yesterday. "It's a larger town. The roads are probably filled with empty vehicles. Give me a GPS location."

Hamid gave him the coordinates. *"Kamal, I am not certain how much longer I will be here. I fear my head will be adorning Kasra Amol's front walkway soon."*

Kamal clenched his jaw. "We all must die sometime, Hamid. If you're going to die, die on your feet."

"You are the warrior, Kamal, not I."

"Then leave this phone with your successor in case I need anything else." Kamal ended the call. He had no more patience for the sniveling of bureaucrats. He put the phone in his pack but left it on in case the helicopter pilot needed Command to track him.

He looked at his watch. The helicopter would be arriving in fifty minutes. He was anxious to get the last leg of this mission underway. He decided to check his weapons and magazines one more time, maybe repack his gear to pass the time.

He reached for his rifle and realized his right arm was over his head, his hand scratching his scalp in an unconscious motion.

CHAPTER TWENTY-SIX

Sarah kept her speed under forty for most of the trip. The Mercedes was sure-footed, but the blanket of snow could be covering any number of obstacles, and hitting something at forty was a lot more survivable than hitting something at seventy, especially on slick roads.

Duckett was going through the gear that the Iranians left in the car.

"They're using American weapons—5.56 and 7.62," he said. "There are also some spare magazines we can use."

He climbed over the seat into the front.

"What about that laptop?" Sarah asked.

Duckett picked up the laptop and turned it over, inspecting it. "It's a fucking Chuwi."

Sarah gave him a blank look so he explained. "Chinese model. The Chinks have been copying our tech, putting their brands on them, and selling them to embargoed countries. It wouldn't surprise me to find out they've got a hand in all this bullshit, too. Fuck, maybe even the Russians. All the axis of evil getting their turn at bat. Fuckers."

He opened the lid and hit the power button. An image of a red, empty battery flashed for a couple of seconds and turned off.

"Shit, it was off the charger last night. They must have left it on when they came to the fight. Bastards thought they'd be right back. We showed them."

"Did you forget Charlie was killed? Robin was shot? Aaron and Leonard were nearly killed? Would have been, if it wasn't for Frank showing up. We got lucky is what happened. What's with you? Why are you so agitated?"

Duckett held his tongue for a minute. Sarah could see he was itching to get something out.

"I'm just frustrated that we haven't been able to get the drop on them. Every time we meet, we're reacting. It would be nice to get the upper hand for once."

She nodded her head. "So, let's figure out how to do that. Look, I know we're not the ideal counter-commando unit, but this group is what we have to work with."

He let out a long sigh. "You're right. People have faced longer odds than this before. We'll sort it out."

It took a little more than an hour to get to the supply depot. Duckett wanted to jump in the Homeland vehicle and head right back, but Sarah insisted on doing a once-over of the building to ensure they had grabbed everything of value.

While Duckett pulled the Homeland vehicle around to the entrance, Sarah entered the access code and opened the door. She walked through the pantry, putting a few cans of soup and vegetables in a duffel bag. She added a bag of rice, but since they'd cleaned the place out the night before last, that was about all that was worth taking. Duckett joined her as she made her way to the rear of the building.

"I wanted to check out the radio before we go. That's how we communicated with people before El Paso. Maybe we can get some updates or recruit some help."

Duckett nodded. "Worth a shot, but we can't take too much time. I'm going to check out the armory and see what we have left in there."

Sarah flipped on the power switch and watched the lights come on across the panel. A digital readout began scrolling through numbers. It had a small "MHz" label at the bottom. She knew that meant it was displaying frequencies. Charlie had done this before, and it just cycled through and repeated. He had tried stopping on specific frequencies, but it never connected with anyone. It stopped on a number and blinked. That didn't happen before.

She pressed the button on the base of the microphone. "Uh, hello? Is anyone there?" She released the button and waited. Nothing. She saw a button labeled

SCAN and was reaching for it when a woman's voice crackled through the line.

"*Someone is here. Who's there?*"

"Uh, I was hoping to find police or something."

"*Who is this?*"

"I'm no one, really. Just, uh, never mind me. I'm going to go now." Sarah reached for the scan button again.

"*The party's just getting started. Don't go yet.*"

Sarah stared at the speaker, waiting to see what the woman would say next.

"*I'm in Scottsdale. Name's Beverly. Who are you?*"

"Sarah, in Durango. Some sort of supply depot."

"*Oh, us too, sweetie. Are you one of Ian's people?*"

"No, I don't know anyone named Ian."

"*Oh, I see. Well, how are things in Durango, sweetie?*"

Sarah bristled. She did not like being called names like *sweetie* or *hun*. Robin was the only person she'd let get away with that since she was ten.

"Call me Sarah. And things here are fucked. The Iranians are trying to kill us."

"Careful," Duckett said from the doorway, holding a massive rifle. "We don't know who she is. Could be a spy. Hell, she might be around the corner for all we know."

"*Iranians, huh? We've got North Koreans here. I guess the cockroaches all come out at night, huh? Well, Colonel Tisdale will be interested that Iranians are here.*"

"Who's Colonel Tisdale?" Duckett asked.

Sarah pressed the button on the mic again. "Who's Colonel Tisdale?"

"He's from the Air National Guard base in Phoenix."

Duckett walked over and leaned the rifle against the side of the desk. "Let me in there." He caught the scolding look from Sarah and added, "Please."

Sarah stood, and Duckett sat down, pressing the talk button.

"This is Sergeant Duckett, United States Army, First Armored Division. What is the status of the fighter wing out of Tucson?"

"Honey, I'm sure I have no idea. I'm in some sort of supply depot myself, was brought here by a client of mine who took off for DC a few days ago."

"So how do you know Colonel Tisdale?"

There was a long pause, then a man's voice came through the speaker.

"Sergeant Duckett, this is Staff Sergeant Jones, Arizona Air National Guard. First Armored is out of Fort Bliss, if I'm not mistaken."

"You're correct, Sergeant Jones. Is there a question in there?"

There was a long pause, and then, *"What are you doing in Durango, and what's your interest in the fighter wing?"*

"Fucking weekenders," Duckett said without pressing the talk button.

"I can understand why he'd be suspicious," Sarah

said. "Didn't you just say we have no idea if they are who they say they are? He's probably telling her the same thing."

Duckett sighed. "I guess." He pressed the transmit button. "Just curious if there's anything there that can help us, Sergeant. We've obtained some critical information that we need to get into government hands, and we're having a hard time with that, thanks to our new friends."

"What kind of information?"

Duckett growled in frustration. "A map with the location of all of these facilities, for one thing."

"We already have that. We've been posting it to the Internet whenever we can get a signal, but someone keeps taking it down."

"We also have intel about a possible immune civilian and other intel on the infection. Whatever is in there, the Iranians are desperate to get their hands on it."

"You still haven't told me how you wound up in Durango when you're assigned to Bliss."

"Okay, short version; I was out on a mission retrieving medical supplies for a lieutenant. I spotted the Iranian team HALO to Beaumont medical and observed their movements. When they left the city, I followed them."

"So, you're AWOL. Why should I trust you with any information?"

"Jesus!" Duckett said. "Listen, Jones. First, anything you tell me won't go far because I'll probably be killed in the next six hours. Second, fuck you and your AWOL bullshit. I'm one less mouth to feed in El Paso, and I've been way more useful in the field. Help us, don't help us, I don't give a shit, but time's wasting here. We need to get the fuck out of this bunker because this is where the Iranians are most likely going to try to re-acquire us."

A few second's pause indicated that SSgt Jones was thinking about whether or not to trust them. Finally, he responded.

"There's not much I can tell you. We've lost contact with the 162nd Fighter Wing in Tucson. I'll talk to the brass and see what we can do. Best I can offer right now. We have our own set of problems to deal with."

"All right, Sergeant. It is what it is. Duckett out." He turned to Sarah. "We should go. If someone was listening in on that, we could have inbound as we speak."

Sarah pointed at the rifle. "What the hell is that?"

He smiled. "This is a Barrett fifty caliber anti-materiel rifle. She's coming with us, and I need your help with a couple of other things we missed before."

THE APEX of the driveway was more than large enough for the Blackhawk to land. The trees surrounding the area made it tight, but the pilot brought it in without trouble. Kamal ran from the house to the helicopter and climbed in. The pilot lifted off as the team in the cargo bay gave Kamal a headset.

He gave the pilot the coordinates that Hamid had given him, and the helicopter turned south.

"How long to get there?" Kamal asked.

"About twenty minutes."

He addressed the new team of *niruhaye vizheh*. "I am Kamal Baraghani."

He looked at the man closest to him. "Mohammad Ahadi," he said. They continued around the group.

"Hossein Mahmoudieh."

"Reza Rashidi."

"Abbas Al Madani."

"Ahmad Pahlavi."

"Mehdi Ebrahimi."

"Ali Firouzja."

"Tarik Mirzaei."

Kamal assessed them. They looked the part, every bit as fit and equipped as his team had been several days ago. "Here's the deal. This group of Americans has in their possession a package of information that Command needs. It's related to the disease that is burning up the planet, and we do not want the American government to get their hands on it. With it, we have a strategic advantage that will put what is left of the powers of the West on their knees, begging for mercy. Without it, Iran and her people will be more meat for the grinding, and the infidels of the West will rise from the ashes.

"You might think I'm being overly dramatic. Do

not underestimate these people. I don't know you, but I knew my team, and I would put them against anyone. They're all dead."

"Maybe the Americans got lucky," Mohammad said. "After all, they know the land here."

"We've had three contacts with them, in three different locations, and at every one, we lost someone. That's not luck, that's a pattern. In 1941, the Japanese didn't invade the West Coast of the United States because..."

"Because they were weak-willed, yellow women," Reza interjected, "who lacked the will to deliver the death blow."

"*Because*," Kamal continued, "there would be a rifle behind every blade of grass. They were right. Every one of them is armed, even their women. I'll repeat, do not underestimate them."

"Maybe it was their leader," Ahmad said, bringing the subject back to the previous team.

"If you think because your family name is Pahlavi you get special treatment, think again. If I fall, you can try your hand at leading this mission, but until that happens, hold your tongue."

"What's wrong with your head?" Tarik asked.

Kamal realized he was scratching his scalp again. He brought his hand down to his side. The new team cast furtive glances at each other. "Check your weapons," he said. "Ensure everything is ready to go."

He set his pack on the deck and fussed with a couple of items while stealing a glance at his fingertips.

They were bloody, and he could feel detritus, probably skin from his scalp, under his nails. He just needed to hold it together a little while longer so he could complete what he came here to do. Just a little longer. He looked up and saw Ahmad staring at him.

He doesn't know. He can't know. He'd kill you if he suspected. Kamal sat up, drawing his torso to its impressive full height and glared back at the team's leader. After a few seconds, Ahmad looked away.

CHAPTER TWENTY-SEVEN

Duckett was behind the wheel of his purloined Homeland SUV. The flat-black, unmarked vehicle stood out in sharp relief to the snowy surroundings. The temperature had warmed to thirty-three degrees, but the snow hadn't melted from the roads. Even though the trip over to Durango was uneventful, he still kept the speed under fifty just in case. He glanced over at Sarah, who took advantage of the time in the passenger seat by reading through Frank's translation of the El Paso documents.

"Anything interesting in there?" he asked.

"There's a bunch of medical jargon I don't understand. Something about mutative variation between six release sites. It says the behavioral characteristics of the vector in nature are changing, mutating. Sanjay said *the efficacy is beyond expectations* but that *generational mutations are higher and more varied than is either optimal or within limits of control.* I'm not a biomedical professional, but none of that sounds good for humanity."

"No, it doesn't. And six release sites? That's proof it's intentional. It sounds like they've lost control of it. These fuckers started something they don't know how to finish."

"Sanjay as much as said that in the first page we read," Sarah agreed. "They opened Pandora's Box, remember?"

"So, is it a virus? I mean, Ebola was the worst thing ever, right? The boogeyman of diseases, ninety percent kill rate, no cure, blah blah blah, and once it hit the first world, they had a treatment in a few months. This shit makes Ebola look like the flu."

"It doesn't say. It just refers to 'the vector' but doesn't say if it's viral, bacterial, fungal, or something else."

"But it was the NORKs and the Iranians, correct? I mean, it's written in Korean, but Sanjay wasn't Korean. So, he's communicating with them. And we know we have Iranian hit squads on the loose, so they *have* to be working together."

"He doesn't name anyone, at least not in the part I've read through. But like you said, I think the evidence is pretty clear. There is something in here about wanting proof that his family is still alive, which is interesting. It reads like he was doing all this under duress. Would he really destroy humanity to save his family? Seems shortsighted."

"What would you do if it were Jack? If you had to do something horrible, but it would save his life?"

"I wouldn't destroy the world."

"And you don't have kids, either. He was probably more worried about them than his wife."

"Do you have kids, Duckett?"

"Me? Fuck, no, not that I know of, anyway. But my sister does. She said when she saw her daughter, everyone else, including her husband became secondary. Her number-one priority was protecting that little girl. And as far as that goes, as her uncle, well, there's not a lot I wouldn't do to keep her safe. There are about a hundred million dads and uncles in this country that will tell you the same thing, I guarantee it. There's a difference between doing something bad just because you're evil versus doing it because you feel you have no choice. Don't get me wrong, I'm not defending him, because destroying humanity is so far removed from killing someone to protect a loved one, but it does put him in a slightly different light."

She went silent for a moment, reflecting on their exodus from El Paso when she made a vow to herself that she would find the people responsible for what happened to Jack, and that when she did, she would make them pay. Was that so different from what Sanjay had done?

Yes, it is. They started it, and I'd be making them pay for their sins.

Duckett stole a glance at her. "You think I'm full of shit, don't you?"

"No, I don't. I was just thinking about something."

"Well, I am, sometimes. I know I tend to talk too much once..."

"Once what?"

"Once I get comfortable around someone."

"So, you're quiet if you don't like people?"

"Yeah. Something like that."

"Well, aren't they lucky?"

Duckett laughed as he made the turn onto Highway 151 going south, toward the entrance to Chimney Rock.

"Looks like Leonard and the others are already there," he said, pointing at the tracks in the snow, winding their way like two snakes into the distance.

"THERE'S NOTHING THERE," the pilot reiterated. *"Just infected wandering along the roadway."*

Kamal dialed Hamid's number. After several seconds, the line connected. "Hamid, I need the location on the van."

"This is Amman, Hamid's attaché. He left me instructions to watch the vehicles and be ready for your call."

"Where's Hamid?"

"Hardly important to you at the moment. Here's the location on the van."

Kamal scribbled the coordinates on a scrap of paper and passed it to Mehdi. He put his hand over the phone and said, "Hand this to the pilot." Mehdi turned and passed the note to the crew chief. He gestured toward the cockpit and the man nodded, unlatching his harness and letting the machine gun hang from its mount. He shuffled a few paces and tapped the pilot on the right side, passing the note to him. Kamal returned to the phone call. "Okay, and you said you were tracking the other vehicle. Where is it?"

"They've returned to the safe house in Durango, where you had your second defeat to a group of partisans."

"Watch yourself, Amman."

"You're in no position to—what do your Americans say?—talk tough to me, Kamal. If you fail again, it will be the last time. Be certain of that."

Kamal ended the call before he said something he'd regret. He scanned the faces of the new team he was working with, wondering which one of them had been given the order to kill him if the mission failed. Maybe all of them had.

"Kamal, the coordinates you sent up are right where we are. There's no van."

He opened the mic. "There has to be."

"There are no vehicles, Kamal. Just infected."

"Kamal, is it possible that the Americans knew about the tracking device?"

He turned to face Ahmad. *Of course, it's Ahmad.* Aloud he said, "Anything is possible. As I said, don't underestimate them."

"Okay, so what about this. What if they took it out

of the van, connected it to some sort of power source, and put it on one of the infected."

Kamal thought it over for a second. While he didn't like Ahmad, it wasn't a bad thought. He opened the mic again. "Are any of the infected carrying something?"

"I'll swing around, you can look for yourself."

Kamal lost his balance as the Blackhawk banked hard. He grabbed at the bulkhead for support, leaning into it so he wouldn't fall.

The aircraft leveled off. Ahmad went to the gunner's window and looked at the couple dozen infected who were reaching toward the helicopter, flailing their arms and screaming. "I see one with a blue bag hanging from his neck!" He grasped the 7.62mm machine gun from the stunned gunner and opened fire.

The team jostled for position to look out the small windows in the door. On the roadway below, infected were torn apart by the relentless fire. The infected carrying the bag fell over, dead, and Ahmad raked the bag with another burst. He opened his mic. *"Call Command and ask them what they see now."*

Kamal placed the call. In a few seconds, Amman answered. *"This is getting tiresome. What is it now?"*

Kamal clenched his jaw and spoke through gritted teeth. "Where is the van now?"

"I told you, it's—wait, that's odd. It was there moments ago, but I don't see it now. What happened on your end?"

Kamal disconnected. He had no further use for the

smug assistant in Pyongyang. He opened his mic. "Get us to the safe house in Durango."

"Roger."

The helicopter and its Apache escort turned to the west and sped up, gaining altitude to clear the mountains and valleys along the way.

CHAPTER TWENTY-EIGHT

The Homeland SUV wound its way up the trail toward the upper parking area. The heavy spring snow was three inches deeper than it was on the main roads, even though the difference in altitude was only a few hundred feet.

Leonard and Cedric greeted them at the top. The black van was already parked in the space closest to the trail leading to the kivas. They had put white hospital sheets across the top of the van and hanging down the sides. They shut them in the doors to anchor them.

Duckett put the vehicle in park and climbed out and pointed to the van. "What's up, guys? Trying to camouflage it?"

"Yeah," Cedric said. "I figure it can't hurt to try and make them a little less visible."

"You know they probably have night vision, FLIR, all that shit, right? Sheets aren't going to do anything."

"But it could help if they're looking with the naked eye, right? Like I said, it can't hurt."

Duckett shrugged and turned to Leonard. "Can you help with the boxes back here? We have some stuff we need to get set up."

He put his pack on, then grabbed the big .50 rifle and the can of ammunition to feed it. Sarah already had her backpack on and was carrying the first box toward the kivas.

Cedric whistled when he saw the Barrett. "Now that's some artillery! If you can bring that into the game, we may stand a chance if they come for us."

"Oh, they'll come for us," Duckett said. "They've been after this information for too long, risked too much, to give up now. The question is, how many of them are there? Do they have reinforcements? And if so, how many? Those are the things we need to be ready for."

Leonard and Cedric grabbed the last two boxes. The quarter-mile walk would typically have taken five minutes but walking through almost a foot of snow made it slow going, and it was nearly ten minutes before they got to the first kiva.

"This kiva will give us good cover," Duckett said. "Assuming they come from the parking area, we'll have good field of fire on the trail. They'll know that, so we need to try to keep them in our kill zone.

"Going left won't be much of an option for them, especially with the snow. The slope is steep enough that they'll slide right off the edge. It's not a huge fall, but it's a bone breaker. No, the bigger risk is that they go right, behind this ridge of rocks. The rock and the trees will give them good cover and concealment, and they'll be able to swing around this flank. Bad for us."

"So, what do we do?" Sarah asked.

Duckett pointed at the box Leonard was carrying. "We use the claymores in that box to force them back toward the trail. There's enough wire to set up a few of them. I'm thinking one back here on the remote detonator," —he pointed at the start of the rock ledge— "one here in the middle on a trip wire, and one here on this end, also on a remote. They trip the middle one, they can go forward, into another one, backward, where they also get blasted, or over the ledge back into our field of fire."

"What if they go farther to the right?" Cedric asked. "Away from the blast zone? Couldn't they still come around and flank us?"

Duckett considered it, looking at the terrain. "It's possible. The slope does drop away, but maybe not soon enough. We can set another couple trip wires in that direction. That should address that as well as we can.

"Now, we need to plan for some of them to get past all of that. That's where this kiva becomes a liability. This thing is basically an ancient version of the Octagon. If they get inside here with us, it's going to be close-quarters combat, hand-to-hand, and they'll kill us all."

"I've been trained in CQC, and hand to hand,"

Cedric said. "I fought in Desert Storm, and I've taken out several meth labs on the Res. I can hold my own."

"That's great, Cedric. You and I can die first and the others second. Seriously, if they get past the claymores and start up this last slope, we need to fall back. All they'd need to do is toss a couple grenades in here, and we're all toast. And we know from the other day that they're fond of grenades.

"So, we fall back to these box rooms." He walked around the kiva and gestured to the rock walls separating each of the five-foot by ten-foot stone walled areas that separated the two kivas. "They'll provide good cover, and we can go from room to room without a lot of exposure. We should put a rifle in each one so there's a fully loaded weapon within reach at all times. We have a few extras."

Duckett walked over to the edge of the second kiva.

"If they get past that, and there's any of us still alive, we can fall back to the last kiva. We can put one more claymore at the base of the bench here. The last survivor can probably safely detonate it as long as they're on the bench, and don't mind going deaf."

"*Last survivor?*" Leonard asked.

"Yeah," Sarah added. "I don't like the sound of that 'probably.' Would we be better off just heading out on the road? They don't have trackers on us any longer. We could just head, I don't know, back to El Paso? Give the information to the people there? Or out west to Phoenix! We know there are military people there. We can give the packet to them and be done with it."

255

"I like that plan, actually," Cedric said. "You two go, and the danger follows with you. The people of this area have sacrificed enough for you, I think."

Duckett looked around, squinting at the sun sinking low in the west. "Okay, I'll tell you what. We get the defenses set up, we hide out here for the night. If we make it through to the morning, Sarah and I will leave. For now, I think we should hunker down here."

Around the group, heads nodded in agreement with the plan.

"Great," Duckett said. "Now, I need help to get the defenses in place."

CHAPTER TWENTY-NINE

"Where is Hamid?"

Kasra Amol stared daggers through Amman, attempting to will him into giving up his superior. Amman, however, was not wilting under her gaze. This intrigued the woman.

"Amman, if I have to ask you again, your head will be on a spike in place of his. Does he pay you enough for this level of loyalty?"

The muscled attendants on either side of her tensed, waiting for her to give the order. Killing Nampoo Yi had been so much fun that they were eager to rip another person to pieces.

"In point of fact, he doesn't pay me. Imam Al-Mahdi furnishes me with everything I need. And I have no loyalty to Hamid Sari. You will find him in a barrel on the back of a flatbed truck, Truck 175, heading to Seoul for resupply. His barrel will be the one in the middle, against the cab."

Kasra gave a nod to the attendant on her right, who then turned and hustled from the room. "Seon will verify your story. In the meantime, tell me, Amman, why do you have such confidence? I'm curious. The gazelle runs at the sight of the lion, but a gazelle that stands its ground would, for a moment, confuse the lion. The lion might wonder, was there more to the gazelle than met the eye? That's where we find ourselves."

Amman smiled broadly. It seemed to Kasra that he had more than the usual number of teeth in his mouth. It unnerved her for a moment.

"One would be forgiven, then, if one wondered which of us was the lion and which was the gazelle."

"There's no confusion about that order, Amman. Not from me, anyway. Maybe *you* are confused, but I can disabuse you of that issue in short order."

"Maybe we are both lions, then, Kasra," he said, taking a chance and using her name without being given permission. "You can have Hamid's head. I don't care. But I have something to offer you. Something in which you will be greatly interested."

Seon returned and whispered in Kasra's ear. A grin spread across her face, making it Amman's turn to be unnerved.

"Security forces stopped the truck, Amman. They opened ALL the barrels. Hamid isn't in any of them. You have lied, and now your head belongs to me."

"Haste makes waste, Kasra. As I said, you will want

to hear what I have to offer you. Regarding Hamid, he is a snake, but his mind is not feeble. Your reputation for persuasion—*well deserved*, I might add—had a great effect on Hamid. I'd wager he suspected you would convince me to turn on him and paid the driver to stop and let him out along the way. Question the driver, and I'm sure he'll confirm it."

"My reputation has an effect on Hamid's mind, but not on yours? Is that the implication?" Kasra was ready to give the kill order to her attendants.

"No, no, not at all. I am well aware, and a great believer, in your... *gifts*, shall we say? But I also attribute to you an element that Hamid was too simple to see."

After a moment's pause, Kasra gave in. "I'll play your game for another minute, Amman, and then you'd better deliver something of value for the time I've wasted here."

"You're too smart to kill someone with a solution to your problem."

"What problem is that?"

"The missing notes from Sanjay, and the search for a cure."

She narrowed her eyes at the man. *Damn him, now I want to know what he has to say. I've misjudged this man. He is bright, and he knows it. I do hate that.* She nodded to Seon again. "Check with the driver. See what he says." She turned back to Amman. "You have until Seon returns to tell me something of value."

"I'd rather wait, if you please. You see, I am not a liar, and the earlier implication weighs on me. Once my honesty is no longer in question, I will gladly tell you what I have to offer. You will not regret it. If you do, well, you still get to have me killed, I suppose. But I will at least die as an honest man."

"You are a curiosity, Amman. An Iranian man with a spine. We'll see if you have a brain to go with it."

The next few minutes passed in an uncomfortable silence. Neither Kasra nor the remaining attendant seemed to breathe. Kasra stared directly into Amman's eyes. He tried holding her gaze but blinked after only a few seconds. She didn't react, and neither did she blink. She sat motionless, to the point that Amman started to wonder if she were human at all, but rather a robot designed by a Korean tech company.

Thankfully, Seon returned and whispered in her ear.

"Well, that was an overreaction, Seon. I don't think a dim-witted truck jockey knew who he was ferrying. There was no need to kill him. Send some fruit to his family." Seon, seemingly confused, bowed and left the room again.

"Well?" Amman asked. "My integrity has been restored, I take it?"

"Oh, yes. It seems Hamid included a note in the roll of cash he gave the driver, instructing him to stop the truck after ten minutes and let him out of the barrel. He does not—*did not,* I should say since he's dead now—know where dear Hamid went after that.

So, now I need to issue a national alert to find him. But we still have unresolved business, you and I."

"We've been wasting time searching for a cure, Kasra."

"I'm at a loss, I'm afraid. I thought you were a *smart* man. With no cure, death eventually comes to our door."

"Let it come. We should be looking for a way to protect *our* people while leaving *their* populations vulnerable to the plague. If we develop a cure, eventually it will leak out to the Americans, and we're back to a level playing field. We want them fighting two enemies: the disease and us. Ideally, they'll be so focused on the former, they won't spend much time on the latter."

"And you think you know a way to accomplish this feat?"

"I have ideas, yes. But I need the resources to develop them."

"And I so happen to have resources that could help you, is that correct? It seems there's a symbiosis forming here, Amman. I'll admit your concept intrigues me." She looked him over, scanning him from head to foot. She found her lust for blood was gone, and a different lust was taking over. She turned to the remaining attendant. "Hyuk, leave us."

The large man bowed and left the room, pulling the doors closed behind him.

"Now, Amman, before we go any farther down this

road, you will learn where the balance of power rests in this relationship."

Outside the chamber door, Hyuk stood guard. As Seon returned, Amman's cries seeped through the ornamented steel security doors. Without asking any questions, Seon took his post at the opposite side of the entrance.

CHAPTER THIRTY

DURANGO, COLORADO. MAY 9

"Most of the food and almost all of the weapons are gone," Hossein reported.

Reza approached next. "They made contact with the supply depot in Scottsdale, but no one else."

Ahmad took in the new information. The Americans had gained entry to the safe house without brute force, stolen most of the valuable supplies, used their communications equipment, and left before the team arrived. He began to suspect that Kamal was right and that the Americans had been underestimated. *It makes sense*, he thought. *We're not dealing with the spoiled Facebook warriors that our PSYOPs teams used to cause division amongst the populace. We're dealing with the survivors—trained, independent, more resilient than the average American. No one ever took that into account.*

"Let's get ready to move," he said to the team within earshot. "There's nothing to gain by staying longer. Their trail grows colder by the minute."

He strode outside where the remainder of his team, plus Kamal, was busy picking off the infected that had come to investigate the sound of the Blackhawk touching down.

"Kamal," he called out and waited for the giant man to walk over.

"What is it?" Kamal snarled at him.

"What did you find in the Mercedes?"

"Nothing. They took the weapons and ammunition, they took the laptop, they took the food. Everything."

"And yet they left the satellite uplink plugged in and powered on. Curious, no?"

"What are you driving at, Ahmad? I'm getting tired of your shit."

"We were lured here, Kamal, or rather, you allowed us to be lured here. They were smart enough to remove the GPS tracker from the van but left the SatLink active. You've allowed yourself to be played for the last time. I'm taking command of the mission now."

"Like hell..."

The silence of the weapons around them suddenly seemed conspicuous. Out of the periphery of his vision, Kamal could see one of the team had a rifle trained on him, and he assumed others did as well. He relaxed his shoulders and softened his posture.

"Fine, Ahmad. I just want to get that package and kill these Americans. I don't care who gets credit."

"Very good. Let's go." He pointed a finger in the air and waved it in a circular motion. "Mount up!"

The team boarded the Blackhawk, and a moment later it was airborne.

Ahmad slid around the forward set of seats and went up front to the pilots. "I've assumed command of this mission. You will no longer take orders from Kamal Baraghani. Do you understand?"

Both men affirmed that they understood.

"Good, now, tell the pilots in the Apache that I want them doing a widefield search using all available technology to look for the Americans. We can start by following the tracks in the snow leading away from here. Understood? I want them found, gentlemen!"

He returned the cargo area, scanning the faces of all the men. They were alert and ready for action. He noticed Kamal scratching his head again.

"Kamal!"

The big man was startled. "Yes?"

"Are you okay? I've seen you twice now scratching your head. You know the symptoms of the infected, right?"

"Of course, I do, Ahmad. Don't be stupid." He dropped his hand to his lap, conscious that the other men were watching. "I caught a little shrapnel in the battle in Durango," he lied. "It's a small wound, and it's healing. It just itches. I am not infected. Test me if you like!"

Ahmad studied the man for a moment. He was sweating, but it was hard to imagine a situation where a man that size would not be overheated. He seemed alert and was indeed not confused. Still, it would bear watching. Plus, they had none of the equipment they needed to do the test, and he suspected Kamal knew that.

"No, that's okay, Kamal. You understand my caution, of course. After what happened to your man."

"Of course, I do understand, Ahmad. Just focus on finding the Americans."

Ahmad nodded and locked eyes with his number two, Hossein. He flicked his eyes to Kamal and back to Hossein, who returned the signal with an almost imperceptible nod. The meaning was clear; watch Kamal and take him out if necessary.

CHAPTER THIRTY-ONE

CHIMNEY ROCK, COLORADO. MAY 9

Duckett and Leonard walked back to the first kiva. Sarah stood on the east side of the rim, looking toward the highway.

"Anything happening?" he asked.

"No. Well, nothing along the road. We got rifles planted in the storage rooms and…"

"Storage rooms?" Duckett asked.

"Yeah, that's what those rectangular rooms were used for by the ancients. Storing food and supplies. Like, you know, rifles."

"Okay. I don't care what we call them, everything's in place?"

"Yes."

The sun peeked out from behind the clouds long enough for the bottom to edge its way behind the mountains to the west, stretching out the shadows and instantly dropping the temperature.

"It's going to get cold tonight," Duckett said. "Does everyone have enough shirts and jackets to layer? I'm really glad we swiped a bunch of stuff from that supply depot now."

Cedric had his patrolman's coat and gloves, so he was set. The others took a few minutes adding long-sleeved shirts and hooded sweatshirts to their ensembles and rearranging holsters and vests and ammo pouches to new configurations.

Leonard climbed out of the kiva to look around in the last few minutes of twilight. "Car coming!!" he shouted.

The others came running to him, where they could see a car approaching the turnoff from the main highway. As it slowed to make the turn, a new sound started bouncing off of the landscape.

"Shit," Duckett exclaimed. "Choppers!"

The car forgotten, he wheeled around, looking for them.

"There!" he shouted, pointing to the northwest. Two helicopters, flying low, coming out of the valley that Highway 160 ran through.

"You think the Arizona Air National Guard sent them?" Sarah asked.

"No clue. They're flying our equipment. That's an Apache in the lead and a Blackhawk following it, but I'm not going to send up a signal flare until they do something that tells me which side they're on. Everyone stay low, don't move. They're not looking over here, just don't call attention to yourselves."

"Where are you going?" Cedric asked.

"To get the Barrett."

The helicopters continued to follow the road, headed east, banking first to the left, then to the right as they followed the curves.

"They're following our tracks in the snow!" Sarah exclaimed. "If it's not our people, it will lead them right here!"

Cedric had a pair of binoculars against his eyes. "That car is Susan Red's Travelall. She's either coming up here or going back to Arboles. Either way, if she doesn't get around that curve, she'll be spotted by them."

They watched helplessly as the helicopters followed the terrain, cresting over the last hill and banking back to the right. The noses tilted forward as they descended toward the Highway 160 intersection with 151.

From their vantage point atop Chimney Rock, they could still see the Travelall, but they could not tell if the helicopters could see it or not. Susan had made it around the curve, putting her on the other side of one hundred feet of a hillside that the people in the helicopters would need more altitude to see over.

The helicopters passed the intersection, following Highway 160 toward Pagosa Springs.

"Oh, that was close," Sarah said.

Cedric let the binoculars hang from the strap around his neck. "Yes, it was. But now I'm worried about what's in store for Pagosa Springs. There are only a few cops left there."

In the valley to the east, the helicopters both banked hard toward the south and gained altitude. Susan's SUV had almost reached the turnoff into the Chimney Rock monument. The Apache picked up speed and pulled away from the Blackhawk. It belched fire from the gun mounted on its underside. Puffs of dirt and gravel erupted all around the Travelall, launching chunks of asphalt into the air, gravity bringing them cascading down on the hood of the car. It was too late for the SUV to stop, so it hit the new ruts in the road, lurched sideways, and went off the side. Susan managed to keep it on all four wheels but quickly got stuck in the thick bushes and rocky terrain that lined the road. The passenger door opened, and a person half fell, half jumped from the vehicle.

"It's Aaron!" Leonard exclaimed. "Why is he out of the hospital?"

"Probably wanted to come help us," Cedric replied. "I'm sure it's the same reason Susan is driving him."

Susan exited her side of the SUV and ran into the trees, beckoning Aaron to follow her.

The Apache turned and lined up another attack. It went into a hover, the gun on the belly belching fire again, tracer rounds lighting a path toward Aaron.

On the ground, Aaron ran toward the trees, but the first ten feet of timber exploded, earth and splintered wood erupting in all directions. Aaron was knocked off his feet. He crawled to a big rock and rolled over, lying back against it. Overhead, the Apache turned, the huge 30mm gun aimed directly at Aaron.

He raised a pistol at the Apache and started firing.

CHAPTER THIRTY-TWO

EAST OF DURANGO, COLORADO. MAY 9

The two helicopters banked and turned, following the roadway a hundred meters below. The Apache had the lead. The trail was easy to follow. Only one set of tire tracks led into the safe house, and one set led out.

"If we're lucky, we'll see tail lights before long," Ahmad said.

"We don't even know what kind of vehicle they're driving," Kamal warned.

"Then we shoot them all. They may be skilled, or lucky, or some combination, but they can't stand up to the Apache's gun, Kamal. This is one gunfight where we're at an advantage." He considered the multiple failures Kamal had led, which led to his request for reinforcement and additional firepower. "Thanks to your request, I would add, Kamal."

Kamal stared at Ahmed and fantasized about biting

into his neck, ripping the blood vessels open, and drinking the warm, salty blood. He shook his head, clearing the thoughts away. *I am many things, but I am NOT a ghoul,* he admonished himself.

The Blackhawk banked one way, then the other. Kamal's equilibrium was out of balance again, and he fell hard into the man next to him. Mehdi, or Tarik; Kamal wasn't sure which.

"Careful," the man said, pushing Kamal off him. Kamal mumbled an apology.

The pilot called Ahmad on the headset.

"There was a side road behind us. The Apache gunner saw tail lights on that road."

Ahmad opened his mic. "Let's go after them."

The engine revved and the Blackhawk rose sharply then banked hard to the right. It was only a few moments before they had overtaken the vehicle. The Blackhawk overshot it to allow the Apache to get a better angle, going in a wide arc around the scene.

Ahmad opened his mic again. "Tell the Apache to fire a burst from the thirty, a few meters in front of the car. If they have it with them, we don't want to destroy the package in a direct strike."

The message was relayed to the other helicopter, and a few seconds later they could hear the *zzzzr-rrrrppp* of the 30mm gun firing a burst. Ahmad's face lit up as he watched out the window.

The car wasn't hit directly, but chunks of asphalt were blown into the air by the inch-thick high explosive rounds, showering the vehicle with debris and forcing it off the road. After a few seconds of trying to drive through the brush, the SUV stopped, and a man got out and started running.

"Apache wants to know what to do about the runner," the pilot said.

"Does he have a backpack?"

"Negative."

A heavy-set woman emerged from the driver's side and ran into the stand of pine trees directly in front of the crashed SUV. Ahmad could not see if she was carrying anything, either.

"Male runner is empty-handed, no pack."

"Take him out."

The gunner in the Apache took aim and released another burst, ripping the ground to shreds.

The man had been blown off his feet but wasn't killed by the burst of fire. He crawled to a nearby rock and flipped over, lying face up, and raised a pistol at the Apache. Ahmad started laughing. He turned to the rest of his team.

"The American thinks he's going to shoot down the Apache with a pistol!"

They all started laughing. Ahmad looked back out the window as the Blackhawk slowly circled. He opened his mic. "Finish him off, then look for the woman in the woods. Once they're neutralized, we'll set down and search the vehicle."

The Apache lurched to the side and began to spin.

"What is happening?" he asked the pilot.

"They're taking fire."

"Yeah, I see the American shooting his pistol."

"No, this isn't small arms. The GFAS from the Apache says it's coming from the mountaintop to the east."

"No, no, this can't be happening!" Ahmad said. The Apache continued to spin, the nose dipping down, and it crashed in the open space in front of Chimney Rock. The Ground Fire Acquisition System identified another threat on the mesa. "Get us up there."

The pilots increased their speed and gained altitude, moving the craft farther away from the mountain, then they banked right and moved to the south.

"We saw three people up there, but there could be more. There's a parking lot with several vehicles. The people are halfway between the parking lot and the tall spires on the north end of the plateau."

"What's our best point of entry?"

"I can get you on the south side pretty easy."

Ahmad left his mic open while he instructed his team. "Get ready to go. Mohammad, Hossein, Abbas, and Tarik, you'll fast-rope in and advance to the north. Reza, Mehdi, Kamal, and I will deploy to the north end and we'll meet in the middle. Kill anyone you see. But be careful of their bags and gear. If we damage any of the information contained in that packet, this is all for nothing. Ali, you stay on board and direct fire from the machine gun to keep them occupied. Pilots, do you copy?"

"We copy. Give us the go for insertion."

Ahmad looked every one of his men in the eye; even Kamal, who was a sweaty mess. "Are you ready?"

As a chorus, they cried out, "YES, SIR! ALLAHU AKBAR!"

He keyed the mic one more time. "Let's go."

CHAPTER THIRTY-THREE

Duckett returned with the Barrett and dropped to a knee. He extended the bipod arms and moved to a prone position, got his eye behind the scope, and lined up a shot. He pulled the trigger. The gun roared, sending a half-inch thick projectile at the Apache.

Nothing happened. He changed his aim and fired again, this time seeing a hole in the windshield of the helicopter. He fired several more rounds as quickly as he could get the scope back on target.

"You guys need to get down, get to cover," he shouted as he changed magazines in the big rifle. "The Apache has a system that detects ground fire. They'll be locking on to us soon and launching missiles."

"I don't think so," Sarah said.

Duckett looked back down at the Apache as it began to spin, losing altitude and crashing in the meadow below.

"Holy shit! I did it! I hit the pilot! That's the

longest shot I've ever made! That has to have been three-fourths of a mile!"

"Where's the other one going?" Leonard asked.

They watched the Blackhawk pull away to the east and loop around to the south end of the mesa.

"Probably dropping troops. Everyone get to your positions. Remember, shoot to kill, use the rock walls for cover. Try not to get stuck in the kivas, or you're going to find yourself in a cage match with a trained killer. It's a bad place to be, believe me. Keep track of your rounds and swap mags when you get low or grab one of the extra rifles. Just don't get caught with an empty mag. Does everyone have the headsets and police radios Cedric gave us?"

When everyone gave him an affirmative answer, he said, "All right. Switch them on. Just breathe, keep the bad guys in front of you and pull the trigger."

The helicopter left the mesa and made a wide loop, starting out heading west, then angling to the north.

"Okay," he added. "They'll be here in a few minutes. This will all be over soon, one way or another. Fight until you can't. Then fight some more. If you go down, go down spitting fire and lead. Make them regret coming to America." He trotted off to his position, where the clackers for the claymores were waiting.

"*Coming To America*. I love that movie," Leonard said. "If we make it through this, I'm watching it first chance I get."

"I can't wait to see it," Sarah said. She went to the

southern kiva and got into position, standing on the stone bench that circled the inside base of the structure. From that position, she laid her rifle on the lip of the kiva. Using her arm, she swept snow into foot-high piles on either side of her rifle. She saw Leonard look at her quizzically. "Just some concealment. If they're using infrared, it might give me a second where they can't see me, and I get the drop."

"Will that work?"

"It can't hurt, right? I mean, they'll still see me, but they'll see a sliver of heat and not my whole head, right? At least that's my theory."

He nodded and did the same thing from his spot farther down the bench.

Cedric walked over to his son. "Leonard, I don't want you to take any unnecessary chances, okay? Shoot, and when they get close, move. Shoot and move, don't give them an easy target. I'll be over here to the right, in the storage rooms."

"Okay, Dad. We'll get through this. We have to avenge Grandpa, right?"

"Just focus on surviving. Don't worry about revenge."

"Okay."

After Cedric left, Sarah got the young man's attention again. "Leonard, see that spot where the mesa narrows and the path skirts the drop-off?"

"Yeah, I see it."

"Well, that's the bug-out zone. If they get that far, you run up the steps and out the back of the kiva. I'll cover you. Once you get clear, turn and cover me. Okay?"

"Yeah, got it. So, what do we do now?"

"We wait."

Sarah checked her rifle for the tenth time, ensuring it was loaded and the magazine was full, then let it hang from its sling. She checked the pistol on her hip and counted the magazines in her tactical vest. She cupped her hands and blew into them to keep them warm.

The noise from the helicopter hadn't disappeared. It had faded, but was growing louder, coming their way from the north. Sarah turned to see if she could spot it, but it wasn't running any lights. Besides, it was on the far side of the twin spires of rock, so they might not be able to see it no matter what. It remained there for a minute, then drifted away to the east. Now she could see its dark shadow rising above the mesa and holding in place. A thought flashed through her head.

If we can see it, they can see us!

She dropped down inside the kiva, below the vision of the Blackhawk to the east. "Leonard, get down!" she called out. He nodded and hopped off the bench and ran over to Sarah's position.

"What's going on?"

"We were in plain sight of the people in that helicopter. I didn't want them telling the others where we are, or worse, shooting us!"

Duckett's voice came through on the comms. *"Folks, things just got more complicated. I think that*

Blackhawk just dropped people on the north end. We're trapped in between them. Look sharp and be ready to fight in both directions."

Sarah pressed her talk button. "Roger, Duckett. Hey Cedric, can you see the main trail to the south?"

"I sure can, Sarah."

"Good, because we had to hide from that copter. Call out if you see anything."

"Will do. I'm behind a stone wall in the storage rooms so that thing can't see me from where it is, but I've got a clear view of the trail."

"Good. We're going to get out of here and move to the storage rooms on the west side of the second kiva. It will give us a better view to the north and more cover from the copter."

She tapped Leonard on the shoulder. "You ready?" He nodded, and they stood with their backs to the wall of the kiva. She was about to tell him to go when an explosion from over the ridge stopped her. The Iranians had set off the claymore! Her hands no longer felt cold. It was time to start the fight.

CHAPTER THIRTY-FOUR

CHIMNEY ROCK, COLORADO. MAY 9

The Blackhawk dropped low on the south end of the mesa. Two of the long, thick ropes spilled out either side of the cargo bay, and two men rolled out and slid down them to the ground below. Another two followed, and the ropes dropped to the ground. The Blackhawk glided back, away from the mesa, rolled to the left and took off in a wide arc that would end with it re-approaching the mountaintop from the north, behind the two towering monoliths that gave the monument its name. Four more members of the team would rope in there, and the two groups would make mincemeat of the Americans.

As it left, Ahmad's voice crackled into Hossein's headset. *"Once you get to the parking lot, you're going to see a trail where the Americans have walked. I think that will leave you exposed, but there's a ridge of rock you can use for cover as you approach their last known position."*

"Roger," he said in response. He relayed the instructions to the rest of the team.

The four soldiers resituated their gear and headed off through the brush, winding upward through a draw that was thick with pine trees and snow.

It was slower going than they anticipated, taking nearly fifteen minutes to travel a little more than a kilometer to the parking lot. Gasping for air after fighting through the snow and the altitude, they approached the vehicles with caution, half expecting the Americans to be waiting inside. A cursory inspection found them empty.

Hossein lifted his night vision and pulled out a pair of binoculars, also equipped with night vision technology. Ahead he saw the path Ahmad had spoken about. The snow was tamped down as the trail left the parking lot and disappeared over the hill. A hundred meters ahead it reappeared, climbing fifty meters over the next half kilometer and disappearing again at the top of the rise. Two-thirds of the way to the top, he spotted the ridge of rock jutting up through the snow. Ahmad was right; that would give them a concealed approach to the top.

He passed the binoculars to Mohammed and told him what he'd seen. "Look ahead and tell me if I'm missing anything. Each of you take a look, so you're familiar with our route."

Abbas and Tarik took their turns staring across the sheet-covered hood of the SUV. None of the men had anything to add, so Hossein stashed the binoculars, lowered his night vision goggles, and they set out on their path.

The sound of the packed snow crunching under their boots seemed deafening. *Another reason to go around the side and advance through powder,* Hossein thought.

The trail went steadily up for two hundred and fifty meters, leaving them out of breath again, then it dropped down a steep decline for ten meters. Right where it began another upward rise, they diverted from the worn path and moved into the concealment of the vertical ridge of rock.

To the north, Hossein heard the Blackhawk approaching and knew the other team was being dropped off. Soon they would meet in the middle of the mesa, surround the Americans, kill them all, get the package, and get to someplace warm and dry.

They crept along, stepping lightly in the foot of fresh powder, working along the stone barrier. Mohammad was first, then Abbas, then Hossein, with Tarik bringing up the rear. Each man stepped in the tracks of the one in front of him.

Hossein fought his adrenaline. He wanted to get around the far side of this trail and get into it with the Americans, but he knew they had to move slowly and not give away their location so they could surprise them. Kamal had warned them about underestimating the infidels, and while Ahmad wasn't impressed with him, Hossein had a lot of admiration for Kamal Baraghani and didn't take his warning lightly.

He was watching his steps, making sure not to make more noise than he had to when he noticed a change in the pattern of the snow. It was hard to tell with the night vision, but it looked like the powder had been groomed, brushed smooth by something. *But what? A pine branch? And why?*

These thoughts rushed through his head in a millisecond, and it clicked. He saw Mohammad's foot descending into the disturbed snow.

"Mohammad don't..." he started.

The night air exploded. The whine of shrapnel whizzing past him let Hossein know that he was in harm's way. Something struck him in the right shoulder, likely a ricochet from the rock wall on his right side.

Mohammed was torn to shreds, taking the brunt of the blast. Abbas was down, injured, but not dead. Hossein was flat on his back, but Tarik, farther back than the others, was still standing when the second blast went off behind them, sending blood and bits of flesh sailing past Hossein. He rolled to his stomach in the snow, using Abbas as a shield, and turned to look back.

Tarik was dead. Hossein, by a massive stroke of luck, had been almost entirely shielded from both blasts by the bodies of his men. A quick assessment of his right arm told him that it was hurt but was functional.

He tried to reach the helicopter, but his radio had taken a hit. His earpiece had even been torn from him.

"Abbas, can you hear me?"

"Yes," the man replied, louder than Hossein wanted. "My ears are ringing, but I can hear you."

Hossein wiggled closer to him so he could talk directly into his ear. "How hurt are you? Whisper, I'm right here."

Abbas didn't need to do a complete assessment. "My leg is useless, Hossein. My left leg. I can't feel anything below my knee. I think I need a tourniquet."

Hossein fished the pouch from the pocket on Abbas's vest and removed the tourniquet. He grabbed Abbas's ruined left leg, noticing the dark stains in the snow all around them. With the tourniquet in place, he pulled Abbas backward and leaned him up against the rock wall.

"Kamal was right, the Americans are not to be underestimated. They anticipated we would come this way. They're trying to force us onto the main trail where they can pick us off."

"You mean pick YOU off, Hossein. I'm not going anywhere."

"Well, yes, me, I guess."

He heard the Blackhawk above them, to the west, providing overwatch. "Soon they'll have plenty to contend with, and I will surprise them from another direction. You stay here and kill anything that tries to get past you."

Hossein pressed the switch to activate the infrared strobe on Abbas's helmet, then turned on his own.

Now Ali in the helicopter would be able to tell them from the Americans.

He patted Abbas on the shoulder. "Remember, kill anything that comes this way. We'll come to get you when it's over."

THE BLACKHAWK COMPLETED its big arc and headed back to the Chimney Rock mesa. It hovered just beyond the second of the tall stone spires, out of the Americans' direct line of sight.

Reza and Mehdi rolled out of the sides, sliding down the thick rope and landing on the rocky terrain below. Ahmad grabbed the line and looked over at Kamal. He half expected the big man to lose his grip under his tremendous weight and kill himself on impact. It wouldn't bother him much to lose him, other than his size and strength would be an asset in the fight ahead.

"Ready, Kamal?" he shouted.

Instead of answering, Kamal dropped out the side of the Blackhawk and disappeared. Ahmad smiled and dropped out, sliding down the rope and landing harder than he wanted to. He felt a pain shoot up from his foot to his hip, but he shook it off.

Ali dropped the ropes from the Blackhawk, and it peeled away, circling around to the east and climbing another hundred meters to get a better view of the mesa.

Ahmad gathered the three other men together. "Turn on the IR tags on your helmets so Ali doesn't shoot you by mistake." He looked at Kamal before adding, "That would be a real shame. Okay, let's move out. Everyone on me, let's get this done."

They struck out on the path toward the Americans. It was slower going than he would have liked, but Ahmad was not going to let the snow stop him from completing this mission. He plodded ahead, moving as quickly as he could, while also being conscious of the steep drop to his left should he lose his footing in the snow.

In the distance, an explosion boomed through the night air. He stopped the line and listened for gunfire, hoping the other team had thrown a grenade and was engaging the Americans in a firefight, but there was nothing but the rotors of the helicopter to his left.

A second explosion rang out. He pressed the call button on his radio. "Hossein, do you copy?" Silence. "Hossein, do you copy?" Silence. "Blackhawk, do you see anything?"

A few seconds went by, then the pilot replied. *"I see a strobe southwest of the Americans, heading downslope away from their emplacement."*

"Only one strobe?"

"Affirmative. Just one."

Ahmad looked back at Kamal. The huge man was breathing hard and adjusting his helmet. His warning not to underestimate the Americans made Ahmad's skin flush. He shook it off and started forward again. He called back to his team.

"Let's go end this!"

CHAPTER THIRTY-FIVE

With the first explosion echoing in her ears, Sarah told Leonard to move. He ran up the steps out of the kiva while Sarah drew her rifle up and checked the main trail to the south, then the access points to the east and north. When he was clear and in position, he clicked the talk button for his radio.

"Sarah, go!"

As she ran up the steps, a second explosion rocked the mesa. Even with just the moon to light the night, she saw a plume of snow blown skyward on the other side of the rock wall.

Shit, that was only a hundred and fifty feet away! They're right on top of us!

She ran past Leonard, into one of the rectangular masonry rock-walled rooms. She turned and covered Leonard's sprint to a similar room farther down the row. She pressed her talk button.

"Duckett, what's happening over there?"

"They hit the trip wire. No one moved forward, so I blew the rear mine in case any survivors tried to retreat. I'll see them from my spot if any come forward, and I'll hit them with the third one."

"Great. They got pretty close."

"That happens in battle sometimes."

She bit her tongue and didn't return his sarcasm. Instead, she looked around the area, watching for movement.

Cedric opened his mic. *"Get ready, the helicopter is moving closer. I think the second group is almost here."*

"TWO ON THE MOVE, out of the big circular things and out of sight on the far side of them."

Ahmad was trying hard to remember what he had seen of the top of the mesa when they took their long arc from south to north. Two big circles dug into the ground, with several rectangular structures to the side of them, facing west. "How many do you see in total?"

"None right now. I'll have to move into a position overhead to see them."

"Do it! You'll need to be there to lay down suppressing fire anyway."

The helicopter dipped its nose slightly and moved forward.

Ahmad checked over his shoulder. The others were still kept up with him, even Kamal.

"We've got three in the rectangles; one between the two circles and two on the west side."

Good, Ahmad thought. *We can come up, take them out, and be done in minutes. We just have to get there.*

Booming gunfire echoed off the top of the mesa. Ahmad looked up and saw the flashes and tracers of the gunner returning fire. Ahmad keyed the transmitter. "What's happening up there?"

"There's a fourth American up here. We missed him before. Looks like he's got one of the fifty-caliber rifles the American military uses. We're good. He punched a couple holes in the skin, but he's running now."

Ahmad turned to the rest of the group. "Pick it up, we need to get up there *now!*"

"WE NEED TO MOVE. That helicopter is giving them our positions, I'm sure," Sarah said over the radio. "Duckett, what's your status?"

"I'm good, had to un-ass from my hide, but I'm in one piece."

Sarah ducked into another of the storage rooms. The helicopter was over her shoulder, and the wall between them was a full five feet high. She crouched down and peeked around the corner long enough to see Leonard take up a spot similar to hers.

The helicopter began firing on them. It loosed a burst at Sarah, the rounds splintering rocks and cascading pieces down on her. From somewhere to her south, she heard the big Barrett barking again, and the fire redirected toward it.

She ran from her spot and hustled to the base of a tree, hoping it would give her some cover from the overhead fire.

She spied a shadow moving along the far edge of the second kiva.

"If any of you are walking along the kiva, hit the deck now." She released the talk button, and the figure kept creeping. She raised her rifle and fired. The silhouette dropped, and she saw others pop up. She ducked and scurried closer to the rock walls just as several rounds from suppressed rifles ripped through the limbs and smacked into the trunk of the tree where she had been hiding.

She heard a pop and a hiss, and the area was bathed in light from a flare someone had fired. Standing in stark relief a hundred feet away was the giant Iranian who had grabbed her by the neck in Durango. She felt a bolt of fear, the memory of Shane's head snapping sideways as the big man shot him point-blank playing through her head. He was wearing night vision goggles, but he pulled them off and dropped them.

She was brought back to reality as rounds from the machine gun in the helicopter danced around her, snapping against the stones in the wall in front of her. Either a bullet or a fragment of rock tore a gash in her left bicep, and she dropped to the ground. She tried rolling to the side but found herself wedged against a pile of loose stones hidden under a blanket of snow. The icy cold felt good on the wound on her arm, but she knew she needed to get up before the gunner in the helicopter found her again. She grunted as she pulled herself into a crouch and ran back toward the storage rooms.

THE HELICOPTER HAD BEGUN FIRING on the Americans. Ahmad told them to make the final push onto the flat area where they were hiding. He went first, taking direction from the pilots in the helicopter, making his way toward the closest American's position.

Rifle fire erupted from his right, and he heard the hiss of rounds passing by his head, then the thump of one hitting the ballistic plate in his vest. He hit the ground immediately and listened to the rest of the team returning fire. He felt as though an ox had kicked him. His hands moved over his torso, checking for wounds and blood, but he found none.

A *pop* from ahead and to his left was a flare being sent up. The light flashed in his night vision, and he shut his eyes and lifted the goggles to the top of his head. He cursed the Russians for selling outdated equipment to his army. He knew they had optics that prevented the flash he'd just felt, but there was none of that tech in their war chest.

Reza was next to him then, asking if he was hurt. Everything snapped back into focus for Ahmad.

"I'm fine. Get fighting, go! All of you, you know your mission!"

The pain in his chest was intense. He found a pocket on his vest and removed two items. The first was a narcotic painkiller, which he snapped open then jammed the needle into his side. The pain abated almost instantly. He let out a sigh and opened the other item, a vial containing an acrid powder. It consisted of a mix of cocaine, some sort of smelling salt, and powdered adrenaline. He inserted it into his left nostril, squeezed the bulb and inhaled. He let out an involuntary *Ahhhgh!* and repeated the procedure on the right side.

He tossed the vial to the side and flipped over to his stomach, scanning the area in front of him. After a false start, he was about to get into this fight.

DUCKETT FIRED the flare and ran to another spot he'd scouted. He looked across the plateau and saw several of the black-clad men scurry after removing their NVGs. He had a suspicion that their equipment would not be up to the US standard. In any case, his team needed the light. Now the field was more level.

One of the men stood tall, despite the high visibility. He had to be the one Sarah described to him in Durango when they were hiding from the infected in the pre-formed concrete. If he wasn't seven feet tall, he was damn close. His massive beard made his head look like it was two feet wide. Duckett raised his rifle and got the sights on him just as the gunner from the helicopter strafed his position. A piece of stone from the wall next to him dropped on his head, blurring his vision and knocking him off balance. He staggered sideways and never saw the second Iranian man fire at him. He felt rounds hit his leg and abdomen, and everything went black.

CEDRIC SAW the top of the stone wall spraying powder into the air as the bullets hit it from above. He wasn't sure who was on the other side of that wall, but in the light of the flare, he saw a black-clad man rise, seemingly from nowhere, and start shooting. He sighted in on the man's torso and started squeezing the trigger. Three, four, five rounds hit the man in the back, neck and finally, the side of the head just behind the temple.

He crouched and stepped over the foot-high remains of the section of the wall that used to separate two of the ancient storage rooms. He pulled back into the shadows of the archeological ruin to get his bearings on what was happening. He could hear gunfire from the other side of the kiva, so he knew someone else was engaged in battle. Knowing it could be Leonard, he ran clear of the masonry walls and sprinted around the north side of the ruins.

The gunner in the helicopter sprayed a line of

7.62mm rounds, chasing Cedric with it, finally over-taking him. He tumbled to the ground, ending on his back. He tried to get up but was unable to move his legs. He saw the dark blood soaking into the snow where he'd fallen and knew this was bad. Strangely, it didn't hurt.

He recalled as a boy, when his grandfather passed away, asking his father what happened when people die.

"No one knows, except those who have died, and they don't tell us anything about it."

"What do you THINK happens?" he had asked.

"I think if we've lived well, we see friends and family from long ago. Maybe we get to feast and dance with them, as was done in the old times."

"What if we haven't lived well?"

"I think we're sent back to try again. Maybe as a person, maybe as an animal."

All of this ran through Cedric's head as his blood poured into the snow. He felt his eyes closing and was powerless to stop them. He saw streaks of light just as they closed. *Was that real?* he wondered. He heard an explosion. It seemed like the world he knew was coming apart.

His mind grew calm. The sounds of battle faded away. Cedric knew he had lived a life of service to his people, protecting them as best he could. He was ready to see his ancestors, his wife, and his grandfather. He smiled, and death welcomed him.

CHAPTER THIRTY-SIX

Amman and Kasra were alone in the Command room. He had just laid out his plan for the next phase of the purification of the world.

"And you're confident you can make this work?" she said, the doubt in her voice evident.

"Yes. We had some promise in the Brazilian labs before things got out of hand. It would be easy to start that back up. With your blessing, of course."

She leaned back in her chair and tented her hands, her index fingers placed over her lips. Her eyes narrowed, and Amman could tell she was thinking, moving the pieces on the chess board in her head.

A female communications officer entered the room and approached Amman, carrying a satellite phone. "I have the pilot of the Blackhawk as you asked." She bowed, extending the phone.

Amman stuck his hand out. "Thank you."

She handed him the phone, turned on her heel, and marched out of the room.

"This is Amman Yaziri. You can speak freely—what is the mission status? I see. Yes, that's good. Give me one minute."

He covered the mouthpiece with a hand and turned to Kasra.

"Is it your wish to continue this mission or terminate it and restart the work in Brazil? Now is the time to decide."

Kasra ran her tongue over her teeth, pausing to push it against the point of one of her canines which, Amman knew, were prominent and sharp. The bite on his neck was still sore and needed disinfectant applied to it. The human mouth was filled with bacteria, and she used hers liberally all over his body.

"Terminate it. We no longer need that information. I want it all destroyed. Burn them all down and destroy everything."

Amman smiled, feeling like a predator himself. He took his hand from the phone and addressed the pilot again. "We have a new directive. Terminate them. ALL of them. Yes, them too. And burn everything to ash, all traces of it. Not one shred of that information can be found."

He ended the call and turned to Kasra. "It's done. We're committed to this new course of action."

She one-upped his predatory smile, sending a chill up his spine.

"You'd better hope this goes as well as you say it will, or we'll be using YOU as the next test subject. Now—back to my chambers. I'm not done playing with you yet, my little mouse."

Amman swore he saw a tail flickering behind her.

CHAPTER THIRTY-SEVEN

ABOVE CHIMNEY ROCK, COLORADO. MAY 9

The pilot stashed the satellite phone in a pouch and motioned for the co-pilot to lean in.

"That was Command," the pilot said. "They want everyone killed and everything burned." He nodded toward the gunner's position. "Start with him."

The co-pilot moved to the rear. The pilot heard a single gunshot. He eased the bird to the west and heard the machine gun start up once more. His stomach was knotted up, disgusted by what they were doing, but it was well known what happened if you disappointed Command.

Alarms started going off in the cockpit. The pilot realized too late what was happening, and his last thought was that he wished he never volunteered to learn to fly the big American helicopter.

CHAPTER THIRTY-EIGHT

Leonard ran from spot to spot, trying to hide from the helicopter and find an angle to fight the Iranians. He had outpaced Sarah when they left their first hides, so he wasn't sure where she was. When she fired her rifle to start the battle, he looked in her direction, then in the direction she was shooting. He saw the silhouettes of the men coming from the pueblo trail below the ancient village that had become their battleground. A flare went up, illuminating the entire tableau.

Gunfire erupted on the southeast side of the ruins, with the helicopter peppering rounds down on them. He had a moment of fear for his father, who was over in that direction but forced himself to focus on his own situation. There was nothing he could do from here to help his father.

He saw a figure approaching, and it wasn't any of his people, so he aimed his rifle and fired, squeezing the trigger a half dozen times. The figure dove to the ground, kicking up a fantail of snow, and rounds started zipping back at him, hissing as they passed him by.

Leonard returned fire, pointing the gun toward the spot where the muzzle flashes had come from, then he sprinted from his position, hearing his father's voice saying, "Shoot and move, shoot and move." He kept firing as he ran past the place where the man in black was, and as he passed him, Leonard felt a bullet rip into his left leg. He fell, hitting the ground hard despite the cushion of the snow. He tumbled, and he slid on the snow toward the kiva. His momentum carried him over the edge and into space for a second before he landed hard on the kiva floor. The wind was knocked out of him, and he lost his rifle in the fall.

The man in black was on the edge of the kiva, looking down on Leonard. He pointed his rifle at the young man, and Leonard winced, waiting for the final shot that would end his life.

Overhead, a streak of light flew past, coming from the southeast, a loud *whoosh* accompanying it. The streak hit the helicopter, detonating in a massive explosion that broke the aircraft into multiple pieces, raining burning hunks of debris down on the northwest side of the mesa.

The black-clad figure had turned his head to look at the spectacle, just for a second, then turned back to finish off Leonard. Instead, Leonard had his pistol aimed directly at the man's face. He fired three shots, and the man fell forward into the kiva.

The Iranian solder landed on Leonard. His rifle was pinned between them, and Leonard felt his ribs break as the weight of the man drove that rifle into Leonard's torso. He gasped for air, each breath now bringing horrible pain and forcing him to take fast, shallow breaths. He realized he was hyperventilating but was helpless to stop it, and his vision faded to black.

SARAH SAW Leonard go down and fall into the kiva as the Iranian chased him. She fired several shots at the man in black but missed.

Overhead, the helicopter had moved slightly to the west, and the gunner was shooting, but the target was nowhere near her, so she got up and ran a few steps to get closer to the Iranian. As she raised her rifle to fire again, something streaked out of the dark sky to the southeast and slammed into the helicopter.

The explosion was incredibly bright, drowning out the light from the fading flare, but quickly dimmed as the pieces of the helicopter came apart and fell to earth.

Thank God it wasn't directly overhead, she thought. With one less thing to worry about, she ran in a crouch to the kiva's edge and saw the Iranian lying on top of Leonard. He wasn't moving, and there was blood all over the place in the snow around them. She crouched down, trying to lower her profile, and scanned the area, looking for targets. She pressed the talk button for her radio.

"Is anyone else out there? Duckett? Cedric?" There was no reply. "Anyone?" Again she was greeted by silence. Fear began creeping into her bones as she realized she was alone with an unknown number of enemies who wanted to kill her.

Gunfire from the right chased the fear from her. She raised her gun and returned fire, not aiming so much as trying to get some rounds near the shooter to get them to duck their head long enough for her to find cover. She scurried to the east edge of the kiva, returning fire until her magazine was empty.

She dropped the magazine and pulled a fresh one from a pocket on her vest. It didn't come out cleanly, and she gave it an extra tug. It came free, but the momentum was enough to make her left foot slip out from under her, and she rolled to the side, tumbled in the air for a second, and hit the ground hard on her left shoulder. She felt the *pop* as something broke, and pain radiated all the way up and down her left arm. It hung limp, useless. She used her feet to push herself back to the bench, then she tried to use that to leverage herself upright.

AHMAD SAW Reza cut down the man who fired the

flare. That had been a nice trick, getting them to ditch their outdated night vision, but the man paid for it with his life.

Then one of the Americans shot Reza. Ahmad stalked him, but just as he was going to shoot, Ali strafed him from the helicopter, robbing him of his first confirmed American kill.

Mehdi was engaged in battle with another of the Americans, but Ahmad had no good angle to join in, and besides, it was over almost as quickly as it started. The American was shot and fell into the pit. Mehdi was going to deliver the coup de grace.

Then the missile whipped past them and took out the helicopter. Several thoughts flashed through his head in quick succession.

Where did that come from? How are we getting out of here now? Where is the package? Where is Mehdi?

The last thought returned his focus. He wasn't thinking as clearly as he usually would because of the painkiller and the wake-up powder, but Mehdi had been standing there, and from the time he looked at the exploding helicopter and returned his gaze to the edge of the pit, Mehdi had disappeared.

He saw a woman creeping over to the edge of the pit where Mehdi had been. She must have shot him. He raised his rifle and put the sights on her, but his hands were shaking. He cursed the effects of the medicine and laid the barrel of the gun atop the stone wall for stability. After reacquiring the sight picture, he fired several shots at her.

She fired back right away, getting a round close enough to spray dirt and bits of rock in his face. As he got ready to fire again, she fell sideways into the pit, and he heard her scream. *That* made him smile. He got up and walked over to the big circular pit and saw the woman crawling to the opposite wall. Her left arm was slack. If he were a wolf, he would be licking his lips.

SHE HEARD A THUMP, and one of the Iranians was in the kiva with her. He walked toward her, calm, but with purpose. He glanced down at Leonard and the other Iranian and shook his head. He gave her a *tsk tsk*.

"So much death and pain," he said in heavily accented English. "And for what? You're going to give me the information we seek, and you're going to die anyway. You could have made this much easier if you had given up when you had the chance."

"Fuck you."

"You Western whore! This is why you will all die! You don't know your place. You're profane. You and the rest of your decadent race will soon be dead, either from our hands or from the creeping death that devours your land."

Tears welled up in the corners of her eyes, in part from the pain in her shoulder, and in part from the anger she felt toward this man. "I said fuck you!" she screamed and drew her 9mm pistol.

Before she could even get her finger on the trigger,

he grabbed her hand and twisted the gun away, quickly taking it from her. He headbutted her, knocking her off balance. She fell against the wall.

"Where is the package? Tell me, and I'll kill you quick. Or die slowly," he leered at her, a twisted smile spreading across his face, "with my seed spilling from you."

She stared at him defiantly but said nothing.

He slapped her with the back of his hand and laughed. "I can do this all night, whore."

He turned to his right when a heavy thump announced someone else had entered the kiva. "Oh, Kamal," he said in Farsi. "You're here in time to help me beat the location of the package from this whore."

Kamal's scream startled both of them. She saw the giant from Durango fifteen feet away. His rifle hung slack from its sling. He opened his mouth and bellowed the sound they all had learned to fear.

He was infected.

CHAPTER THIRTY-NINE

Since leaving El Paso, it seemed to Ian they'd gone from the frying pan to the fire over and over. He promised his team some R&R if they got out of their last hairy-assed situation, and truth be told, he was looking forward to a few days of downtime himself.

Then the call came in from Scottsdale. They were needed again, and right away, so Ian, against his every desire, found himself geared up and riding in a Blackhawk steaming north. Toby's voice cut in on the comms, interrupting his angry introspection.

"I've got a good picture, good tone."

"Light 'em up, Tobes."

Toby pulled the trigger on the MANPADS. The missile fired from the tube, dropping the launch motor thirty feet from him, and the flight motor took the missile toward the target at sixteen hundred miles per hour. Five seconds later, a fireball erupted in the southern Colorado sky.

The big man sprinted toward the cargo area of the idling Blackhawk and tossed himself and the MANPADS inside.

"Go, go, go!" Ian commanded the pilot. The helicopter lifted off and made straight for the mesa of Chimney Rock.

Toby looked at Kinsey and Ian with a giant grin on his face. "Bada bing, bada BOOM!"

Kinsey rolled her eyes at Toby's commentary. "It's like you've never seen a Stinger take out a helicopter, Tobes."

"From four clicks out? That was a helluva shot!"

"We're two minutes away. Get your game faces on." Ian was all business.

Toby put on a pouting face. "Fuck, Ian, let me enjoy the moment."

"With all we've been through in the last few days, I want to enjoy a fucking bed and a fucking pillow. Let's just whack some more Iranian pieces of shit and get the fuck out of here."

"Easy, boss, you're cursing much more than normal. These people need our help. And according to Scottsdale, they have some important information."

Ian glared at Kinsey. As usual, she calmed him down. It seemed like she was always chilling him out, but right now she was on his last nerve. Everything was on his last nerve. But he knew she was right. They were in a position to help these people, and so they would. It's what they always did. "Fuck it, whatever. Sixty seconds."

Ian opened his mic to talk to the pilots. "We're ready to rock back here."

"Roger. We'll do a quick assessment to check for threats and then drop you in. If we can land, we'll do that. Otherwise, you'll rope in."

"Roger, out." He took the headset off and put on his helmet, then adjusted the night vision. He put his hand out with a thumbs up. "Ready!" he shouted to Kinsey and Toby. They each returned a thumbs up of their own.

"Everything's green!" Kinsey confirmed.

Toby was his usual over-exuberant self. "Ready to rock out with my cock out!"

"Toby!" Kinsey admonished.

"You can jam out with your clam out! We're all about equality here!"

Kinsey laughed, and Ian shook his head. *Last. Fucking. Nerve.*

AHMAD TURNED and raised his rifle to shoot Kamal, but the big man reached him first. He grabbed the smaller Iranian. "You're a flea," he said in Persian. Ahmad pushed back against him, but at just under two meters tall, he was no match for the giant. Kamal twisted Ahmad's head, snapping bones and tearing muscles. He kept spinning it until he had turned it two hundred and seventy degrees.

In the dying light of the flare, Sarah saw the man's

skin split open and vertebrae, rent muscles, and blood vessels were protruding from the tears. The impossibly large man dropped the limp rag doll and turned his focus on Sarah.

She scrambled around, looking for her pistol, but wasn't fast enough. The man grabbed her by the throat and lifted her off the ground. He pushed her against the back wall of the kiva, banging her head into the rocks and holding her high enough that the tips of her toes barely scraped the surface of the stone bench.

He growled something at her in Persian, which of course she didn't understand. His grip on her throat was so tight she couldn't tell him she didn't speak his language. She tried to breathe, but her airway was closed off.

"Where is package?" he growled again, this time in English.

She tried to speak but couldn't make a sound. She was getting light-headed and realized he was probably restricting the blood flow to her brain in addition to cutting off her oxygen. She started beating at his arm, but it had no effect on him.

He leaned in close to her. She could feel his hot breath, but since she couldn't breathe, she could not smell it. *I bet it's awful. What are you doing? You're dying, and you're making fun of his breath? What's wrong with you?*

She shook her head the little bit that she could. She felt her heart beating impossibly fast in her chest. It seemed like it was beating hundreds of beats per minute. *Is that possible?*

The man tilted his head back and roared, screaming like the infected did. Sarah was reminded of Jack, who in his last moments, was semi-lucid one second and biting at the air the next. This man was a horror show, a real-life Jekyll and Hyde, battling for control of one enormous body.

Her good right hand beat at the immense man, pounding his chest. Her fingers found something on his vest. Something long and round, with a loop of fabric holding it in place. She wrapped her fingers around it and jerked on it, trying to pull it free. Her fingers found a snap, which she tugged open, and the knife slid free from the sheath.

Kamal, somewhere in his diseased brain, realized what she'd done. He snapped his head down, locking eyes with her. Her vision was graying out—or was that the flare dying?—just as she drove the knife up as hard as she could.

It pierced his neck in front of his Adam's apple, driving upward, bisecting his esophagus, the point entering and getting lodged in the brain stem.

He dropped her immediately, and her head banged against the stones all the way down as she fell to the bench. She inhaled, screaming as she did so, making a noise that freaked her out. She could not breathe deeply or quickly enough.

Kamal staggered backward, his hands flailing at the knife handle but missing it every time. His feet got

313

tangled up with Ahmad's legs, making him stumble. He spun and fell forward. His body was stiff, like a tree, and he landed hard. The knife handle was under him when he hit, and the ground drove it all the way through to the pommel, the blade popping out the back of his head.

Sarah wheezed, gulping air, her throat burning. She vaguely recognized another helicopter hovering overhead, whipping snow and ice particles around the kiva like a million tiny daggers. A figure approached her. *No, no more!* she screamed inside. *No more!!*

She reached around, looking for her gun, and she found something metal under her ribs. It wasn't her gun. It was odd shaped and had a cable attached to it.

The detonator for the claymore! She laughed out loud, immediately regretting the pain it caused in her throat. She knew the mine would probably kill her too, but she remembered Duckett's words; *fight until you can't, then fight some more.* She held the device up and started to squeeze it.

CHAPTER FORTY

PAGOSA SPRINGS, COLORADO. MAY 12

S arah cracked her eyes open, squinting against the light. She didn't understand *why* it was light, but she knew she had Iranians to kill. She squeezed the detonator as hard as she could but winced when her fingernails dug into the palm of her hand and then winced again as her throat protested the sound she made.

"Calm down, honey!" an unfamiliar voice commanded. "You're safe, hon, you're okay. You're in the Pagosa Springs Medical Center. You've been here for a couple of days."

Sarah relaxed and lay back against the pillow.

Holy shit. I made it. And please, don't call me 'honey.'

She tried to sit up, eyes wide open and realized that her ribs were killing her, and her left shoulder was radiating pain, too. "My friends," she started, but her voice descended into a cough that brought tears to her eyes.

"Don't talk, okay? Lie back. Your friends are all here too. I'll get... some of them for you, okay?" The nurse wheeled a C table over to Sarah's bed. "Here's a glass of water. I'll get you some ice, too, and let the doctor know you're awake. Just relax."

While the nurse's footsteps faded down the hall, Sarah tried to adjust her position, but her ribs protested. She felt some discomfort in her groin and reached under the gown to see what was causing it. She found a catheter and the drain tube leading to the urine collection bag.

Gross.

As she was looking at the drain tube, she noticed bruises and cuts all the way around her wrists.

What the hell? What happened to me?

The nurse returned a few minutes later with a glass of ice chips. "Here you go, hon. These should feel good on that throat. The doctor will be here in a few minutes to chat, and get you all caught up on everything, okay?"

Sarah nodded. She wanted to know what had happened to everyone else. The nurse said her friends were here, but Sarah picked up on the pause when she said she'd get "some" of them. That was ominous.

She heard multiple footsteps outside the room and a stern voice. "You'll be able to talk to her later. Go away for now, or I'll have you kicked out of the building!"

"You do that, the gennie comes with us," a male voice said.

"Shut up, Tobes. You get us kicked out, and I'll never speak to you again," a woman replied to him.

"Promise?" he jabbed back, his voice already sounding farther away.

"Hello!" the man with the stern voice called out from the door. The harsh tone was gone.

Sarah turned her head and winced. It seemed everything in her body hurt. She tried to say "Hi," but the only sound that escaped her throat was a dry rasp. She gulped a drink of water before she went into another coughing fit.

Jesus, it even hurts to swallow. Fuck me.

"Becky!" the man called out.

The nurse, who must have been just outside the door, said, "Yes, Doctor?"

"Grab a whiteboard from the front desk. One of the ones by the printer. Be sure to get a marker and eraser too."

"I'll be right back!"

The man walked into the room and slid a chair over to the side of Sarah's bed.

"Hi, Sarah. I'm Doctor Spengler." He extended his hand, and she offered hers for a quick handshake. "I know you have a lot of questions. Once we get that whiteboard, you can ask them.

"You've suffered extensive trauma to the neck and throat. You had a collapsed jugular vein that we had to go in and reopen with a stent. It will dissolve in a few months, maybe more, so no additional surgery will be needed.

"The hyoid bone—that's here," he tapped the area above his voice box, "has been broken, but not displaced. That's good news. It will heal with no need for surgical repair. However, you're going to need to be very careful with movement. No fighting for a few weeks, I'm afraid." He gave her a kind smile. "Until then, I can tell you that you *will* get your voice back, but that will take some time. A week or so, maybe less if you can rest your voice for that long. The bruising will take a couple of weeks to fade. You're fortunate; I've never seen neck trauma this bad in someone who lived.

"You also have a separated left shoulder. I couldn't detect any ligament tears, but we did have to manipulate the clavicle back in place. That's going to hurt for a while, I'm afraid. When you're mobile, we're going to put you in a sling to keep it rested. It'll take three to six weeks for it to heal, again, depending on how much you're able to rest it.

"Lastly, you have a couple of cracked ribs. I'm sorry to say that they, too, will be painful for a while, but since they're not displaced, they should heal on their own. So, that's all the bad news. You can pepper me with your questions in a minute."

The nurse returned with the whiteboard and handed it to the doctor, who passed it to Sarah. She took the pen and wrote.

What happened to my wrists?

"Ah. When you came in, you had multiple open wounds and were covered in blood, and not just your own. We sedated you, cleaned you off, patched you up, and we tested you for the infection—and it was negative. However, due to the extent of your injuries, we had to be sure you didn't have a latent infection that didn't present at your screening, so you were restrained. You, ah, you're a fighter, Sarah." He pointed to her bruises. "You did that yourself. We ended up sedating you until we were sure you weren't infected. Honestly, that was probably for the best, as your throat, that hyoid bone, your shoulder, and ribs have had a couple days of complete rest."

She erased the question and wrote more.

Who made it? How did I get here?

"Ah. Well, I don't know who all was there. I can tell you who came through here, but you'll have to forgive me if I miss anyone. Susan Red made it. She suffered a concussion and hypothermia. Your friends Ian, Toby, and Kinsey brought you here in a helicopter, along with Wayne and Leonard." He noticed the puzzled look on her face. "You don't recognize those names?"

Leonard and Susan yes, others no.

"Ah. I don't know what to tell you about that. They're the ones who came off Chimney Rock alive. Wayne was in bad shape, worse than the rest of you. Ian took the helicopter back to Albuquerque and brought us another generator and a few hundred gallons of fuel so we could keep all the systems going to keep the rest of you all alive while we performed surgery on him. If they weren't your friends before, they are now. You're all they're talking about—something to do with being a giant slayer. Though I will admit, that Toby is hard to deal with."

Cedric Naranjo?

"No, I'm sorry, he didn't make it. He was DOA. So was the other young man, Aaron."

Duckett?

"Oh yes, he's okay. That's Wayne. You didn't know his name?"

Sarah shook her head but was obviously relieved.

Want catheter out. Want IV out. Want to see Duckett and Leonard.

He chuckled. "Okay, I'll have the catheter taken out. We'll disconnect the PICC line, but when you're in bed, you're on the IV for a couple more days at least.

Once the nurse is done, I'll let Toby and Kinsey wheel you to see your friends. No walking, you hear me? And I want you back here in thirty minutes, or I'll have you sedated again. Deal?"

She gave him a thumbs up. He patted her leg and left.

CHAPTER FORTY-ONE

Kinsey pushed the wheelchair into Duckett's room. He was groggy but awake. "Hey, Sarah! It's damn good to see you!"

She scribbled on her whiteboard.

I'm so glad you made it! Thought you were dead!

He looked at the whiteboard and glanced at Kinsey. "She's not supposed to talk for a few days. Doctor's orders," Kinsey said.

"Holy shit, are you okay? I didn't know you were hurt this bad!"

Will be fine. I'll be singing in no time, <u>Wayne.</u>

He seemed perturbed. "So, you know my name now. Great. Let the jokes begin."

She giggled and immediately regretted it. Kinsey passed her the glass with the ice water and bendy straw, and she took a long sip to lubricate her throat. She scribbled another message on her whiteboard.

Don't make me laugh. Hurts throat.

"Sorry," he said, sounding genuinely contrite. "I see you've met Kinsey."

Sarah nodded.

"Did she tell you she and I met before? In El Paso?"

"I haven't told her anything yet, Duckett. Didn't want to go through everything twice."

"Okay. Well, remember I told you that Ram and his friend Jesse were escorted out of Beaumont by some hard-assed broad?"

Sarah nodded.

"Meet the hard-assed broad."

Sarah's eyes went wide, and she scribbled on the whiteboard and turned it to Kinsey.

Where is Ram?

"He bailed on us in Scottsdale," she said. "Wanted to find his family, and we weren't going back to Cali. So, he and Jesse took off. Left us in the middle of the night without so much as a goodbye."

"I can buy that," Duckett said. "He was a pain in the ass to deal with. Heaven help anyone—or any*thing*— that gets between him and his family, though." He affected the tone of an infomercial huckster. "But wait, Sarah, that's not all."

She raised her eyebrows and shrugged her shoulders in a *Well?* gesture.

"They're the ones who killed Sanjay. In a way, they set this whole thing in motion."

"Hey, we had no idea it would lead to all of this business," Kinsey added right away. "Besides, *your* man stole the packet with the goodies in it."

"Yeah," a voice from the doorway chimed in. "Apparently, Sanjay tried sending all of that information to the NORKs via a secure VPN, but the network didn't cooperate, and your guy stole Plan B from the front desk. And when I fragged Sanjay, that put a rip in their condom."

"Toby, get in here. She can't turn her head," Kinsey ordered. "And tone down the asshole routine a notch. No one's impressed in here."

"And Sarah can't talk yet, so go easy on her," Duckett added.

Toby wandered around to the far side of the bed so Sarah could look at him without craning her neck.

"Okay, Romeo, relax," he said to Duckett, who

blushed at the implication. Toby pointed at Sarah and smiled. "You," he said, "are a tough mother fucker."

"Tobes, Jesus." Kinsey's frustration was showing. She shook her head as she turned back toward Sarah. "Can you believe I have to work with this guy?"

"No one makes you stick around, Kins," he said. "Besides, she totally is a tough MFer. Did you see the size of the Iranian she iced? He was a BFI." He looked around, his eyes smiling. No one said anything. "Big Fucking Iranian? BFI? Anyway, I don't know if *I* could have taken him, and she did him with his own knife, no less. And then she was going to blow us both up with that claymore!"

Sarah wrote on the whiteboard.

I was? I don't remember that.

"Yeah, you were. You held up the detonator and started laughing like the damned Predator when he started his mini-nuke in the first movie." He laughed at the memory. "No offense, but that's what you sounded like. I'm just glad I got to you before you could trip that thing. You were going to fight to your last breath, man. Mad respect, Sarah."

Kinsey laughed. "Sarah, that's as good as it will ever get coming from him. That's high praise."

"High praise indeed, and well deserved." Another voice in the doorway made everyone's head turn, except for Sarah's, who winced when she tried to look.

"Ian, get in here. Sarah can't turn her head," Kinsey repeated for the newest guest.

"Sorry, Sarah. I'm glad to see you're up and moving. Seemed touch and go for a while there. You too, Duckett. I heard all you lost was a lot of blood, some belly fat, and your spleen. You don't need that thing anyway. You got real lucky. How's the leg?"

"Well, I won't be dancing any time soon, but it's not like my card was filled, to begin with, right?" Duckett stole a furtive glance at Sarah when he said it, so quick it could have been subconscious. "But yeah, it beats the alternative. Regardless, it's good to be above ground."

Ian nodded. "Every day above ground is a good day anymore. Anyway, I just wanted to stop by and see how you all were getting along, and to say thanks for bailing us out of a jam."

Sarah scribbled on her whiteboard.

I think you have that backward.

"Oh, no," he said. "The Iranians pulled those choppers off the battle we were fighting in Albuquerque."

"Yeah," Kinsey added. "We had a real situation on our hands there."

Ian clarified her statement. "We were cooking up a real shit stew. Your shenanigans up here gave us an ounce of daylight."

"And that's all we need," Toby bragged. "Just that one chance, and we can get it done. Pulling you guys off that mountain was the least we could do in return."

Sarah did more scribbling.

How'd you know where to find us?

"We got back to the supply depot in Albuquerque, and the folks at the one in Scottsdale had left word about your conversation with them. Turns out they re-established contact with the 162nd Fighter Wing, and it turns out the 162nd still has a few working drones. They were watching your events unfold. We—well, *I*," Ian corrected himself, "was just about to pass out when we were voluntold to come to your rescue. Turns out, you had taken care of business on your own and just needed medivac."

"I got to pop one Iranian," Toby interjected. "He was all fucked up, I think he fell while wandering around after your claymore ambush. Injured or not, I'm counting it."

Sarah wrote on her whiteboard some more.

What happens now?

Ian looked at his team. "Depends on these two. The local police have hinted that they'd like our help clearing the infected out of this area. We're not in the military, so we can do what we want when we want, and I think that would be a good thing to do. Having a safe place to medivac people would be nice. And besides, it's easy work with a population density as low as this. We need the R&R. After that, we plan to go to DC and see if we can help sort some shit out."

"DC, huh?" Duckett asked.

"Yeah, why?" Ian replied.

"That's a question that sounds like plans could be changing," Kinsey said.

"Well, you know we got all that info about the disease. I don't know if it's going to be valuable or not, but I would think the boys at Fort Detrick would be interested in seeing it." Duckett let that settle for a second and added, "Fort Detrick is practically next door to DC."

"USAMRIID? I've always wanted to see that place," Toby said.

Sarah held up her whiteboard.

What is 'you Sam rid?'

Duckett spelled it out for her. "USAMRIID. It's an acronym, stands for United States Army Medical Research Institute of Infectious Diseases. They're the ones who sorted out the anthrax letters back in 2001. If it's scary and contagious, they're involved."

"You think this info you got is related to a cure?" Kinsey asked.

"Dunno. It doesn't say so in plain language, but maybe it could at least point them in the right direction. Or not. They'd have to be the judge of that, but the Iranians went to a lot of trouble to try and kill us for it, so it must be worth something, and it does us no good here."

"We'll think about it. In the meantime, Kinsey, Tobes, let's chat about this pied piper business the locals want help with."

"Sarah, you want me to wheel you back to your room?" Kinsey asked.

Yes. Need favor when you have time.

"Name it," Kinsey replied.

Need TV, DVD player, and* Coming To America *on DVD. Maybe you can find them in Durango? I promised Leonard we'd watch it.

"I'm sure that can be arranged," Kinsey said, smiling.
"I'd like to sit in on that. I love that movie."
"Who doesn't?" Toby added.
Sarah smiled and scribbled on her whiteboard. This time she turned it to Duckett.

I'll be back. Don't disappear on me.

He smiled. "Wouldn't dream of it."

CHAPTER FORTY-TWO

Five new holes were lined up in a neat row, with simple pine caskets in them. Susan and Sebastian went to Durango to retrieve the bodies of Shane and Marcus and brought them back to be buried with the rest of the team that fought the Iranians. Pastor Adam Chavez stood before the group and addressed them.

"Everyone present has lost someone important to them." He gestured to four holes already filled with dirt. "These four men died trying to protect our community from the scourge of this horrible disease, only to be cut down by murderous individuals." He gestured to the five open graves. "Still more people, some familiar to our community, others who were strangers, but fate made them a part of our community, fell to the same evil force.

"Officer Cedric Naranjo was killed on Chimney Rock. He was a familiar face to everyone in the towns of Arboles, Allison, and Tiffany. As a member of the

Southern Ute Police Department, he fought for and gave his life for his people. As did Shane Frost, killed in Durango, and Aaron Valdez, who also lost his life at Chimney Rock. We will be forever indebted to strangers to our community, Marcus Freemont and Charles Washburn, also giving their lives in the pitched battles against the hostile invaders.

"For that is what these people were. In speaking with many of you, I have learned America is under attack and has been since this disease took root in March. I won't bore you all with talk of Revelations, the end of times, because I don't believe that's what we face. We face an enemy using a weapon that is new to us but not new to this planet.

"Ancient Mesopotamians in 1500 BC sent victims of tularemia into the lands of their enemies, triggering an outbreak. The Greeks poisoned the wells of their enemies. Hannibal of Carthage, around 180 BC, threw clay pots filled with poisonous snakes onto the ships of his enemies. One can imagine what Samuel L. Jackson would say about that."

Many of the people present laughed. Pastor Chavez smiled and continued. "The Romans continued this legacy, poisoning wells and using pots filled with scorpions rather than snakes. Until now, however, the Mongols held the record for using disease to kill their enemies. Through the middle ages, they harbored people and animals infected with the plague in their caravans and sent them into enemy lands—by foot or, just as often, by catapult. The result was the death of twenty-five million Chinese and one-third of the people of Europe. Russia threw plague-ridden corpses into Swedish fortresses in the 1700s. Europeans used smallpox against native peoples in North America, South America, and Australia. Whether intentional or just by incidental exposure, the effect was the same. Millions died, and conquest was made easier.

"And so now another tribe is using this same technique against us. Only this time the death toll is global and orders of magnitude larger than those that came before.

"I tell you this not to say the end is near, but to tell you that the world has been here before and survived. We of Native American descent are still here. There are still Chinese people despite Genghis Khan's best efforts. The descendants of his European conquest are here today as well."

He gestured at the graves behind him once more. "The five men behind me came from different places but laid their lives down for the rest of us, without hesitation."

He gestured at the people in front of him. Some were sitting in wheelchairs and some were standing, but all bore some sort of injury. All were sporting some combination of bandages, casts, and bruises. "And many of you were ready to do the same. Because of men like them, and like you, the arc of history has shown that those who hide behind cowardice shall not defeat those who fight for a righteous cause. And their cause—*your* cause—*is* righteous. While we who yet live grieve for those lost to us, be assured they are rejoicing in their glory, for greater love hath no man than this, that a man lay down his life for his friends.

"And now, let us bow our heads in prayer."

IAN HAD the group gather in the lobby at the medical center while he asked the woman behind the front desk for a cart or a table. She directed him to the break room up the hall. Susan pushed Dominic in his wheelchair, while Lori pushed Leonard in his, and Kinsey pushed Duckett in his. Sarah walked beside them with her left arm in a sling. Sebastian pushed Robin in her wheelchair. They gathered in a semi-circle and waited for Ian.

He returned a few minutes later with a stainless-steel cart rolling on large, black, solid rubber wheels. He dug into his backpack, lining up shot glasses on the cart. Toby must have seen this before because he went and pulled a bottle out of the backpack and began filling the glasses until all of them—sixteen in total—were filled. Kinsey passed them out to the group, keeping one for herself. Ian picked up a glass and held it up.

"While we were liberating Durango from the infected, I liberated some inventory from a liquor store. We may be the good guys, but we're also cold-blooded capitalists, and we don't do any job for free.

"While we're all together today for the funerals, I wanted to have a toast. There are five glasses left here on the table, one for every person you guys lost. I didn't know them, but I've known hundreds like them. Young and old, they died with their boots on, fighting the good fight. Never forget!"

He drank the shot down. Everyone followed suit, with Leonard coughing and spitting some back up.

"You're cut off," Toby said to laughter.

"Tastes like gasoline!" the young man replied.

"Blasphemer!" Toby joked

"Who wants another?" Ian asked.

Dominic eyed the mostly empty bottle of Glenfiddich. "I would, but I don't want to drink the last of your bottle."

Ian grinned. "I have four cases in the truck."

The old man dug into his coat pocket, retrieved a flask, and held it out. "In that case, fill 'er up! I've run dry."

The instinct of the staff was to stop the revelry, but Doctor Spengler told them to let the mourners continue. "After everything they've been through the last couple of weeks, they've earned this," he said. "It'll help their spirits."

He walked over to join the group and pay his respects for one round. One turned into two and eventually that turned into telling the nurses he was off duty, and they needed to get Doctor Rodriguez if any emergencies came up.

CHAPTER 43

Sarah sat next to Duckett's bed, where she'd been spending more time over the last few days. The bruises on her neck had faded down to pale yellow streaks, and her voice was getting stronger by the day, though Doc Spengler still wanted her to go easy on extended use of her vocal cords.

The group had been up most of the night talking and telling stories about their fallen comrades. It had been a bittersweet gathering.

Today was different. Her head was killing her, and the ibuprofen hadn't kicked in yet.

She took solace in the fact that Leonard, in a wheelchair at the foot of the bed, was in worse shape despite being a decade-plus younger than her.

"I don't know how you guys drink that stuff," he complained. "Even mixing it with soda didn't help."

"Give it time, kid. You just need a flask like your gramps has, and you'll be hitting it all the time."

335

Duckett laughed as Leonard's skin tone changed from brown to a sickly greenish hue. "Get him a bucket," he advised Lori.

She grabbed the trash can and shoved it under Leonard's hunched-over face. It was touch and go for a minute, but he held it together.

"You're not gonna ralph, are ya, kid?" Toby said from the doorway. "I can make you a Bloody Mary if you want. Little hair o' the dog will cure you."

"That does sound good," Sarah said. "If you're serious, I'll take one."

"Make it two," Duckett added.

Lori chimed in. "Four. I'll drink his if Leonard doesn't want it."

"Fuck me. I guess I'm raiding the stash I picked up in Durango. I'll be back in ten."

Everyone except Leonard laughed as Toby groused his way down the hallway. They heard him say, "I suppose you want one, too! Jesus, I'll just make them for everyone! Fuck me!"

Kinsey walked up to the door. "What's he on about?"

"He offered to make Bloody Marys and is pissed we took him up on it," Lori said.

"Ooh, that does sound good. I could use a little hair of the dog."

"That's what he said, too," Sarah said.

"Oh, fuck me. I'm starting to sound like him? That ain't good," Kinsey lamented. Everyone laughed, even

Leonard. "Listen," she continued, "We're bugging out soon, back to Albuquerque. The depot there, where we came from, is no-shit fifty times the size of the bunker you found in Durango. They've gathered a bunch of civilians there, survivors from the area, mostly, but some travelers who got held up on their way to El Paso. Anyway, they're conscripting people for a civilian company, maybe even a battalion, to start clearing the city. They want someone to train them, get them in fighting shape."

Duckett had a sinking feeling where this was going. "Why are you telling me?"

"Well, the people in Scottsdale have been talking with this Air Force colonel—Colonel Hoisin—and they want you to be that someone. Said your AWOL status would be taken care of if you agree."

It was Duckett's turn to utter a *Fuck me*.

"Hey, I'm just giving you the heads-up, so you can do what you need to do. I'm a hired gun, for fuck's sake. As a merc, I'm not one to pass judgment if you tell them to pound sand. I can't see them spending the resources to look for you when they have other, much larger, battles to fight."

"Yeah, but they sent a flight crew and a bird full of mercs to come pull us off Chimney Rock. I have a debt to pay. Plus, I *am* technically AWOL."

"Like I said, giving you a heads-up."

Duckett looked at Sarah. "What do you think?"

"Why are you asking me? I bailed on the First Civilian Division in El Paso, remember?"

"Would you go with me? See if two wrongs can make it right?"

"I'd consider it. I mean, Charlie would probably have gone, right? And he's not around for me to worry about, so I'm kind of alone now."

"You're not alone," Leonard said. "You can stay here as long as you want. Then I can keep an eye on you."

Sarah smiled as his eyes began to water. "Don't cry," she said. "Let it turn to something else. Let it turn. Let it tuuuuurn."

He laughed and wiped his eyes. "Nice *Red Dawn* reference. We have to watch that next. But I was trying to be serious."

Now her eyes watered. She thought about all the times he checked in on her when they were in El Paso. He'd make special trips from Beaumont Medical Center to give her updates on Jack's condition, but she knew he was looking in on her and Charlie because he missed them and wanted to ensure they were doing okay. He was a very caring young man.

And Jack! She felt a sudden sense of shame that she hadn't thought of Jack in several days. He hadn't even been dead for a month. How was it that she was so unfeeling that she'd started to forget him already?

"Hey, you okay?" Duckett asked.

"Yes," she said, looking at him, then at Leonard. She wiped her eyes. "No. I don't know."

The same rolling cart from last night slid into the doorway, loaded with glasses of Bloody Marys.

"Thank God," Sarah said, grateful for the focus to be taken off her.

"Sorry," Toby announced as he began passing them around. "No celery. You're just going to have to stir them with the bendy straws."

Leonard sniffed the contents of his glass and wrinkled his nose.

"Oh, just take a drink," Lori teased. "The Bloody Mary has been around as a hangover cure since the 1920's. Six generations of alcoholics can't be wrong."

He took a sip, swished it around a little, and swallowed. "Hey, that's good. What all's in it?"

"I'll tell you later," Lori promised. "Just drink."

CHAPTER 44

ARBOLES, COLORADO. MAY 31

The Blackhawk's motor began its wind up, signaling the group that it was time to go.

"I can't believe you're going to leave," Leonard said.

Sarah grabbed him and gave him a fierce hug, mindful not to pull him off-balance as he used his cane for stability. "I'll miss you most of all, Scarecrow."

"You always do that. Quote movies when you get emotional."

"It's my defense mechanism, I guess. But you love it."

He smiled. "Yeah, I do. I love you, Sarah. You're like a big sister or something. Please be careful. And come see me sometime."

She squeezed him again and gave him a kiss on the cheek. "I'll be careful. You too, mister. Next time you see an abandoned package in a lobby somewhere, leave it alone."

He grinned sheepishly, embarrassed by the kiss. "No promises."

She released him and turned to Lori. "You're sure you're going to stay? You're AWOL too, you know."

The young girl grabbed Leonard's hand. "I'm sure. No one's looking for me. I'm sure, if anyone is even counting heads, they've assumed I was killed by the infected at Beaumont. I'm not AWOL, I'm MIA. And I'm not leaving Leonard. Besides, they need help at the medical center in P. Springs, so I'll still be serving, just in a different way. Take care, Sarah." She grabbed Sarah and gave her a long hug.

Susan Red was next in line. Sarah smiled at the stout woman. "Way back when you strip-searched me so we could cross the Reservation, I never thought we'd be having a teary goodbye in front of the Pinion Hills Motel Café."

"I did," Susan said. "Well, not this, exactly, but Dom told me we'd see you all again. He's not wrong on these things. I've learned to go with it."

"Probably wise," Sarah said, and she gave Susan a hug.

Sarah turned to Dom, still in his wheelchair, but more because he liked being pushed than out of necessity. "How about it, Dom? Will I see you again?"

He stood up and leaned close to her. "I said, those months ago, that my son should let you through the roadblock, let you pass through our lands even though I saw the sickness in your husband's spirit. I said that I saw in him a purpose. I did not know what that purpose was, but I think now that it was to bring you and this group together. It was to form these bonds. Now your fates are entwined. Now you all have a purpose you did not have before. I think that was his legacy to you."

A tear slid down her cheek. "I think of him less and less, Dom. What's wrong with me?"

"Life and death are moving faster than before," he said. "There's no time to waste being concerned with the dance between them. You must take each day as it comes or regret losing what precious moments remain. As a wise man once said, 'I don't have time to bleed.'"

She half laughed, half sobbed. "Did you just quote *Predator* to me?"

Dom's wrinkled face smoothed out in a broad smile and he gave her a wink. "One of my favorites."

She smiled back at him. "Mine too. But you didn't answer me. Will I see you again? Can you see that?"

Dominic stared at her for a minute. "I see you here, in this valley. You will return." He saw movement out of the corner of his eye. It was Duckett, sitting with his feet hanging over the side of the Blackhawk's doorway. He tapped his watch, indicating it was time to go.

"Now, Sarah Washburn," Dom said as he sat back down. "Get to the choppa!"

EPILOGUE

S arah took a drink of Ian's Glenfiddich. Before they left for the East Coast with copies of both the original Korean version and the English translation of the Sanjay Documents, as they now referred to them, he made her promise to watch over his stash since he couldn't take it all with him. She'd been watching over it, all right. Real close.

She was thinking about the Mercedes she and Duckett had abandoned in Durango. It had a certain symmetry; Jack stole the Mercedes from his boss in Denver at the beginning of the outbreak, the Iranians stole it from them, they stole it back from the Iranians and left it abandoned for someone else to take. She hoped someone had found it and used it to get to safety.

When they emptied all the gear from the Mercedes into Duckett's stolen Homeland SUV, they'd taken the Iranians' laptop, too. She'd almost forgotten about it, what with the morning PT and afternoon close-quarters combat training. Duckett had really been riding her ass in there, even though she was starting to feel like a real soldier. She thought she'd made significant progress, but he was all over her, criticizing her every move. Thinking about it, she grabbed the glass and took another pull from the honey-colored liquor.

Fuck it.

Duckett had been given a field promotion to First Lieutenant and owing to her experience with the Iranians, he made her a Corporal. She joked with him that after all they'd been through, she should be a Sergeant at least. He took her aside and told her that he was going to be training people for combat, not just against the infected, but against human forces as well. He would not be able to show her any favoritism or preference. If he treated her differently than the others, he would be shortchanging her training, and that could get her killed. He wasn't about to let that happen. He said that by the time basic training was over, she probably wouldn't like him anymore.

She joked that would imply that she liked him in the first place, and he seemed genuinely hurt by the comment. Things had not been the same between them after that. She took another drink of the liquor and looked at the confiscated laptop.

She didn't know the language on the keyboard, but amongst the gear that was in the base in Albuquerque, she finally found a power cord that fit the socket on the back. When she plugged it in, the little light for the battery turned red. Holding her breath, she pressed the power button, and let out a *whoop* when it beeped and brought up a blinking cursor. It didn't go any farther than that, so she assumed it was asking for a password.

"What now?" she asked aloud, her voice echoing in the empty tech room. "What could it be?" She kept talking to herself as she worked through the problem. "Any of the Iranians could need it. And there were..." she counted in her head for a minute, cataloging the dead bodies they'd left all over the southern part of Colorado. "Eight of them, originally. What would it be that any of the FIs would know?"

FI, pronounced "fee," had become shorthand for Fucking Iranian, and she used it without thinking about it. She got a thought and flipped the machine over. The serial number was 4543948. Could it be that simple? She jotted it down on a piece of paper and flipped it right side up and punched in the number. Holding her breath again, she pressed enter. The screen went black for a minute, then the OS splash screen popped up. A window opened, and a fast-moving string of commands sped its way up the screen.

"Haha! Fuck you FIs!"

A second later another window opened, and a conference room table appeared on the screen. An empty chair faced the camera. She could hear people talking, but she couldn't understand them, so she turned the volume up. When that didn't help her decipher any of the conversations, she said, "Who's there?" The conversation stopped in the room, where ever it was. She heard gasps, then chairs moving, and then a woman with striking, almost feline features walked to the chair in front of the camera and sat down.

IN THE CONFERENCE room in Pyongyang, no one noticed the video console beep, but when the woman said, "Who's there?" the people around the table gasped. Most of them didn't speak English, but the few who did, knew that a random English-speaking woman popping up on the encrypted conference app wasn't good. Kasra Amol stood and strode over to the control chair. If she was upset, she didn't show it. Still, several people pushed their chairs away from the table, ready to make a fast retreat from the room if necessary.

Kasra pressed the green button at the console, and the video image of a white woman in military clothing appeared on the main screen. "Hello, to whom am I speaking?" Kasra purred in Korean.

The woman on the other side of the video said, "You'll have to speak English, sweetie. I don't speak... whatever that was."

Kasra smiled her predatory smile. "Of course," she said, her English flawless. "I said, to whom am I speaking." She hated having to repeat herself.

"I'm Corporal Washburn, Alpha Company, First Battalion, First, er, Third Civilian Division—You know what, I'm US Army. That's all you need to know. Are you one of the assholes who launched this attack on us?"

Kasra's face melted into a scowl. "You're impolite for someone in possession of stolen equipment. The United Nations will not be pleased to hear about this. I demand you return it immediately."

"Fuck me," Corporal Washburn said. She held up a glass and wiggled it, golden liquid sloshing around. "Excuse me, Miss Manners, I've been drinking a wee bit. You didn't answer my question. You're them, right? The assholes, the shit stains, that attacked us?"

"Corporal Washburn, I will repeat, you are in possession of stolen equipment. I demand you return it to one of the United Nations security zones immediately!"

"Yeah, no shit it's stolen, Chuckles. I had to kill a guy to get it. Big fucker, too. BFI. Big Fucking Iranian. Speaking of, you don't look Iranian, but you don't look exactly Korean either. You look like a cat. Whatever, I don't give a fuck where you're from. Why'd you do it? Give me that much at least."

Kasra stared at her, wondering how she got the laptop, how she got the code to unlock it. Someone must have talked. It had been months since they had operations in the field. Had they captured someone and held them prisoner this whole time? Or did it belong to someone who had been taken recently? The impertinence of this American had Kasra fuming, but she refused to show any emotion.

"Whatsamatter, Kitty Cat? Got your own tongue?"

347

Corporal Washburn laughed at her own joke and poured more liquor into her glass. "Well, I'll tell you something, Whiskers, you'd better send some more guys because we've run out of them over here. I want to stack more bodies next to the ones we've already burned. Or, you could save the time and come on over yourself and let me put a knife through your skull like I did with BFI. Because I won't rest until all you fuckers are dead."

Kasra lost her composure. She screamed and slammed her fist down on the red END button so hard sparks flew from the console.

IN THE TECH room in Albuquerque, Sarah jumped back when the stone-faced woman screamed like a banshee. She thought for a moment the woman would actually come through the computer screen like the girl in the movie *The Ring*. The conference window went black, and wording appeared in another language. It didn't look like the Korean from the Sanjay Documents. Must be Iranian. She pressed and held the power button down until the machine shut off.

"That went well," she said, and laughed hard. "Dammit, that felt *goooood*."

She took a long pull from the glass, thinking this had to be the last one. Oh-five-hundred would roll around awfully early. She had a lot of training to do, and now she had a renewed purpose.

. . .

THIS IS **the end of the first installment of Sarah's Run. Her story will continue!**

The Five Roads To Texas World is expanding! Look for more adventures from the minds of other Phalanx Authors soon.

OTHER BOOKS FROM UNDER THE
SHIELD OF

FIVE ROADS TO TEXAS

| LUNDY | GAMBOA | HANSEN | BAKER | PARKER |

From the best story tellers of Phalanx Press comes a frightening tale of Armageddon.

It spread fast- no time to understand it- let alone learn how to fight it.

Once it reached you, it was too late. All you could do is run.

Rumored safe zones and potential for a cure drifted across the populace, forcing tough decisions to be made.

They say only the strong survive. Well they forgot about the smart, the inventive and the lucky.

Follow five different groups from across the U.S.A. as they make their way to what could be America's last stand in the Lone Star State.

GET IT NOW ON AMAZON

AFTER THE ROADS

BRIAN PARKER

The infected rule the world beyond the protective walls of the Texas Safe Zone.

Fort Bliss, Texas is home to four million refugees, trapped behind the hastily-erected walls of the Army base--too many people and not enough food.

In a desperate gamble, the soldiers responsible for securing the walls begin searching for pre-outbreak food storage locations. Not everyone will make it home.

For Sidney Bannister, the Safe Zone's refugee camps have become a nightmare that she can no longer endure. She must find a way to leave before her baby is born, or risk never experiencing freedom again.

Follow Sidney's story from the Phalanx Press collaborative novel Five Roads to Texas.

FOR WHICH WE STAND

JOSEPH HANSEN

El Paso wasn't the Promised Land that Ian and his crew had hoped for but it wasn't a total bust either. The concept of a safe haven in today's world was a fool's errand at best. This was the consensus of their tiny band and to keep moving, their only salvation. While others waited in their pens the four from the private security company moved on taking on as many they could help, in hopes that they too would join the fight. Their journey was long and arduous but it was worth it... they hope.

El Paso is where the final evidence that this is more than a simple lab experiment gone wrong. It was too focused with too many players who knew too much too early in the game causing assumptions to be made. Assumptions that gained strength with every step they took until the small troop was convinced that this was not just a simple virus of natural origins, America was under attack.

For Which We Stand is a post-apocalyptic thriller that lends credence to the fears that many share. Is it possible? No one can say, Five Roads to Texas is but one of hundreds end of the world scenarios. We all know it's coming, how and when is the only question.

CONVERGENCE

AJ POWERS

Even in death, life rarely goes as planned.

Having nothing left to live for, Malcom is given a shot at
redemption when a woman named Tessa needs his help.
With death looming, Malcom, Tessa and her children flee
Cincinnati with their sights set on El Paso. They know the
trip won't be easy, but nothing could prepare them for the
nightmares ahead.

Follow these new characters in the Five Roads to Texas
series as they set sail on a harrowing journey to what might
be the last bastion of hope in America.

Book 4 in the Five Roads to Texas series

SIXTH CYCLE

CARL SINCLAIR & DARREN WEARMOUTH

Nuclear war has destroyed human civilization.

Captain Jake Phillips wakes into a dangerous new world, where he finds the remaining fragments of the population living in a series of strongholds, connected across the country. Uneasy alliances have maintained their safety, but things are about to change. --

Discovery **leads to danger.** -- Skye Reed, a tracker from the Omega stronghold, uncovers a threat that could spell the end for their fragile society. With friends and enemies revealing truths about the past, she will need to decide who to trust.

Available on Amazon.

TORMENT

W.J LUNDY

From the War on Terror a world crippling Bio-Weapon is released. The United States scrambles teams of scientists from the Centers For Disease Control. America's top field agent are tasked with collecting samples and developing a cure. In a national laboratory scientists race against the clock searching for a cure. Borders are closed, martial law and soldiers deployed across the homeland.

Thus, begins the greatest outbreak in the history of human kind. A disease so deadly it pushes humanity to the brink of extinction. Entire populations and regions of the United States quickly wiped out, millions falling victim to the Primal Virus. In the wake of the fast spreading pandemic, state and local governments, desperate for answers, rush to provide relief to the devastated and overwhelmed communities. Experts in Bio-Medical Research are desperately summoned to Atlanta and military facilities across the country.

DEAD ISLAND: OPERATION ZULU

ALLEN GAMBOA

Ten years after the world was nearly brought to its knees by a zombie Armageddon, there is a race for the antidote! On a remote Caribbean island, surrounded by a horde of hungry living dead, a team of American and Australian commandos must rescue the Antidotes' scientist. Filled with zombies, guns, Russian bad guys, shady government types, serial killers and elevator muzak. Dead Island is an action packed blood soaked horror adventure.

INVASION OF THE DEAD SERIES

OWEN BALLIE

This is the first book in a series of nine, about an ordinary bunch of friends, and their plight to survive an apocalypse in Australia. -- Deep beneath defense headquarters in the Australian Capital Territory, the last ranking Army chief and a brilliant scientist struggle with answers to the collapse of the world, and the aftermath of an unprecedented virus. Is it a natural mutation, or does the infection contain -- more sinister roots? -- One hundred and fifty miles away, five friends returning from a month-long camping trip slowly discover that death has swept through the country. What greets them in a gradual revelation is an enemy beyond compare. -- Armed with dwindling ammunition, the friends must overcome their disagreements, utilize their individual skills, and face unimaginable horrors as they battle to reach their hometown...

THIS BOOK WAS FORMATTED BY

CARLSINCLAIR.NET